WENDY M. WILSON

When We People the Land

Guernsey Memorial Library
3 Court Street
Norwich, NY 13815
www.guernseymemoriallibrary.org

Copyright © Wendy M. Wilson, 2018

All rights reserved. No part of this publication may be reproduced, stored or transmitted in any form or by any means, electronic, mechanical, photocopying, recording, scanning, or otherwise without written permission from the publisher. It is illegal to copy this book, post it to a website, or distribute it by any other means without permission.

First edition

This book was professionally typeset on Reedsy. Find out more at reedsy.com

Contents

Pronounced Dead	1
The Town Makes Considerable Progress	6
Grubs and Insects	20
A Private Investigation	28
Shaken	37
A Body Surfaces	53
No Signs of Life	64
A Trip to Bunnythorpe	83
Reunited	102
V. Monrad, Esq. J.P.	111
Hidden at the Pa	122
The English Periodicals	133
Treed	138
The Desirable Corner Half-Acre	148
Gathering in the Square	157
Taking the Train	172
The Rutland	180
The Cook and the Lady	186
An Overdose of Chloroform	192
A Cricket Lesson	197
Colonel Whitmore	204
The Consciousness of Plumpness	212
The Diminutive Beast	219
Scandinavian Glee	227

Epilogue: Old Identities	234
An Excerpt from Dead Shot	238
Who is Sergeant Frank Hardy?	253

1

Pronounced Dead

Earache In any form may be quickly relieved (says a medical writer) by filling the organ with chloroform vapour from an uncorked bottle; vapour only, not the liquid; and mamma's bag should always contain a small vial of it, as it is useful in many ways. Ten drops upon a lump of sugar is an excellent remedy for hiccough or ordinary nausea, and I have recalled to life more than one person pronounced dead from sunstroke, with half a teaspoonful, clear, poured down his throat. New Zealand Times, 8 April 1890

"What's he done then, this bloke they're bringing ashore," said the man in the shawl kilt. "Murdered someone?"

"No clue. But we was told you was taking 'im upriver. Must be somefink bad. They didn't tell you?"

"Nah. I just do as I'm told," said the man in the kilt. "But they're a bad lot up there. Don't know why they keep them alive. Not good for anything and they can't let them go."

"How're you going to get him there?"

The man in the kilt nodded to a cart back near the sandhills.

"Put him in that and take him to the river. Then up the river by flat boat. I have some blokes waiting for me on the dock."

"What if he's a fighter?"

The man in the kilt didn't answer. He'd been wondering about that himself. He had a nightstick and cuffs hanging on his belt, and a revolver in his coat pocket. He'd been instructed to kill the prisoner if he made a run for it. With a bit of luck that's what he'd do. Save them all some trouble.

"Hey up," said his questioner. "Here they come."

A shape had appeared through the fog. A rowboat with three people on board. One of them was hanging over the side, vomiting, his arms lashed behind him.

"Give us a hand here please," said a sharp voice. Female.

The two men hurried down to the water and helped pull the rowboat up on the gravel beach.

"Which one is the prisoner?" asked the man in the kilt. "Him as is spewing?"

"Of course," said the woman. "What did you think? Can one of you get on board and help my man get him off?"

"What's the matter with him?" asked the man in the kilt. He was nervous. Lots of nasty diseases came ashore from boats. Typhoid, typhus, malaria…

"We had to give him something," said the woman. "To knock him out."

"And he'll stay knocked out until…?"

"He should be out until you get him to the gaol. He won't give you any trouble."

That was a relief. "What did he do, then?"

The woman ignored him. Her companion helped the two men manhandle the prisoner out of the rowboat and into the shallow water, with the man from the rowboat doing most of the work. The man in the kilt eyed the third person from the boat, and exchanged glances with his helper on the beach. A big brown feller, and what a bruiser. Must've got the prisoner off the Stormbird by himself. The woman wouldn't have been much help. She was tall and strong-looking, but a woman. Handsome, he'd call her, but a bit long in the tooth. Would have been a looker, twenty years gone.

The prisoner was a big man as well. It took the three of them to drag him across the sand and hoist him on his side in the cart. His wrists were bound with a length of rope, and he'd chafed at the bonds until his wrists bled. He awoke, briefly, and said something the man in the kilt couldn't comprehend. "Are you sure he isn't going to wake up before I get him there? It's a fair way…"

The woman lifted the prisoner's head, stared at his face, then let his head fall hard on the boards of the cart. "If you think he's going to wake up, knock him on the head with your night stick. He's tough. You'll want to make sure he doesn't come around competely."

The man in the kilt watched as the pair walked off along the beach, heading for the Heads and the track into town. "Don't think she liked him," he said. "Sounded like she wanted me to hit him on the head even if he didn't wake up."

His companion agreed. "Reckon he did something to her," he said.

The man in the kilt grabbed the prisoner by the head. "Let's get you up the river," he said. "And into one of our best cells. Say goodbye to the world. You won't be seeing it for a while. Maybe never. You're as good as dead."

The man mumbled something again. Something about

someone he'd met? He'd met a something, somebody?

****

He landed on a hard floor head first and lost consciousness, dropped there by human hands. A second to understand he was going down, brace himself, hands out, and then darkness.

He awoke later, face down, his nose bloodied. How much later he didn't know. His head throbbed and his mouth was so dry he couldn't swallow; his swollen tongue stuck to the roof of his mouth. He'd had a rope around his wrists at some point, but his hands were free now, thank God. Lifting his face from the floor, he rolled on his back and saw nothing.

The floor beneath him was hard and damp and lumpy. He couldn't remember how he'd got here—wherever here was. His hand slid from his chest and hit a dirt floor. Not the stamped-down dirt of a cottage floor, but the stony dirt of a dry river bed. He tried stretching out his legs, but was stopped by a wall.

Pulling himself up, he leaned cautiously on one elbow, dry retching through waves of nausea; a faint whiff of chloroform came off his beard. He tried to see through the impenetrable darkness. Was he in a tunnel? He raised one hand and stretched it sideways. Another wall. He was in a space about eight feet by eight feet, with dirt walls and a dirt floor. He tried to stand, but the nausea returned and he fell against the wall, gagging. Leaning there, he reached above his head. Perhaps he'd been buried alive in a tomb of some kind. No. He felt nothing.

Standing with his arm stretched to its fullest extent, he felt wooden slats, spaced out across the top of the hole. The air filtering through the slats was fresh. The cover was a foot and a half above his head, maybe eight feet high to his six feet two inches. He jumped and held himself off the ground on one of the boards, but couldn't budge it. Staring up through the slats he could see a faint trace of clouds against a night sky, obstructed by the shapes of huge trees moving like ghostly ships.

He let go the slats and dropped to the floor. Where the hell am I, and how did I get here? That was the question he had to answer. But first, who was he? Had he lost his memory? Sergeant Frank Hardy. Die Hard…a soldier from Her Majesty's 57th Regiment of Foot, who had fought in India, the Crimea, New Zealand… now living in Palmerston on the Manawatu River, hoping to be married soon.

That stopped him.

Mette. Will she think I've left her? Taken off for another life somewhere? He lost his calm, pulled himself up and pressed his face between the slats, yelling. "Hey. Anyone there? What the hell is this place?"

In response, a howl. Animal or human? He wasn't sure.

He could only hold himself there for a few minutes, but before his arms gave way, he glimpsed the top of a structure, a triangle of halberds, weapons lashed together. Used for floggings with the cat. Not a military prison then — the army had banned flogging a decade ago. Not good for recruitment. What kind of place was it then? A prison? The cat was still used for floggings in prisons. Or was he somewhere private and more sinister?

2

The Town Makes Considerable Progress

After visiting the Scandinavian settlement, so interesting and full of instruction, I rode into Palmerston and arrived there as the shades of eve were falling. Since I was there 18 months before, this place had made considerable progress in the number of stores and buildings. The business part of the township is in the square, around which are the principal stores, and through the centre of which runs the Foxton railway. A very large area of land is devoted to the township, which presents a scattered appearance. The place has a bustling aspect, and has derived its present prosperity from the saw-mills in its neighbourhood and the railway to Foxton. Wanganui Herald, 15 June 1877

Four days earlier

George Snelson, the recently elected Mayor of Palmerston North, New Zealand, held Mette Jensen's eyes in an intense, pale blue gaze, leaning forward to clarify his point. Without meaning to, she leaned away and clasped her own hands behind her back.

"It's vital that the townswomen collect funds for the Indian Famine Relief." The mayor leaned forward to emphasize the urgency. "I'm counting on you, Miss Jensen, to help my wife fundraise at the church. Perhaps a fete in the grounds of the school house? The women of Palmerston could provide biscuits and jam, perhaps some scones, and the children would enjoy a lolly scramble..."

Behind her, Mette heard the door to Robinson's Fine Papers and Books creak open. A large warm hand enveloped both her hands.

"Good morning Sergeant Hardy," said Snelson, releasing Mette from his intense gaze. "I'm trying to persuade Miss Jensen to assist Louisa with a bazaar for the benefit of the poor Indian families who've been hit with famine these last few months. I'm collecting..."

"I'm sure Miss Jensen would be delighted to help." Mette felt her hands being squeezed, and she dug her thumb nail into the soft part between her attacker's thumb and first finger.

"Are you unwell, Miss Jensen," said Snelson. "You're rather flushed."

"Quite well, Mayor Snelson." Mette smiled and made a futile attempt to free her hands. "I have a touch of spring fever now the trees are in bloom, and everyone's planting vegetables and...ouch."

"Yes, indeed," said Snelson. "Palmerston North is a wonderful place in the spring – I'm sure you'd agree Sergeant Hardy. Although it's unfortunate that my wife and I must deal with this terrible fire we suffered. Three thousand pounds... well, never mind. Our little problems, mine and Louisa's, are nothing compared to the poor wretches in India. I must be going, but I'll be reminding you of the baked goods."

Mette noticed that he'd used the new name for the town, knowing he now represented an important and growing town in the North Island: no longer Palmerston, but Palmerston North, because of a town in South Island also called Palmerston. But nobody in town added the North. They'd made up their minds that the name of the town was Palmerston.

She nodded, freed her hands, and escorted the mayor to the door. Frank Hardy came up behind her and they stood in the doorway gazing at the Square, his arms around her waist. The winter mud had dried up and the Square was covered in grasses, except for a path through the middle where a man with a pony trap plied his trade between the Princess Hotel in Terrace End and the Royal Hotel on the Square, sixpence a ride.

A raised boardwalk surrounded the Square on three sides and it was possible to walk all the way from Robinson's Books and Fine Paper to Snelson's General Store without getting your boots muddy. She'd planted seeds of spring flowers along her section of the boardwalk: Sweet William, foxglove, fuscia, pinks. They were starting to appear now, much to her gratification. She leaned back against Frank. "I like this so much."

"The way the town's changing?" asked Frank.

"Yes," she said. "Palmerston is a delightful place to live. But I also enjoy being in love with someone who loves you as much as you love him."

He leaned down and kissed her on the top of her head. "More, I would say. Mette, when do you think we can be married? I'm sick of being a bachelor. I want us to be together. And to think about what comes next, where we're going to live, there's so much opportunity in this country, and…"

"Mr. Robinson…"

"I know." He sounded impatient. "He wants you to stay until his nephew arrives from England in March. But don't you want to be together?"

Mette sighed. She did, of course. But she couldn't just leave Mr. Robinson in the lurch. And the idea of changing her home bothered her as well. Frank seemed to think they could go anywhere, but she was at home here, in Palmerston, near her sister and her friends.

Frank was quiet for a few minutes, holding her close while she leaned back against him. She felt him lean forward. "Your sister is coming."

Mette jumped. Her sister? That would mean Frank would leave. For some reason, he had never warmed to Maren, and was reluctant to stay around when she was there. "Maren is coming here? Why? She never leaves her house now she has three children to care for."

Frank pointed along the boardwalk. "Over there. She has all her children with her, and her husband as well."

Mette released herself from Frank's arms and leaned forward. "And Pieter isn't at work. Very strange. Something must have happened."

"I'll leave you to talk to them," said Frank. "I'll come back later to make sure it isn't bad news…"

Mette's hand went to her mouth. *"Min mor?"*

"Would you like me to stay? I can if you like, to make sure..."

She shook her head. "If a letter came from Schleswig to Maren about our mother, I would have received one as well. It must be something else. You go back to your office. I'll run over if I need to tell you anything."

He pulled her further inside the shop and gave a quick kiss, before her brother-in-law Pieter Sorensen could see him do it, and left, the door flapping behind him. She watched as he strode across the Square, a tall, upright figure with a bounce in his step. He was happy, at least. That was something. She hoped it would last. Sometimes she felt she was so happy it must change.

A minute or two later Maren and Pieter came in, each holding a small baby, with Hamlet trailing behind, his pudgy face disgruntled as it often was since he'd been displaced by twin brothers. Maren and Pieter were smiling. Not her mother then. No one had died.

"Maren, *hvor dejligt at se dig*," she said. She pulled one of Mr. Robinson's cane-backed kauri chairs forward and Maren sat down gratefully, still holding baby Paul. Pieter handed her the other baby and lifted Hamlet up, hugged him and pretended to drop him, sending Hamlet into squeals of laughter and warming Mette's heart. She hadn't liked Pieter much, at the beginning, but he was such a good father to his children, so playful, that she was beginning to be somewhat fond of him.

"We have some wonderful news," said Maren. "Well, bad news as well. Pieter's Tante Gertrud has died, the one who lives...lived in Copenhagen."

"The one I've been writing letters to, for Pieter?" Mette had developed a business for herself since she'd moved into town, writing letters home at sixpence apiece for Scandies who, as she liked to say, could not express themselves well, although in fact could barely write more than their names. There were enough of them in the district to keep her busy.

"Yes," said Maren. "And now she has died and left Pieter all her money, well a large amount of her money."

"Some of her money," Pieter interrupted. "All we know is, I'm one of her heirs. Perhaps it's just a small amount. A few hundred *krone*."

"Wasn't she quite rich?" asked Mette.

"Her husband was a shipping merchant," said Pieter. "He exported cheese and bacon to Canada and America, and brought back tobacco and beaver skins. One of his ships sank two years ago on the way to America and, unfortunately, he was on it. Tante Gertrud wanted me to go back to Denmark and help her manage the business…as you know." Mette suppressed a smile. He had given her credit for once. She felt she knew as much about Tante Gertrud as Pieter, having written several letters from Pieter to her and read the answers back to Pieter. "And Maren and I decided we preferred to stay in New Zealand, where our children could have a better life, even though your mother still lives in Denmark."

Pieter went to the door. "I have to see the lawyer who has her will now. I expect she'll have left me a small amount. Maren and the children will stay with you until I return."

Maren watched him affectionately as he left. "He's trying not to be too hopeful," she said. "Perhaps all she left us was her best china, and it will cost too much to bring it to New Zealand."

"What if it's a lot of money?" said Mette. "Your life might change completely."

Maren closed her eyes and smiled. "I'd like to have a hundred pounds," she said. "I would buy a new bed for us—with a spring mattress—and something better to sit on, like a horsehair sofa to lie down on when I was tired. Also, a perambulator so it would be easier to take the babies for walks, and let them sleep outside in the fresh air. And one of those new coffee machines…and, a family photograph taken at the new portrait studio over next to the Bank of New Zealand."

"You're so practical," said Mette. "I think I'd prefer to go on a holiday, perhaps to Wellington, and stay in a hotel where I could eat good dinners every night and sleep on a really soft bed."

The talk of a holidays and beds reminded Maren of Mette's situation.

"When are you and Sergeant Hardy going to be married?" she asked. "Surely you'll go on a holiday then and sleep in a soft bed."

Mette turned pink.

"Not until March," she said. "As I'm sure I've told you, Mr. Robinson asked me to work in his shop until then. When his son Ernest arrives from England he'll take over from me."

"Poor Sergeant Hardy," said Maren. "That's a long time for him to wait."

"We see each other every day," protested Mette. "It won't be any different when we're married."

Maren leaned over and gave Mette's hand a squeeze. "I can tell from your face it will be different," she said. "You and Sergeant Hardy, you haven't, you know…"

"Of course not," said Mette. "We'll wait until we're married. The same as you and Pieter." Her sister had met her husband on the boat from Copenhagen.

"We arrived in February and Hamlet was born in September." Maren's lips twitched. "Did you not think anything of that? He was born seven months after we married. And he was a large baby, even for nine months."

"But how?" asked Mette. "It was so crowded on the ship. How could you...?"

"Remember the foredeck where all the young couples used to go at night?" asked Maren. "Everyone laughed about it at the time."

"I thought..." Mette started. "Then all of you at the same time, on the foredeck...?"

"I didn't notice," said Maren. "It was a bit like being in a barnyard, I suppose, but it was fun as well. We didn't watch other couples, and they didn't watch us. We all sort of agreed not to, without saying so."

"Georg Dahl was alway after me to go to the foredeck," said Mette, shocked. "You mean he would have expected...?"

"I believe so," said Maren. "Unless he was as naïve as you..." She stood abruptly. "Here comes Pieter. He's walking very fast. I think it must be good news." She leaned closer to Mette, and said quietly, "Don't make him wait, Mette. I'm sure he's a good man, but he's older than you, and he isn't a saint. You don't want to lose him by being silly."

Mette's embarrassment was masked by the arrival of Pieter, who came in shouting, "*Min Gud, ah min Gud.*"

"*Hvad er det?*" said Maren, almost dropping Jens and Paul in her excitement.

"Please Pieter, tell me at once."

"More than..." He took a deep breath and started again. "More than a thousand pounds. I'm not sure because it's krone, but..."

Maren gasped and fell back onto the chair, still clutching the twins who were whimpering in harmony.

"*Min Gud*," she said. "Not just a bedstead and a sofa, but a whole new house…and a feather mattress."

"That's not all," said Pieter, squatting down in front of her, his eyes holding hers. "The house, Aunt Gertrud's house and all her furniture. She left us that as well. We'll have to find a way to sell it all, but the lawyer says it may be worth two or three thousand pounds, with the furniture included - if we can find someone we can trust to sell it for us."

They stared at each other, unable to speak.

"What about your sister?" asked Mette. "Did your aunt leave her anything, or will you have to help her?" Mette had made a trip the previous year to bring back Pieter's recently-widowed sister, Agnete Madsen and her children from Woodville. Agnete had other plans, however, and had gone to live in Wellington with a horrid Englishman, much to Pieter's displeasure. Mette had not much liked Agnete.

He frowned. "She did leave Agnete something, the same amount as she left me, although I'm to have the house completely," he said. "But Agnete will have her money from me a little at a time, and won't be able to touch it herself. I was happy about that."

"That's good then," said Mette. "I wouldn't trust Mr. Williams with any of her money." She remembered the pale-skinned, fawning Mr. Williams and felt a prickle of revulsion run down her spine.

"I should insist she comes to live in Palmerston," said Pieter. "Where I can make sure she doesn't get into trouble with another man. Alone, of course, not with this man she lives with."

THE TOWN MAKES CONSIDERABLE PROGRESS

"Should I write a letter...?"

Pieter rose from his chair. "No," he said. "A letter won't do. Someone should go to Wellington to bring her back." He saw the look on Mette's face, and added, "Not you of course. Not this time. But remember when you told me I should ask Sergeant Hardy to go to Wellington and bring her back? That's what I'm going to do."

Mette's heart sank. Frank would go to Wellington, as Pieter asked, and she wouldn't see him for days. Maybe he'd like Wellington so much he'd want to move there. Sending him down to fetch Agnete had seemed such a good idea when she'd only been a little in love with him and didn't see him every day anyway. But now...

"Come Maren," said Pieter. "I'll take you over to Mr. Snelson's General Store with the children. You can buy yourself...whatever you want. I'll go and talk to Sergeant Hardy. He should fetch Agnete as soon as possible, get her away from Mr. Williams."

They left in a flurry of noise and wailing babies. A minute after they left, Maren poked her head back in the door and said with a mischievous smile, "For your wedding present I'm going to buy you a nice new iron bedstead with a spring mattress." She closed the door, leaving Mette with a bright red face.

She sat there for several minutes thinking of Frank. Perhaps Maren was right and she wasn't being fair to him, making him wait. She could leave Mr. Robinson now if she wanted. He'd said so. She wasn't the only person in town who wanted such work, although perhaps the only one who loved it as much as she did, surrounded always by wonderful books. They could get married soon, if she just left her place at the shop. And then they could be together...

Thinking of it made her body feel strange, and she stood up and walked around the store stamping her feet, feeling the hobnails on the bottom of her boots reverberate up her legs.

Someone was outside reading the notice she'd posted in the window, offering to write letters in either English, Danish or German, and to translate any documents as well. He wore a large broad-brimmed hat which partly concealed his face, and she couldn't see much more than a silhouette, but he looked familiar. She knew some people needed encouragement to come in and talk to her, so she opened the door and looked out, smiling.

He turned, and for a moment her heart stopped.

It was Gottlieb, Gottlieb Karlsen, who had attacked her in her bed just a few months ago, and who Frank had killed with a tomahawk when he'd ambushed them in the Manawatu Gorge. It was not possible he could be here. What had happened to the tomahawk in his head? Was it under his hat?

He smiled back at her, a wide, toothy smile, and took off his hat, revealing a tomahawk-free head.

"*Guten tag, Fraulein,*" he said. If it was Gottlieb, she thought, her heart now pounding so loudly he must be able to hear, he had grown himself some new teeth. Or maybe they were wooden...she'd heard...

"*Guten tag,*" she managed to reply. She held herself upright with the door jamb and knew if she let go she would fall in a heap on the floor of the book shop. She'd seen Gottlieb Karlsen, a tomahawk wedged in his head, fall to his death in the Manawatu River. She'd worried about what would happen if his body surfaced, but not if he himself....

"Ah, then you are the person who will translate letters?" he asked in German.

She nodded, unable to speak.

"Could we talk?" he asked. "Inside?"

She nodded again and he followed her into the book shop.

"I'm here on a quest," he said. "Allow me to introduce myself. My name is Frederic Karlsen. My brother was Gottlieb, Gottlieb Karlsen—you knew him perhaps?"

Another nod.

"My brother went missing just a few months ago. He managed a road crew in town."

No, he did not, thought Mette, taking a deep breath. But never mind.

"I live in Australia," Gottlieb's brother continued, "In Melbourne, where I am a merchant. But when I received a letter informing me that my brother was missing I closed my dry goods store and left for New Zealand as soon as I was able. He's my only family, you know, and I had to find him, in spite of...."

Mette's frozen muscles started to relax. His brother, and a brother who sounded much more normal than Gottlieb. She could manage that, even though the resemblance was frightening.

"Were you hoping to retrieve his things?" she asked.

He shook his head.

"Not at all. In fact, I doubt very much that he had anything to retrieve. No, what I had hoped to do is find where he might have gone, or where his body rests, if he's dead."

"He's probably dead," said Mette cautiously. "He's been missing, as you said, for some time. People believe he is dead."

He shook his head emphatically. "I won't believe he's dead

until I see his body. Perhaps he was kidnapped, or lost in the bush."

"You should talk to Constable Price at the police station," said Mette, her voice shaking.

"I've spoken with Constable Price," he said. "He gave me some foolish story about a vengeful Maori who was killing people all over New Zealand. I don't believe for one minute that he killed Gottlieb. Why would a Maori do that? What I need is a private investigator, an expert. Not one with connections to the police who clearly have something to hide. Do you know such a person in this town?"

Yes, I do, Mette felt like saying. And he was also the person who killed your brother when your brother attacked us in the Manawatu Gorge. Instead, she said, "I'll ask around for you, if you wish."

He agreed, and left, saying he would return the next day at the same time to see what she had discovered.

She was not supposed to leave the shop unattended for any reason, but felt she must. She locked the front door and ran towards the Royal Hotel. Frank would know what to do. He always did.

She was still half way across the Square when she saw Frank walking towards the Foxton tram, which cut across the corner of the Square, wearing his blue greatcoat, a carpet bag in his hand. She was too out of breath to call out to him, but she lifted her skirt higher and ran as fast as she could. She was barely a hundred yards away when the tram pulled away from the station. She could see Frank sitting in a seat at the rear, his back towards her. Gone. Off to Wellington to fetch that stupid Agnete, she was sure.

She bent over, struggling to catch her breath, rubbing the

stitch in her side, then continued towards his office at a slower pace. Will Karira, the Maori constable and Frank's partner at the agency, would be there. She would ask him what she should do, instead of Frank. Surely he would have a suggestion.

3

Grubs and Insects

He edged around the pit with his hands against the dirt walls to see what kind of cell he was in. His foot kicked against a pail in a corner. Empty, but clearly there for slops. Nothing else, however. His windowless cell was devoid of furniture, or anything that might be used as a weapon…

He still wore his greatcoat, but the new large-bore Colt Deringer revolver he'd purchased at Gardner and Co. in Wellington was gone from the inside pocket; so was his money clip with Pieter's ten-pound advance and all his own ready cash. His fingers closed over a small velvet box. The brooch he'd bought Mette at Te Aro House on Cuba Street – a butterfly fashioned out of blue enamel – an impulse buy because it reminded him of what she'd said to him the day he asked her to marry him. It was a beautiful piece, and he knew she'd love it, but as a more practical matter, it had a sharp heavy pin made of steel. He tested the point with his thumb and drew blood.

Something skittered across the floor; a weta the size of his palm crawled across the toe of his boot. He impaled it with the pin, the sharp point sliding easily through the hard, outer shell of the insect. One decent weapon then. And with wetas on offer he wouldn't starve if they forgot to feed him. Not as easy to eat as huhu grubs, but still with some sustenance. He flipped it off the pin. A tree weta, which meant it probably came from a tunnel in the dead trunk of a tree buried in the wall of his cell.

He slid the brooch into his shirt pocket and dug inside his coat again. A box of Vestas. Just a couple left, but something. Down in the dust at the bottom of his pocket he found a small twist of humbugs—another purchase from Te Aro House. He opened the packet and sucked on one to help the dryness in his mouth. That was it for his coat. His trouser pocket yielded a few coins: a shilling, two pennies, a halfpenny, and a couple of farthings. He wasn't going to be able to bribe his way out of this predicament.

He edged around the cell, feeling the wall from top to bottom, seeking a gap or entry. It was damp in places, and hard, the soil held in place by heavy totara beams.

He'd been kidnapped it seemed. But why, and by whom? When had it happened? He could remember being at sea on the steamer from Foxton to Wellington. Had he returned from Wellington? Yes, because he remembered boarding the steamer, the S.S. Stormbird, with Pieter's dreadful sister Agnete and her two pasty-faced children. She'd boarded with a large steamer trunk of clothing, wearing a crinoline that barely fit through the doorway of the cabin she'd insisted on taking on the saloon deck. She already saw herself as one of the Royal Princesses: Vicky or Louise. He'd badly wanted to tell her that her tiny inheritance would not elevate her to the *crème de la crème* of society, even if Palmerston had anything that could be described as society, which – thankfully – it did not. That was one good thing he could say about the town.

God. Agnete Madsen. He already had his doubts about Mette's family, and now Agnete was added to the mix. Perhaps he and Mette should move to Napier, or Auckland – or even the South Island. As far away as possible. He'd heard Christchurch was a growing metropolis, as well as being the most English town in New Zealand, and free of conflict with the natives. Dunedin might be even better – further away from Wellington as well.

His exploration of the wall yielded nothing. He sat on the floor, leaned against the wall, and thought. What had happened in Wellington? Anything unusual? He'd booked into the South Sea Hotel on Lambton Quay, after reading in the *Evening Post* that it had a splendid billiard table, thinking he might need to entertain himself for a few nights while he searched for Agnete Madsen. But as it happened he'd found her within days. Wellington was small, despite the fact it had been the capital of the colony for over ten years – under 20,000 people.

He'd started by asking at the hotel for an Englishman named Williams who kept semi-respectable women in his home who were not married to him or related to him; one suggestion led to another, and by the second day he'd tracked her down. She was living in a rundown tin-roofed boarding house built of wooden planks, on Oriental Parade, not far from the Te Aro Swimming Baths. She'd been surprisingly pleased to see him, and when she heard she was about to inherit some money was ready to fetch her valise and leave right away for Palmerston. He'd had to remind her of her children. Obviously, Mr.

Williams had not been as generous as she'd hoped.

He closed his eyes and dozed, waking with a start to the sound of a trapdoor opening. He staggered to his feet.

"Hey there, you, who are you? What am I doing here?"

A rope sling holding a basket of food wrapped in leaves was lowered down to him. He grabbed the basket and the sling was pulled up and out of view. He strained upwards, but could see no one, and no one spoke to him.

"What the hell is going on. Why am I here?"

A bucket on a hook dropped down, empty, and hung there. He stared at it, then understood its purpose. Slops. He grabbed the used bucket from the corner and switched it with the new one, watching as the old one disappeared slowly into the darkness, not seeing anything.

He opened the basket of food. At least whoever had him didn't intend to let him die here. The basket contained the most basic of food for survival – potatoes and kumara, the sweet New Zealand potato – and a bottle of water with a glass stopper. Famished, he ate quickly, and spent the next few hours with his guts roiling, regretting his haste. He hoped that wasn't to be his food for the day. When he was in the Armed Constabulary back in '68 and '69 he'd got by on less, at times nothing but water, but he'd become soft, used to three meals a day.

Daylight came and the sun rose and bore down on him through the branches. The strength of the spring sunlight was weak, but his underground cell became heated; the woody scent of totara and pines wafting through the bars added to the miasma. He thought he could also detect the faint smell of blood, a smell he associated with a slaughter house – or with flogging, of the kind he'd seen so often in the army.

The smell and the heat got to him, and eventually he vomited into the slop bucket. When he was done, he took off his greatcoat and laid it in a corner. Now he could see the true extent of his prison, the dirt floor, the walls reinforced with crossed slabs of wood. He thought of the sawmills back in Palmerston, busy cutting such planks on their sharp blades.

The sawmills reminded him of Mette. He could see her once more as she was the first time he saw her, barely three months ago, standing in the forest clearing with her sister, laughing, her blond hair gleaming in the sunlight. She was beautiful, although she didn't believe it herself, because her beauty was in her animation and came from within. She was the perfect woman, like Patmore's Angel in the House, the goddess of the family – their family of course, the one they would create, not the family she already had. After that first time, when she'd run from the Maori warrior Anahera in the bush and into his path … all he wanted after that was to protect her, to keep her safe. It was an odd feeling. Women didn't usually have that effect on him. Perhaps it was because she was younger than the women he'd previously been involved with, more dependent on him.

And what about Anahera? The rebel Maori warrior had descended on Palmerston a few months ago, determined to revenge himself for the deaths of his two small nephews and the kidnapping of his sister. They'd caught him and he'd been sent up the Wanganui River to the secret Armed Constabulary gaol, known to be impossible to escape. He was probably still there. Could he have organized Frank's kidnapping from his prison cell?

Surely it would be impossible for Anahera to organize a kidnapping from his gaol. He'd be separated from other prisoners, and without enough of the English language at his command to recruit a corrupt guard. Besides which, the man was terrifying. He was not someone who would charm a guard into helping him. Terrorize a guard, perhaps, but that didn't work when you were in solitary confinement, and guarded closely by experienced men. However, others in the gaol could be in contact with the tribes in the King Country, up the far reaches of the Wanganui River, where the Maori King Movement had drawn a line beyond which Europeans could not go if they wanted to stay alive. Maybe the Movement had developed some kind of forward base closer to Wanganui and were holding him there? Could they be using him to facilitate a prisoner exchange? He hoped not. No one would consider him worth swapping for Anahera.

The day dragged by, and as the sun went down, the ritual with the basket and the slop bucket was repeated: more potatoes and water, and a chunk of mutton that was mostly fat. Two meals a day — enough to keep him alive.

As his cell darkened he heard the skittering sounds of wetas once more, and used one of his precious matches to find the tunnel. Half way up the wall nearest to the trapdoor, the flickering light from his match lit up a small colony of females and juveniles, and one male who hissed at him angrily. He used the last of the flame to locate a rock, and shoved it deep into the tunnel. That would keep them in there while they dug around it, and make sure they didn't crawl over him as he slept. They weren't dangerous, but they could bite, and he needed his sleep.

He dozed off thinking about his stay in Wellington. He'd had a brief and somewhat curious encounter at the South Sea

Hotel, with a colonel belonging to one of the British regiments in India. He seemed to recognize Frank, although Frank had no memory of ever meeting him. Why would someone from India have anything to do with this? He hadn't been in India for almost twenty years, when he was a raw recruit. Surely nothing from that long ago could be coming back to cause trouble for him now?

He stretched out on the ground, which was as hard and uncomfortable as a metalled road. It was not the soft bed he was used to these days, but he knew from his years of campaigning that rest was vital, and would help keep him ready for opportunities. He lay back on the hard, uneven ground, his head on his rolled-up greatcoat and dropped instantly into a heavy, dreamless sleep.

The sun rose and the distant, familiar sounds of a military camp drifted down to him. His first thought was that he was still at war in Taranaki, but then reality hit. Still in his underground prison. He got up and stretched, then threw his coat in the corner opposite the slop bucket. The click of a key pushed into a lock and turned signalled that food had arrived, and he was instantly alert. He had to find who had him before he could understand why he'd been taken.

The trapdoor creaked slowly open. He stood underneath, ready to receive the basket of food, and ready to discover who had him. The food came towards him slowly; he braced himself. Slowly, slowly. Then his hands were around the basket. He gave it a sharp pull, sending it tumbling across the dirt floor, and then leapt upwards, grabbing at whoever was there.

His hands connected to an arm. Gripping it, he pulled down

hard, putting his weight behind it. A brown arm, small, and soft, a woman's arm. The surprise almost caused him to let go, but he held on and pulled the woman down further. Her whole upper body was through the trapdoor, her hair tumbling over his face.

"Who are you? Why are you keeping me here?"

She began to wail. *"Te tauturi, te tauturi."*

Boots thumped towards them in the dirt, followed by the ominous sound of carbines being engaged.

"Let her go," said a voice. "Or you're a dead man."

He continued holding the arm for a few seconds, then grudgingly let it slip from his grasp and stepped back. The woman was pulled up by unseen hands, still wailing loudly.

"That's better." An Irish voice. He recognized the accent. "Now sit down and be a good boy now."

He lowered himself against the wall and sat on the earthen floor. They could see him, but to him they were just vague shadows. Above him the carbines were disengaged, followed by muffled words. He heard them leave, but the shadow of one man remained, like a ghostly presence, leaning over the grate.

"Got me eye on you, mate," said the Irishman. "Don't try anything like that again or I'll shoot youse in the leg, hobble you for good."

He picked up the kumaras and potatoes and brushed the dirt away. He knew that voice. Who the hell was it?

4

A Private Investigation

Wiremu—Will—Karira, lately a Maori constable, and Frank had opened a small private enquiry office in the new building next to the Royal Hotel: Die Hard Enquiries, Inc. They were building up a steady list of regular clients to keep them in business – tracking down stolen horses, delivering legal papers, patrolling hotels at night and such. Mette arrived at the agency out of breath, and ran up the steps, down the hallway and through the swinging half door to the office. Karira was at his desk, buffing his boots with dubbin, the *Manawatu Times* beside him, open at the cricket scores. He dropped the cloth and jumped to his feet.

"Mette, what's…Frank just left. He's gone to Wellington to fetch your brother-in-law's sister. He didn't have time to say goodbye – he had to rush for the tram. But he told me to tell you he'd be back in three or four days. I'm sorry, I…"

Mette sat down at Frank's desk, which faced Karira's, dropped her head into her hands and started sobbing.

"He'll only be gone a few days." Karira moved uncomfortably in his chair. "He'll be back before you know it."

Mette brushed the tears away with her fingertips, sniffing.

"I'm sorry, Will," she said. "I saw Frank leaving, and I so much wanted to talk to him, about…something terrible has happened. You remember Gottlieb Karlsen? The Scandi man who went missing in October?"

Karira nodded. "The road worker?" He looked at Mette, his soft brown eyes guileless.

Mette nodded, avoiding his gaze. Had Frank told Karira about what happened? The expression on his face suggested he knew something.

"His brother's here," she said. "Gottlieb Karlsen's brother. His name is Frederic Karlsen and he's come all the way from Australia. He wants to hire an investigator to find what happened to Gottlieb. I'm supposed to find someone who can help him and let him know tomorrow. He doesn't speak English and needs someone to translate. He thinks I'll be that person."

"Hmm," said Karira. "That's awkward."

Mette looked at him warily.

"Frank told me what happened," he said. "I swore I wouldn't tell anyone, and I won't."

"Everything?" said Mette, her voice shaking. There were some things she wanted no one to know about. She didn't even want to know about them herself, but had no choice. She'd struggled hard to forget the terrible attack in the night, and the attempted rape, and the only time she felt completely safe now was when she was with Frank.

Karira shrugged. "He attacked the pair of you in the Gorge, and Frank killed him with Anahera's tomahawk. It was clearly self-defence, but I have no intention of making Frank—or you—go through a trial to prove that it was."

"Thank you Will," said Mette, her eyes filling with tears. She wiped them away with the back of her hand, sniffing. "Then what should I tell him? Do you know anyone else who can help him search for his brother's killer, without letting him know the truth?"

Karira picked up a delicately carved greenstone paper knife from his desk and twirled it between his fingers, looking thoughtful. "I'll take the case," he said finally, stabbing the end of the paper knife into the wooden desktop. "I'll take him on a nice little tour of all the places his brother spied on women, and have him talk to my Uncle Hakopa, who heard the complaints, and we'll talk to the men who worked under poor Sergeant Jackson before he was murdered by Anahera. They watched Karlsen go down to the river bank to spy on the women from the Pa. When I'm done with him he'll think—no, he'll know—that his brother was the worst sort of man to be found in New Zealand."

She was in the bookstore the next day when Frederic Karlsen arrived, followed shortly by Karira. Karlsen looked Karira up and down, frowning and said, "I thought you would bring that sergeant...Sergeant Hardy, is it? Mr. Snelson at the general store told me about him. He would seem more suitable..."

"He's away," said Mette, glad that Karira didn't speak German. "Mr. Karira is his partner. He can help you just as well. In fact, he probably knows the district better than Sergeant Hardy."

"Aah," said Karlsen, giving her a knowing look. "Then this Hardy, you wouldn't recommend him so much then? You think this Maori fellow will be able to talk to the local rascals better?"

Mette bit her lip and smiled, itching to give Karlsen a good slap.

The two men talked at one another, using Mette as an intermediary, and then sealed the deal with a handshake and a five-pound note for Karira, which was to be the advance. As he handed over the note, Karlsen asked, "He isn't related to that Maori who killed people, is he?"

"*Nein*," said Mette. Then, in English to Karira, "Mr. Karlsen wonders if you are connected to the Maori who killed several people a few weeks ago."

Karlsen watched Karira with narrowed eyes, waiting for his answer. Karira shook his head firmly.

"Sergeant Hardy and I did our best to catch him," he said slowly, exaggerating the words, as if Karlsen was a bit slow, as Mette translated. "He almost killed us, up behind the sawmill. But we caught him and he's been sent away now. He may even have been the man who killed…made your brother disappear."

Karlsen frowned. "That's what Constable Price said, but it isn't true."

"How do you know?" asked Mette nervously in English. "I mean, *woher weist du das?*"

He leaned forward confidently. "Because the boy who works behind the counter in the general store told me. He said no one in town believes the Maori killed Gottlieb."

"Who do they think did kill him then?" said Mette, forgetting that she was trying to pretend Gottlieb might still be alive.

Karlsen looked carefully in either direction, leaned forward, and said in a dramatic whisper, "The Armed Constabulary."

It was so far from what Mette expected that she almost burst into laughter.

"Why would they do that?"

"Because he had discovered they were secretly selling alcohol to the natives and they wanted to shut him up."

"Not a bad theory," said Karira, after she'd translated for him. "Better than the one where he was killed by an enraged Royal Mail coachman with a tomahawk, at least. Shall we run with that one? An Armed Constabulary conspiracy?"

Karlsen saw that Karira had accepted his idea and he nodded and smiled. "*Gut, gut.*"

Mette crossed her fingers behind her back and said, "Mr. Karira thinks that's a possibility."

"As good as any other possibility that isn't the actual truth," said Karira, smiling at Karlsen, who smiled back again.

He shook hands once more with Karira and left.

For the next week, Mette continued working at Robinson's Fine Papers and Books, longing for Frank to return, and receiving frequent updates from Karira on his investigation. She was unable to leave the shop and go with Karira and Karlsen as a translator, so they did the best they could, talking at each other slowly and loudly, neither listening to the other. Karira would drop by with his update at midday, and later in the day Karlsen (she could not think of him as Frederic as he was still a little bit Gottlieb in her mind) would come in and be given the translation she and Karira had decided on between them. A visit to Karira's Uncle Hakopa, who talked angrily about how Gottlieb had spied on the young women from the Pa, was translated as Gottlieb watching the river to see the alcohol being sold to the natives.

"I didn't intend him to take that from our conversation with my uncle," Karira said apologetically, after Mette had told him about a discussion she'd had with Karlsen. "I want him to understand how depraved his brother was, but he drew the wrong conclusion. He understood the words 'Armed Constabulary' when my uncle mention them —Uncle Hakopa suggested Karlsen should go to them I believe. That, with your suggestion of Gottlieb spying on someone at the river allowed him to conclude there was a plot against Gottlieb." He picked up a book from the book shop table and waved it at Mette. "It sounds like something out of *Tom Brown's Days at Rugby*, or *Masterman Ready*, Gottlieb crouching on the river bank listening to the plotters, determined to unmask them to the world."

For a disloyal minute, Mette wished that Frank knew as much about books as Karira, but she pushed the idea from her mind. Karira would always be around, and she could talk about books with him. In many ways he had become like a brother to her. Frank had other things she loved about him.

"What other evidence has he seen that shows his brother was killed by the Armed Constabulary to stop him revealing their plot to sell alcohol to the nati…to the Maori," asked Mette.

"Remember that raid by the Armed Constabulary back in August?" said Karira. "When they found a large cache of liquor? Karlsen heard about that from his source behind the counter at Snelson's General Store. He thinks that the Constabulary kept some of the bottles and sold them off to my people." He picked up one of Mette's recipe pamphlets and flipped through the pages. "We don't even drink alcohol, most of us. It's insulting, actually."

"Perhaps you should tell him…" She stopped. Hop Li, the cook from the Royal Hotel, and an old friend of Frank's, had come rushing into the shop, looking upset. Mette had never seen him even slightly troubled about anything, and her heart dropped like a stone in her chest.

"Something has happened to Frank," she said.

Even as she said the words, she did not believe them herself. It was just like when she thought the news about Pieter and Maren's inheritance was going to be that her mother had died. A minute of intense worry and then an explanation that was terribly important of course, but did not involve the death of someone she loved.

"Mrs. Madsen just arrive from Wellington, with her children," said Hop Li.

"And Frank?" said Mette and Karira in unison.

"Gone," he said. "He disappeared from boat. He didn't come down gangplank."

He was too distraught to tell them much more, so Karira and Mette ran towards the tram station leaving Hop Li in charge of the store with instructions to tell anyone who came in that Mette was away for five minutes. Mr. Robinson would not be happy if he found out, but that was the least of her worries.

They found Agnete Madsen supervising a sullen tram conductor as he tried to hoist her steamer trunk on Pieter's dray, with assistance and conflicting instructions from Pieter. At any other time, Mette would have been amused at the scene, but not now. She strode up to Agnete and demanded, "Where's Frank?"

Agnete gave her a long, cold look, then shrugged.

"He left me to come from Foxton on my own," she said. "With my two small children and all my luggage."

"What do you mean he left you alone?"

"I explained all this to the Chinaman," said Agnete. "Didn't he tell you?"

Mette shook her head. Had Frank gone somewhere? What had happened?

Agnete sighed. Clearly, Mette was testing her patience.

"We were supposed to meet him at the top of the gangplank when we arrived in Foxton," she said. "We were on the SS Stormbird in cabins at opposite ends of the saloon deck. But I waited and waited and he didn't come. In the end, they – the crew – made me disembark. I found my own way to the tram, with the help of a very nice Scotsman, and here I am. I must say I'm not at all happy that he abandoned..."

"He would never do that," said Pieter sharply. "That is why I asked him to come and fetch you. I trust him completely."

A tiny bit of warmth started to melt the icicle wedged in Mette's heart.

"He didn't disembark from the steamer, then," said Karira. "I'm going to Foxton to see what they can tell me."

"Thank you Will," said Mette, her voice husky. She turned to Agnete again. "Is there anything Mr. Karira should know before he leaves? Anything important?"

"Goodness, I don't know, I'm sure," said Agnete. Mette noticed that her English had become very...English. She'd been practising her elocution during her time with Mr. Williams.

"Anything?" said Karira. "I don't want to go running off to Foxton and find out that Frank was following up on something, and everyone knew..."

Agnete put a finger to her pursed lips and said, "Hmm. Well, I saw him talking to a man on the boat. A very large Maori man."

Mette and Karira looked at each other. "Not..." she said. He finished her thought.

"Surely not Anahera?"

"What did he look like, this large Maori man?" asked Karira.

"Like a Maori," said Agnete, like that explained everything.

"Not dressed like a Maori, however, but fashionably. He wore a dark suit, and a bowler hat, you know the kind, with a rolled-up brim and high crown. Mr. Williams dressed like that, but I would never expect it of a Maori. A Maori in a suit seems very strange to me." She was apparently oblivious to the Maori in front of her, dressed in a fashionably cut dark grey suit.

"Did he have *te moko*– I mean facial tattoos?" asked Karira, ignoring the insult.

Agnete shook her head. "I didn't see anything like that. He wasn't the savage kind of Maori, you know. He looked quite respectable. Almost European."

"I'll go to Foxton," said Karira, glancing at Mette, one eyebrow raised. He took off towards the rear of the Royal Hotel, where he kept his horse in the paddock.

"What a nice young man," said Agnete. "Very well spoken for…"

Mette interrupted her. She was tired of listening to Agnete's foolish comments.

"Yes, he is, a very nice young man. I like him very much. And he is a good friend to Frank, my, my…" A little sob left her throat before she could stop it from happening.

Pieter touched Mette's arm awkwardly. "I'm sorry Mette," he said. "I'm sure nothing has happened to Sergeant Hardy. Everything will be explained when Mr. Karira returns. There'll be a good reason for all this, I'm sure."

She hoped he was right, but in her heart, she knew he was not. Something terrible had happened to Frank. He would never disappear without letting her know. He wasn't that kind of man.

5

Shaken

He awoke on the third morning feeling better; the queasiness he'd experienced the first day had gone. His food came with the morning light, as he'd begun to expect, but with one difference: now the woman was accompanied by men with carbines; he heard the bolts click into place as the trapdoor was unlocked. The knowledge did not help him understand where he was, how he'd come there, and, most importantly, who had brought him here and why.

The carbines pointed to a military encampment, but why would he be in a place like that? Could he be in the Armed Constabulary prison where Anahera had been taken? Not likely. He couldn't imagine they'd keep prisoners underground, or use whipping posts with crossed halberds. The Armed Constabulary was an honourable organization, especially now with Whitfield in command. They wouldn't break the rules in that way. Would they?

He spent the morning standing on the upturned bucket attempting to unlock the trapdoor with the butterfly brooch. If it came to it and he had a chance to escape, he might be able to do it that way. But the trapdoor was high above his head and he'd have to pull himself up and push himself through without any leverage from below. Not something he felt he could do without weeks of pulling himself up and down on the planks above him to increase his strength. And he didn't intend to be in this hole long enough for that.

He thought again about Wellington. Who had seen him there? What had he stumbled into that had lead him to this place?

His search for Agnete had taken him to Oriental Parade in the shadow of Mount Victoria. A slovenly maid answered the door of the run down boarding house and called out to her mistress without moving from the door, eying him up and down, deciding whether he could afford to enter. Agnete Madsen was not happy to see an envoy from her brother, but changed her mind when she learned there was money to be had.

"Five hundred pounds?" Agnete clutched her breast with both hands. Pieter had asked Frank to mention a lesser amount to stop her from running up debts. "I could live very well in Palmerston with that much, at least for a year or two, until I could get more settled perhaps..." She dropped her head and eyed Frank flirtatiously through her stubby lashes.

He stared back at her coldly, signalling to her that she shouldn't entertain ideas about him. He couldn't imagine why anyone would be interested in her - although perhaps there'd be a Scandinavian man foolish enough to take her on, with her little inheritance.

"I'll tell Mr. Williams...or perhaps I'll leave him a note." She backed into the hallway and opened a drawer, searching for a pen and paper. "He's gone to Nelson to meet a widow who contacted him through the newspaper."

Frank understood her situation without her telling him. She'd been left to moulder in this boarding house alone, while Mr. Williams went in search of fresher meat. Serve her bloody well right. He arranged to collect her in a rented pony trap the next day.

As he left he heard the seven-gun salute of a twenty-four pounder, which had been dragged up Mount Victoria that day to much fanfare and with accompanying populace, to be used as a time gun. He enjoyed the excitement of living in a larger New Zealand city. If he and Mette moved here, he'd have no trouble finding work, especially now it was the seat of government. She'd have to give up her idea of having a garden, as the sections were small and steep, but she'd find something else to interest her: the libraries and book shops, the little coffee shops. She'd love it in Wellington.

He'd collected Agnete and her children in the trap and taken them to Lambton Quay to catch the steamer to Foxton. He'd arrived shortly before midday and helped her, her steamer trunk and her children on the trap. The four of them and the trunk barely managed to squeeze in, and she wondered aloud if she should leave the children behind with the maid. The children stared at her wide-eyed, understanding that their fate hung on the balance.

They boarded the steamer, she went to her room on the saloon deck and he went to the bar, and then ... he drew a blank. Something had happened...he had vague memories of talking to someone about...what? He thought he might have been chloroformed, based on the nausea and the faint smell when he first awoke, but how that had happened he couldn't guess. And he had vague snatches of memory of being in a rowboat and a flat boat. Of being dragged up a hill and pushed into the cell.

He remembered in Scutari once, when he'd taken a young private with a gangrenous leg to the hospital, listening to Miss Nightingale rage against Queen Victoria's use of chloroform during childbirth. Miss Nightingale was not pleased with the idea. She thought a woman should endure the pains of childbirth without the unnatural assistance of chemistry. However, she wished she could use it for men needing to have limbs removed. Chloroform worked very quickly to send the receiver into a deep sleep, she thought, with the added advantage that afterwards the soldier did not remember anything. As it was, she had to make do with a good dose of alcohol and a surgeon who was quick with a knife. The private had lost his leg within thirty or forty minutes, and was undoubtedly spending his days begging in the streets off Golden Square.

Before he found Agnete Madsen he'd spent three nights at the South Sea Hotel. Something odd had happened there. He remembered thinking about it when he first awoke. Something strange. The lingering effects of the chloroform had muddled his thoughts, but now he concentrated on remembering.

On the first night at the hotel, he'd played billiards with another ex-soldier. They'd both fought in the Taranaki Wars and reminisced about that between shots. Both had been at the storming of the rebel Maori stronghold of Otapawa Pa in Southern Taranaki, his new acquaintance with Von Tempsky's Rangers, and they'd had the same misgivings about the attack: a village full of women and children had been used as the launch site for bombardment by the Armstrong six-pounders, and there'd been some killings. They'd overrun the Pa and killed thirty rebels, the rest escaping from the rear towards the river, but eleven Die Hards from the 57th were also killed and two dozen wounded. Afterwards the newspapers came down heavily on General Chute for launching a frontal attack on a Pa he assumed was abandoned. General Chute had responded by leading his troops across the Waingongoro River and destroying seven more Maori villages on a march north. One of the reasons Frank had left the army.

"Are there many such as us in Wellington?" He asked. He'd like to live in a place where he would run into ex-soldiers, men who knew what they'd all been through.

His newfound friend shrugged and shook his head. "Most have settled in the countryside," he said. "With the scrips for land grants and our pensions we can make a good life. I'm hoping to settle near Napier. I hear it's pleasant. You been there?"

Frank had spent the rest of the night regaling him with the beauties of the area, and how the population of Napier was expanding daily with new immigrants from Home.

"Any good for grape growing up there, d'you think? I'd like to start a bit of a vineyard. Not much wine sold now in this country, but one day perhaps...."

"It's not unlike northern Portugal, come to think of it." Frank had not thought of the similarity before. "You might make a go of a vineyard up there, make a decent port wine for the locals. All they're used to drinking is ginger wine so they won't be fussy. Prone to earthquakes up there though. If I were you I'd go to Wanganui. It's a fruit area, and they're already growing grapes there."

He'd not seen the ex-soldier again. He told Frank he was a book salesman and was off to the Wairarapa early the next morning to deliver an order to Marton. Frank hoped he'd turn up in Palmerston one day; he liked the man. If he and Mette moved to Napier, he'd have a ready-made mate.

Later, when he was checking out of the South Sea, there'd been a – what could he call it? A situation involving a self-important colonel, ex British Army. Frank was chatting to the proprietor, an Englishman named Nixon, about life in Wellington, especially for ex-soldiers, when the colonel interrupted them, speaking as if Frank were not there.

"Landlord – I wish to lodge a complaint about the condition of my son's room. The fire wasn't lit and the window was left open. The room was freezing. He almost died of cold"

He'd spoken from behind Frank's back, and Frank had stepped aside to let him move forward, turning towards the man as he did so. He found himself under intense scrutiny from the bulging-eyed, ginger-haired colonel, a look somewhere between shock and dislike, as if he remembered meeting Frank in the past when Frank was taking part in the riotous aftermaths of a battle, or had committed a terrible social *faux pas*.

"And who are you, sir?"

Frank had introduced himself, mentioning his rank and his regiment, as was usual in such circumstances. He couldn't remember ever meeting the man before, and held out his hand towards him. The colonel ignored it, staring at Frank with narrowed eyes. "You were in India?"

"Yes," said Frank. "Back in the late fifties. I don't think we've ever…"

The colonel stared at him for a long minute, then harrumphed, turned on his heel and left the hotel.

"What the hell was that about?" asked Nixon. "Did you murder one of his children?"

"If I knew who he was I might be able to tell you," said Frank. "I can't remember ever seeing him before, let alone meeting him."

"Colonel Humphrey Mountjoy," supplied Nixon. "Ex Indian Army, currently an adviser to the New Zealand government. He served as British Consul in Samoa, and now I hear he has his eye on the governor's job when it comes up next year. But he's an absolute fool, from what I've seen. God help us if he becomes Governor. His wife is the daughter of someone high up in the Admiralty, which should increase his chances. Family is always a determining factor for the English."

Frank shook his head. "Doesn't mean anything to me."

As he left the hotel he saw the colonel and his son boarding a coach. The son was taller than his father, better looking, with a straight athletic body and dark hair, but a sullen face. Frank saw the curtain on the window of the coach twitch, and he wondered if the colonel's wife was inside. She'd have to be handsomer than her husband, to have a son who looked like that.

Sitting in his prison, he tried to think about what he could have done in India that might incur the hatred of the colonel. Nothing came to mind, other than the time he'd been sent undercover to bring back a captain who had gone absent without leave with a native woman. They thought with the proper clothing he could pass for a local, because of the dark skin he'd inherited from his Spanish mother, but it had been tricky and he'd been lucky to get out alive.

Then of course there was the Relief of Lucknow. He'd taken a message from his commanding officer to Lieutenant Mowbray Thomson, in Cawnpore, and arrived just after the Bibighar massacre when all the British women and children who'd been held captive had been massacred. All those dismembered bodies tossed like so much meat into the well...woman and children, one hundred or more, hacked to death by local butchers after the rebel troops declined to do it.

He carried on with the regiment as they marched to Lucknow, all the men in a white rage to relieve the garrison there after so many months, and the slaughter had been ferocious. Not him though. He hadn't killed any of the rebel soldiers. He'd been given the task of protecting a young woman, the daughter or wife of an important person, he couldn't remember who. She'd been a strange woman, high-strung, nervous...Lady...something. She'd broken her ankle escaping from an awkward situation and he'd been sent to bring her out and get her medical attention.

He been helped by her maid, Betty, a sturdy young woman from Devon. She'd been impatient with her mistress for breaking her ankle, and spent hours complaining to Frank what a difficult family she worked for and how much care her lady needed, even without a broken ankle. Frank remembered the mistress as being an attractive woman, fair-haired, an English rose. He hadn't seen either of them after that as he'd returned to his own regiment.

He'd remained in India as the Crown took over from the East India Company in the late fifties, but hadn't kept up with news. Disraeli had recently declared Queen Victoria Empress of India, so he supposed the problems in the sub-continent were done with now. He was there until his regiment, the

57th Foot, were sent to New Zealand in the mid-sixties. The question remained. Was there anything that had happened during those years that would rouse the ire of the colonel?

And was this imprisonment even connected to the colonel? All he'd seen so far was the young Maori woman he'd pulled into his cell; and he'd heard an Irish voice that sounded familiar, and sounds of carbine bolts being shot. Was it an anti-government conspiracy of some kind? Fenians, perhaps? They'd been active in New Zealand in recent years.

Soon after his evening meal arrived he felt a faint tremor underfoot. An earthquake. Earthquakes were frequent in this country, something to be ignored. But this time he was trapped underground. He got up and looked at the trapdoor. If he stood on the upturned slop pail and picked the lock with the brooch pin, maybe, just maybe he could lift himself through the opening if aftershocks made his situation worse.

On the wall near the trapdoor he noticed the tunnel where he'd trapped the weta. If escape became imperative he could force his toe into the weta tunnel and boost himself up. He sat down again and returned to his meal. The frequent earthquakes at worst cracked walls and brought down hillsides. New Zealanders protected themselves from that by building their homes with wood, which swayed during earthquakes but didn't fall. Of course, that meant fires were a hazard instead. He resumed eating and decided not to worry.

A sudden jolt knocked the food basket from his lap and sent the slop pail flying, spilling its contents across the dirt floor. A large crack opened along the wall in front of him, and one of the wooden planks reinforcing the wall buckled, followed by a shower of dirt raining on his feet. He stood, worried. Was he doomed to be buried alive here, with no one ever able to find his body? Would Mette think that he'd deserted her? And what about his father, to whom he seldom wrote? He'd just think his son had forgotten about him, sitting in his cottage on the estate of his employer, with only the badly-painted portrait of his wife to comfort him. He might never know that Frank was dead.

He stepped on the upturned bucket, feeling it push into the dirt with his weight, and picked the lock with the pin. It clicked open and he pushed open the trapdoor with a loud thump. Nothing happened. No one came to close it. He managed to pull himself up above ground level and hold himself for a few minutes before his arms gave way. However, his brief glimpse of the outside showed him things were worse than he thought.

A new smell wafted towards him on the wind, a smell that sent terror into the hearts of settler and Maori alike. Smoke! He was in the bush, and it was burning.

Sounds of men yelling and horses whinnying reached him. He thought he heard women screaming as well, more than one.

He grabbed his coat from the corner of the cell, folded it, and placed it under the slop bucket to stop it sinking with his weight, and to add height and give him better leverage. He threw open to trapdoor and considered his next step. The bucket was still not enough, but by jamming his toe into the weta tunnel he managed to pull himself up enough to get his elbows over the edge of the open trapdoor. He hung there for a minute to consolidate his strength, then, with one tremendous heave, lifted himself up enough to grab hold of one of the slats. From there it was easier, but he was out of breath and gasping, his muscles seizing up, by the time he managed to pull himself out on to the flat area.

He was in a large, sloping clearing with the crossed halberds he had glimpsed earlier sitting menacingly in the centre. Down through the trees he could see a river bustling with activity as men pushed out boats and ran back and forward with supplies. Near the river was an abandoned camp, cooking pots overturned and horses running loose, eyes white with fear. They'd released the horses to let them get away from the flames. A group of Maori women ran from the camp down to the river and back carrying supplies. As he watched, a small totara tree burst into flames, showering sparks on the women, who screamed and beat their clothing.

That sight was bad enough, but the scene uphill filled him with horror.

About a hundred yards away, a row of cells lined a bank between the roots of giant totara, and in each one the face of a man was pressed against the bars. Above them the smoke billowed as the fire raced towards them. They would not be able to see the dark grey smoke yet, but they could certainly smell it. Higher, further up the hill, he glimpsed the outline of a broken lookout tower. The fire must have started up there when the earthquake shook a signal torch loose, or caused someone to drop a lit pipe into dry brush.

"You there, get back in your cell or I'll shoot."

Frank turned. It was the voice he had recognized the first time he heard the carbines being engaged, and now, suddenly, he knew who it was. He turned slowly, his hands raised above his head.

"Wilson?"

The man looked at him, his carbine pointed towards Frank's heart, a man with whom he had once played cards, laughing and joking about bounty heads. Back then, a few short months ago, Wilson was a member of the Armed Constabulary, and apparently still was: he was dressed in a shawl kilt, the bush uniform of the constabulary, and a trooper's hat. If this was a camp run by the Armed Constabulary, they were operating outside the law.

"Wilson?" he said again. "It's me, Sergeant Hardy, Frank Hardy, from Palmerston. Surely you remember me?"

Wilson stared at him blankly, then nodded. But his face was void of emotion. "Yeah mate," he said. "I remember you." He raised his carbine and looked down the barrel at Frank. "Doesn't mean I can let you live though."

Frank had been in close fighting before and knew he should attack before his opponent had time to steady his aim. He didn't wait to reason with Wilson, but threw himself at the sergeant's legs. Wilson stayed on his feet, staggering slightly, but the carbine went off, deafening them both with its noise.

Frank moved before Wilson could raise the gun again – it was a dual action with a second shot already chambered – punching at Wilson's jaw as hard as he could. This time Wilson fell back against the halberd, smacking his skull against one of the axe heads with a loud crack. A line of blood formed on the side of his skull and he slipped to the ground.

Frank was on him instantly, kneeling on his chest. He ripped the gun from his hands and pulled the trigger. The bullet hit the ground fifty yards away, kicking up dirt. He tossed the gun aside and gripped Wilson by the throat. "Now, give me the bloody keys…"

Wilson writhed beneath Frank, trying to free himself. "You're never going to get away. They'll shoot you…"

"I need the keys," said Frank. "There are men up there who're going to die…"

"You're going to let them out?" said Wilson. "Are you insane? You're committing suicide if you go up there. If you don't burn to death those bastards will kill you."

"You can't just leave them to die," said Frank. "You wouldn't treat your dog that way. At least give them a chance, the same way you've done for the horses."

"They're not worth it," said Wilson. "Look Hardy, I'll give you a chance. Start running and I won't raise the alarm. But you can't let the prisoners go."

Frank raised Wilson by his collar and slammed him to the ground. "Give me the damn keys."

He started to lift him again, but Wilson waved his hand weakly and said, "On my belt, underneath me. But it's too late to set them free. The fire is almost… I'm supposed to leave…" He struggled, trying to push Frank off his chest. "They're bad blokes, all of them. Let them burn…"

Frank looked up at the row of cells above them on the slope. The men were screaming now and shaking the bars, pleading to be freed. "I'll get to them," he said. He dragged Wilson onto his front, unhooked the ring of keys from Wilson's belt and backed away.

Wilson staggered to his feet rubbing his head. "You'll die with them you fool. Just be careful who you let out…there's one there…a bad one…"

He took off running down the hill towards the water, stopping to scoop up his carbine on the way. Frank put his handkerchief over his mouth and started uphill towards the oncoming smoke. The men saw him coming and began begging him to release them first, but the only fair way to do it was to let them out in order. He started at the end closest to him.

The first man staggered out and Frank grabbed him by the arm and yelled into his ear, "Run down the hill. Get into the water and swim out as far as you can. When you see flames coming get under the water as much as possible."

The man ran off and Frank released the next one. Soon several of them, a mixture of Europeans and Maori, were tumbling between the trees, down the hill towards the river. The gunshot sounded as the first man he had released reached the water, the noise ricocheting through the trees and back to him from all directions. The runner fell, his legs kicking up behind him, and lay without moving.

"Hell's teeth," he said aloud. "Why not leave them a small chance?"

He grabbed the next two who were about to leave and held them in place, facing him.

"It isn't safe," he said. "They're shooting at us. Go that way." They stared at him with stunned faces, unable to cope with what was happening to them so suddenly. "They'll shoot you down there. Try to reach the water upriver from the boats and get to the other side. That's your best chance."

Even as he spoke another prisoner stumbled past him and ran towards the river. He saw two more bodies fall as a tree above the row of cells suddenly exploded with a loud crack. A spark landed on one of the men and flames shot from him as he screamed in agony. The remaining freed men began running blindly towards the part of the river they could see. They were either going to die in the fire or be shot. But he had to carry on.

He reached the last cell in the side of the hill. It appeared empty at first, and he almost left it locked. No prisoner shook the bars, and he saw only darkness inside. But he thought he heard a noise - the sound of someone speaking quietly. Peering in through the gloom he saw a figure kneeling, his head down as if in prayer. One more, he thought. The last one, and then I can save myself. He unlocked the door, not focusing on the figure. The man did not move, but kept up his prayer.

"For God's sake man, this is no time to pray. Save yourself."

He wrenched open the door and looked in. "Time to go. Quick." His throat felt raspy and he started to cough. "Please…I can't just leave you here to die."

The head raised slowly and the man looked at him. Frank felt a chill run through his veins. Another face he knew well. The last time he had seen it was when the Armed Constabulary were rushing this man away from Papaioea Pa, squatting in a cage that was too small for his massive body. Anahera. Angry brown eyes stared at him from a face covered by moko, etched in the form of an angel – the Angel of Death.

Frank took a step back, but the sound of crackling and an intense blast of heat made him forget about his old foe.

"*Whakaora koe.*" he yelled, gesturing wildly towards the water, but further upstream. "Save yourself. Head away from the boats. Go upriver. The soldiers are shooting us from the river."

He headed downhill at an angle to the boats. Anahera was behind him, running fast, crashing through the undergrowth; he neither knew nor cared what would happen to him. His instinct to survive had taken over. As he reached the riverbank a hundred yards upstream from where the boats where pushing off, Anahera caught up with him. Frank was bent double, gasping and coughing from the smoke, and he waited for the fatal blow on the back of his head. It didn't come. He straightened slowly and looked at Anahera, who returned his gaze, emotionless.

"You should get..." said Frank, gesturing towards the river. "*Haeri atu...*"

Anahera tilted his head backwards and said something. It was drowned out by the sound of a shot; a bullet bounced off the water in front of them three times like a tossed stone. Frank saw a figure standing in the last boat leaving shore. It was Wilson, who had spotted Anahera...the bad one...on the bank. But the single shot was all he had time for. He turned away and screamed at the other men in the boat as they pushed out into the centre of the river.

Turning from Frank, Anahera dived into the water and went under, surfacing a few seconds later in the middle, from where he swam with strong strokes towards the far shore. Frank followed him into the water. He'd worry about what came next when he got to the other side.

6

A Body Surfaces

Karira returned from Foxton the next day, and his news was not good.

"I talked to the men working on the dock and no one saw him disembark," he told Mette. "The Stormbird went on to Wanganui and won't be back in Foxton until next week at the earliest."

"Could you go to Wanganui and talk to people at the port?" she asked.

"I've sent a telegram to the police there," he said. "A constable will meet the boat and talk to the captain and crew."

Mette sat down, her arms wrapped tightly around her body. "Oh Will," she said. "What can have become of him?"

"I did find out one new thing," he said. "It confirms what Agnete said about the large Maori."

"He really exists?" she asked.

"I spoke to a crew member who disembarked in Foxton. He was working as an attendant in the saloon. He said he saw the man Mrs. Madsen described - a large native wearing a high-crowned bowler hat, he said - although he didn't see him speaking with Frank."

"Could he tell you anything about him?" she asked.

"Nothing important," said Karira. "He said he was either a killer or a copper. Said they look the same to him. I'm wondering if he was a special constable. Sometimes the Armed Constabulary hire men from the Native Police to act as guards for important people. The attendant thought the Maori might be guarding someone so that fits with my theory. It seems there was someone important on board, someone who kept to his cabin. He didn't know who it was, and the person didn't disembark in Foxton. I asked about that in my telegraph to the police in Wanganui."

"Do you think it's important?" asked Mette. "How would a special constable talking to Frank mean he would disappear? What would the Constabulary want with him?"

"I have no idea," said Karira. "But I intend to find out. If I had a name for the mysterious person on board the Stormbird, that would be a start. Of course, it may be nothing to do with the Maori constable, if that's what he was. Frank may have disappeared for a completely different reason."

Mette started rocking back and forth. "Oh Will. I don't know how I can bear this."

"Let's talk to Hop," he said. "He has his finger on the pulse of the town. And he'll feed us drop scones with jam. That will make you feel better." Sometimes Will understood her better than Frank. She put the closed sign on the door and hooked her arm through Will's. He patted her hand and said, "Frank will be safe, I know it. Don't worry Mette. He's following up on something and didn't have time to contact us. You know he would have if he'd had time."

Hop Li was fussing around his kitchen mixing up strange

concoctions of fruits and vegetables. He'd planted a kitchen garden with a variety of plants, vegetables and fruit trees – hawthorn, quince and apricot – behind the Royal Hotel and some of it was just coming into season. The kitchen table was covered with piles of rhubarb, gooseberries and strawberries, surrounding a basin of crushed sugar. Mette and Karira watched as he whipped up a batch of pikelets, dropping them on the grill two or three at a time. He served the pikelets hot with quince jam and a dollop of cream scooped from the top of the milk in the billy, which sat on a shelf opened to the outside to catch the cool air.

"Need to keep the milk colder," he grumbled as he mashed sugar into the top milk with a fork and whipped it to a smooth consistency. "Not much ice in this country except in the mountains. Cream goes off quickly. In America, they have ice boxes. Keeps everything cold."

The scones melted in Mette's mouth and calmed her slightly. It reminded her of everything good in the world and for a minute she imagined that Frank was working in his office next door, and not vanished without a trace.

Feeling comforted, she stood to leave just as the door swung open and Constable Price's round pink face appeared. He, too, was a regular in Hop Li's kitchen. In fact, it was becoming the de facto meeting place for the townspeople. He was not there for a social occasion, however, but on an errand, and he managed to shatter her calm with a few words.

"We've found a body."

The three of them stared at him in shock. Was it Frank?

"Who...?" said Karira finally.

"Not sure," said Constable Price. "It's been in the water a long time from what we can see. Can't tell. And no one has been out to bring it in yet. I sent Jimi, my assistant, out there to watch it until we get there."

Karira put his hand on Mette's shoulder, squeezing it tightly.

"It isn't Frank, Mette," he said. "It can't be. He's only been gone a few days."

"I thought you could help me out," said Constable Price to Karira. "You might know who it is, seeing it's in your territory." He looked at Mette and added, "Sergeant Hardy is missing? Is this true?"

"He went to Wellington to fetch Pieter Sorensen's sister and she arrived here without him. We haven't heard from him," said Karira shortly. "What do you mean, my territory?"

"Ah," said Price. "Sorry. I mean the body is in the river beside the Papaioea Pa. I thought it might be someone you know, considering. Would you come along and help me identify him?"

Mette bit her lip and said, "I'd like to come as well please Constable Price. I want to be sure it isn't Frank."

Constable Price glanced at Karira and said, "Of course, if you must. It may be an upsetting sight, you know."

"Miss Jensen is a resilient woman," said Karira, smiling reassuringly at Mette.

"One other thing," said Constable Price. "That Karlsen fellow, the one who's been in town looking for his brother. He overheard me talking about the body with the mayor, and he'd like to come along as well. His brother Gottlieb has been missing for a while, and it may very well be his body."

Mette shivered. She'd thought things could not get any worse. She caught Karira's eye and looked away. Of course it would be Gottlieb's body. Who else could it be? And what would happen to them all once Gottlieb was found? Constable

Price would see the gash in his head made by the tomahawk and would start investigating what he would assume was his murder. And he'd know that Gottlieb had disappeared when the Gorge was closed off at either end by the Constabulary looking for Anahera. It would take no time at all for him to realize that Frank had been driving his coach through the Gorge at the right time, just days after he'd beaten Gottlieb.

They formed a small party, Constable Price and Karira on horseback, Frederic Karlsen and Mette in a borrowed pony trap, as they rode out to the pa.

The state of the pa shocked Mette. Most of the buildings, including the beautiful red-ochre meeting house with the wood carvings on the front, were gone, pulled down by workmen who were levelling the land, making it ready to be sold as sections for smaller homesteads. Further away from the river, the dry winter bush had been burned in preparation for crops, although it would take some time to make it completely ready. On the north side, horses and drays were ploughing land where potato and kumara had once flourished. The palisade with its zig-zag entranceway was also gone, replaced by a heap of rubble and rocks to be used for the road that would pass through the centre. Two small whare, the huts families slept in, still stood at one end, near the river, and a cluster of Maori women and children sat in front of them watching Mette and her group with empty gazes.

They stopped near a small jetty lined with canoes, where Constable Price's assistant waited for them.

"Now then, Jimi," said Price. "Show us where the body is. Who found it?"

A sturdy young Maori girl with dark wavy hair parted in the centre and cascading below her shoulders came from the trees at the edge of the river. She was holding a bundle of washing. "I did," she said. "I was washing clothes further up the river and saw a body rise up and move this way. I followed it until it stuck on the logs out there, then sent my little brother into town to tell Constable Price. It's there, you can see it from here." She pointed out to the middle of the river where what looked like an inflated plaid shirt twisted gently in the current, trapped by a stack of logs swept down from the logging camp. The back of a tow-coloured head bobbed above the shirt.

Karira removed his boots, pulled up his trousers and waded out.

"I can't get it from here, but it looks like another Scandi..." He stopped and looked back at Mette.

"*Min Gud*," she said, her hand on her heart. "Could it be Jens at last?"

Karlsen pushed forward. "No. It's my brother, I'm sure of it. Those are the very clothes he would have been wearing."

How he knew that was unclear, as he hadn't seen his brother for years. But for Mette, it didn't matter if it was Jens or Gottlieb; both were terrible possibilities for different reasons. She translated for the rest of the group and Constable Price nodded.

"Could very well be," he said. "One or the other. Someone needs to go out and pull him in. Jimi?"

"Not me sir," said Jimi. "I can't swim."

"I'll go," said Karira. "But I'm not getting my clothes wet if you don't mind."

He stripped off his shirt and trousers and stood there in his cotton underwear, much to Mette's embarrassment. The young Maori woman was not so shy, and moved forward, eying the near-naked Karira interestedly. "Willi Karira looks better without his pants on than I realized," she said to Mette.

He dived in with a clean slice that hardly broke the surface and came out further into the river, downstream from where the body was caught, and then turned and swam back against the current, making headway.

Mette moved beside the young woman. "Are you from the pa?"

The woman nodded, her eyes lingering on Karira a moment before she turned to Mette. "I'm Wiki, Wikitoria. I saw you here before."

"I don't remember you…"

Wiki smiled. "You were with my grandmother," she gestured with her head towards the group sitting in front of the two whare. "She told me about you, but I saw you across the Marae as well. You were interested in our food and the way we cooked it. My grandmother said they called you Hine Raumati, the summer woman."

"Yes, that was me," said Mette. "My name it Mette." She held out her hand to Wiki, who took it and shook it firmly. In the water, Karira was gradually making headway towards the body. "Do you know Will?"

"Willi Karira and I grew up together," said Wiki. "But he's five years older than me. And he always acted as if he was better than the rest of us. His father was chief…and he went off to England to go to school." She put her hand above her eyes so she could see him better against the reflection. "We were lucky that Moana, the wife of the chief, made us learn English, or…"

"Why are you and your family still at the pa? I heard you say your grandmother and your brother, but is your mother here? Or your father?"

"My mother left to stay with her hapu, her extended family, up north – with Moana. We need to find a place in town before she comes back. And we can't," said Wiki. "Nothing. Nobody will rent to us. That's my grandmother over there, the old woman. And my two younger brothers. The others are just part of our hapu. We don't have much room. I sleep with all the old…with my grandmother and the other women in one whare and my brothers – I have two of them unfortunately – share the other one. The boys have plenty of room. I don't know why they don't let me share with them."

"I could help you find a place," said Mette. "And Will would help…"

There was a shout from the river.

Karira had reached the body, where it was caught in a tumble of logs lodged against a sandbank. He moved the logs, and grabbed the body by the shirt. A pull and it came loose, flipped over and floated free.

"You won't want to look at this," he called to Mette. "I think it's Karlsen, Gottfried Karlsen." She was the only one who understood fully what he was saying, and she turned away and walked back up the bank, stopping at a distance. Her new friend came with her, holding her arm solicitously.

Karira swam ashore, pulling the body with him, or what was left of it as eels had been feasting on the face. But the shirt was intact, and Mette remembered it clearly. The last time she had seen it, the wearer had tried to push her to her death into the raging waters of the Manawatu Gorge. She felt bilious about the thought of seeing him again.

Constable Price helped Karira drag the body to the mud

A BODY SURFACES

flats at the edge of the river and turn him over. The eyes were gone and the skin hung in strips, but it was certainly Gottlieb; the face, with mouth pulled back in a horrible grin, showed uneven, loose and discoloured teeth. On one side of his head a large deep gash cut through his hair, exposing his skull.

Constable Price said the words that confirmed it for her: "Looks like someone hit him with a tomahawk."

Frederic Karlsen stepped out into the mud, ignoring the damage to his boots. "Ah, *mein Bruder, mein Bruder, was haben sie dir angetan?*"

He knelt beside the horrible remains and looked at the mark on the side of his brother's head, where the tomahawk Frank had thrown to save Mette had cleaved it open. Then he looked up at Karira, his eyes glowing with anger, and said in German, "You see? It is just as I told you. He has been killed by a Maori with a tomahawk. And you insisted it was some plot by the Armed Constabulary."

Mette translated. Karira ran his hands through his hair to remove the water and stared at Karlsen in astonishment. "Uh, yes - *ja* -I suppose…"

Once more Constable Price loaded a body into a small canoe and paddled towards home, as he had done with Paul Nissen a few short weeks ago. Mette watched him go, and thought about Jens, her poor cousin and friend. Paul had appeared from the depths of the river, and now so too had Gottlieb. But where was Jens? An idea bumped around at the edge of her brain, a faint memory, but she could not grasp hold of it. Somehow, she knew what had become of Jens, but…

By the time they reached Palmerston, Karlsen had changed his theory one more time. He had merged the two theories, making them into an even larger conspiracy.

"What I believe has happened," he said, staring intently at Mette, "is that the Armed Constabulary have hired a Maori warrior to kill Gottlieb. He is somewhat like a gun for hire in a Karl May novel, only he carries a tomahawk. Now we must look to see if we can find such a man. Perhaps you have saloons in Palmerston, where the gunslingers hang out?"

Mette explained to Karira what the new theory was.

"The good thing is that if he ever comes up with the truth no one will believe him," said Karira. "It will just be viewed as another of his crazy ideas."

Karlsen looked at Karira suspiciously, his eyes narrowing. They'd need to be careful. He could understand more than they realized. German and English were not that different,

Before Mette could say anything to Frederic, a vision appeared on the verandah of the Royal Hotel to distract him: Agnete, wearing a sultan red dress, cut short at the front hem to reveal the toes of her boots, and trailing low behind in a manner entirely unsuitable for the Palmerston mud. The vision was topped off by a pale grey bonnet with a coronet brim and an elaborate puffed crown cap, of a style unseen in Palmerston, although reported on in the *Manawatu Times*. Frederic Karlsen took of his broad-brimmed hat and swept it before him in a deep bow. He was clearly impressed with what he saw and eager to impress in return. His brother was forgotten for the moment.

"Agnete, Mrs. Madsen, allow me to introduce to you to Mr. Frederic Karlsen of Melbourne, Australia," said Mette. Agnete did something strange with her lips and fluttered her eyelashes at Karlsen. If she had a parasol in her hand she could have twirled it, thought Mette, and then the scene would be perfect – or perfectly awful.

She left them to get to know each other and hurried back to the book shop. She'd been gone for almost two hours and knew she had neglected her duties. To her dismay, the "Open" sign was on the door and Mr. Robinson was moving around inside.

"Goodness me, my dear, you look very worried," he said.

"I, I'm very sorry," she said. "But a body was found out by the pa and I was afraid it was Frank, my fiancé."

"You have some reason to believe Sergeant Hardy has come to harm?" he asked.

Mette spilled out the whole story. Half way through he stopped her and insisted that she sit down and catch her breath.

"If only I'd known," he said. "I'm quite able to leave my bookshop in Foxton and stay here for the week. You must be available in case you are called upon. Please do not come in for the rest of the week. And don't worry about money. I'll pay you as usual."

Mette sniffed and squeezed Mr. Robinson's hand in gratitude. He was the nicest man she'd ever met, and she knew he meant well. But staying in her room at the back of the book shop, or with her sister in the clearing, would not help at all. She would just worry about Frank all the time, especially now that she'd seen what the river could do to a body. An image of him floating to the surface of the river was constantly in her mind, and it took all her willpower to push it away.

7

No Signs of Life

Frank came up from the depths of the river into a flaming vortex. The forest he'd just left was consumed by fire, trees exploding with loud cracks. Flames shot out above the water, followed by showers of sparks. A wall of heat hit his face. He pushed himself under the surface and swam as far as he could towards the other bank without coming up for a breath. The flames had not yet crossed the river but the heat was intense. Downstream where the boats had been moored he could see one large canoe engulfed in flames, another sitting empty but for some large smouldering bundles which have once been human. But the rest of the boats were gone. Two bodies floated face down in the water beside the burning canoes, one with steam rising from its back as if the fellow had been on fire and jumped into the river to save himself. On land, there was no sign of life. The chances of any of the prisoners Frank had freed escaping were remote. He hoped the women had been taken off in the boats and not burned to death beside the cooking pots where he'd last seen them.

 He'd surfaced near a clump of kuta reeds, and he wrenched out a stem and broke it at each end as best he could to reveal the hollow interior. With the addition of the kuta tube he could stay under the water for longer periods. They'd called the same stuff sedge when he was a boy, and he'd often swum under the water breathing through the stem for play.

He worked his way downstream, staying submerged for as long as he could with his makeshift breathing tube, keeping a lookout for falling branches and sparks.

Eventually he got beyond the burn, which was moving away from him and upriver, and into calmer waters. He caught the current and floated on his back for a while, letting the river take him downstream, watching for clues to his whereabouts. He'd been captured by the Armed Constabulary, obviously, and they'd taken him to the same prison where they kept their worst offenders. The Wanganui River then, but what part of the Wanganui River? The rumours he'd heard about the mysterious Armed Constabulary prison had not been specific. Beyond the reach of the paddleboats most likely, and up into the ranges, but not so far upriver to be accessible to the Maori King Movement in the upper reaches of the Wanganui River.

What puzzled him most was why he of all people have been taken to that prison. If he'd done anything wrong in his life, it certainly wasn't recently. His life had been dull and without action for at least three years, until he'd run into Mette – or more correctly, until she'd run into him. What they'd been through together had surely not come back to kick him in the head.

After the Armed Constabulary had captured Anahera and taken him away in a cage, his old commander Captain Porter had written to him from Poverty Bay, thanking him for his assistance in the capture. He'd noted that the Poverty Bay tribes had calmed down to such an extent that he was considering a run for mayor of Gisborne and forgoing his duties with the volunteer force.

But more pertinent, why would the Armed Constabulary be involved if this was about the rebellion? He'd heard from other sources that the Gisborne settlers were still worried about Te Kooti, but Titokowaru and his followers had turned to pacifism, and Manawatu was considered safe, other than the occasional peg removal from the settlers' lands and other nuisances.

What was it Anahera had said, just before he dived into the river? One word. Utu? Frank remembered Ringiringi, the army deserter who'd gone over to the other side, to the rebels, telling him what that meant. Revenge? No, not exactly revenge. More like…balance. Had he been saying they were even now? That he would no longer try to kill Frank? Small solace.

He floated further, enjoying the crispness of the water. What about the colonel in the South Sea Hotel and his strange reaction? What was that about? Had something happened in India? Seemed farfetched. His memory was good, and he could not recall any awful event, like the one that drove Anahera, anywhere in his own past. Was it something he knew or had seen? And if it was related to the colonel, was it something that happened in India, or more recently in New Zealand.

The light faded. He dragged himself from the river into a quiet spot in the bush and made himself a place to spend the night. The usual bush fare was there to sustain him, and he chewed on young fern roots and huhu grubs without trying to think too much about what was in his mouth. When he'd done, he flattened some ferns and made himself a rough bed. No need for precautions. There were a few wild pigs in the bush, and rats and possums, eels in the river, but nothing threatening. Man was the most dangerous animal in New Zealand.

As the night turned to total blackness, he lay in his bed of ferns thinking about the events of the past week. Some memories had resurfaced. He remembered being on the Stormbird, and how much he wanted to avoid Agnete Madsen. He'd left the saloon level soon after they boarded and bumped into someone large in the doorway -an image of a meaty hand grabbing him by the shoulder. Had he talked to the man? He didn't know. But the memory of a distinctive hat – a bowler of some kind – hovered in the back of his mind.

The next memory was of a boat; not the Stormbird, but a smaller boat, a rowboat he thought, or a ship's lifeboat. He'd awoken with a pounding headache, and had vomited over the side of a rowboat. That memory was brief, but he thought he'd felt a dress brushing against his leg, the swish of silk. He must be remembering Agnete Madsen. Why would a woman take part in a kidnapping, especially in a rowboat? Had he gone voluntarily? Had someone asked for his help and then grabbed him? That possibility was ridiculous. Enough that he'd been kidnapped; adding someone, a woman possibly, who sought his help before he was kidnapped stretched credulity.

Morning came and he was awakened by the dawn chorus, hundreds of song birds starting their day with their musical chirps. He recognized the song of larks, mingled with those of the black feathered huia, and the aggressive chatter of a parson bird with its call of tui, tui, and it lifted his spirits. Now his clothes were dry, he was reluctant to go back in the water.

A rudimentary track ran alongside the river and he followed it downstream. He'd lost both his boots while escaping the fire, but his feet were protected by thick woollen socks, which made the hike bearable.

The land flattened gradually and he realized he was close to Wanganui. The days were long now, and the light would linger until nine o'clock, so he pushed on, hoping to reach town before darkness came.

The sun still sat well above the horizon when he finally came upon the outskirts of town. He recognized the cemetery, and heard noises coming from a raised area he knew was Cook's Gardens. He climbed up to the gardens, concealed himself behind a row of poplars, and saw a group of volunteers – probably the Wanganui Rifles – practising with bayonets. He didn't know how he stood with soldiers, volunteers or otherwise and stayed hidden. Every small town in the country had such a group of volunteers, and he'd often wondered about the effectiveness of using untrained men like those. Was it worth training them? It would be difficult to instill the military discipline, so necessary during a fight, into a motley group of volunteer shop keepers and farmers. Especially as the hovering presence of physical punishment did not exist for volunteers.

A sergeant, obviously one with some actual military experience, was demonstrating the way to run at a large bag swinging from a pole, plunge in a bayonet, pull the bayonet out and keep going. While some couldn't stick the bag at all, some of the younger men were able to run towards it and stab at it ferociously after stopping first and lining up the bag. One young man who managed to impale the bag performed a fling afterwards, as if the whole thing was a game. Frank wondered what he would do if he was faced with an armed, experienced warrior who continued moving towards him rather than swinging gently back and forward on a pole.

As if reading his thoughts, the sergeant bellowed, "Give it a good swing and hit it again. It isn't going to be so easy when a mad savage is coming at you with a spear."

The young man gave the bag a hard push, and, as Frank expected, was hit by the bag on the rebound before he could get his bayonet in position. He walked back to the line of waiting men to jeers and shouts, his shoulders slumped.

Further away from the river he came upon the playing fields of Wanganui Collegiate. He'd always thought that if he had a son one day he'd send him to Wanganui Collegiate, one of the finest boys' schools in New Zealand. A cricket game was in progress and he stopped to watch, happy to be in a civilized place again where a game of cricket was all men were fighting about.

Shouts of "A six, a six," drifted towards him, followed by a cricket ball coming at him from on high. Without thinking, he cupped his hands and caught it effortlessly. The ball whacked against his bare skin with a satisfying sting. It felt good. Normal.

Two men ran up, both too old to be schoolboys – early twenties, perhaps?

"Good catch, sir," said one.

But the other sneered. "Lucky catch, I'd say. This fellow has clearly never played a game of cricket in his life."

"Give it a rest, Mountjoy," said his companion, a young man dressed in cricket whites, with light brown hair flopping across his eyes. "Begging your pardon sir. This is a game of Old

Boys against the First Eleven, and we're struggling to keep up with them. If you've had any experience, we could do with assistance."

"Only Old Boys in this match," said the one named Mountjoy. "Those are the rules. And look at the man. Surely, Masterson, you wouldn't want our team to be represented by a tramp…"

"If he knows how to play I would," said the irrepressible Masterson. He winked at Frank. "I'm sure he was a cricket player and a gentleman before he was a beggar. A veritable W.G. Grace by the size of him and the beard…"

In response, Frank retreated a few steps, took a run and threw the ball high into the air, watching as it faded towards the inner field, where it was caught by another of the Old Boys, whose team members yelled out their appreciation. The two runners for the First Eleven were doing their bit, running between wickets, tapping the creases at each end with their bats; an Old Boy caught the ball and hurled it at the wicket, knocking the bails off the stumps; whoops and cheers echoed across the field, accompanied by the ref's voice: "Out!"

Mountjoy glared at Masterson, turned and stamped back towards the pitch.

"Sorry," said Masterson, looking apologetic. "Mountjoy is a first-class chump. He thinks because he's new out from England…technically he's not even an Old Boy himself. He landed on us a few days ago and Reverend Harvey took him on as a house tutor, because he went to Harrow, and his grandfather…"

"Never mind," said Frank. "I don't usually dress like this, but I've had an adventure on the river and my clothing has suffered for it."

Masterson looked him up and down. "Do you need a bed

for the night?" he asked. "No questions asked, I promise. My cottage is on the school grounds. Sit with our side until the end of the match and then come back to my place for a meal and a bed. And shoes, perhaps. You look as if you could do with something to put on your feet. Those socks are almost worn through. I probably have an old pair of shoes that would fit you, and socks of course. As you can see, although I'm not as tall as you, I do suffer from very large feet."

"Thank you, that's very kind Mr....Masterson, is it?"

"Reverend Masterson," said his benefactor. "John. I teach Latin at the school, perform the occasional wedding or funeral, and take care of the rose garden in my spare time. Not really an Old Boy, but they tolerate me because I'm good with the bat. Most of these chaps are decent enough. Don't pay any attention to Mountjoy. He's a fool."

Frank watched as the last minutes of the game played out. The First Eleven won without much of an effort, despite the assistance he'd given the Old Boys. The men took him into their midst as if they had known him all their lives – except Mountjoy, who continued to either ignore Frank or scowl at him as if he was a hated rival.

Frank had recognized him, both his name and his face. And he knew who his father was as well. This...fool...was the son of Colonel Mountjoy, the very man who'd been upset by his presence at the South Sea Hotel. He remembered Mountjoy interrupting his own discussion with the proprietor, complaining about the state of his son's room, and then boarding a coach with his son. For some reason the sight of Frank standing at the desk had thrown the colonel off and he had not pursued his complaint. The son had clearly inherited his father's rude nature, but what had he done to set them against him? Was it his lack of status, or were they rude to everyone equally?

He stared at the man, barely a man really, probably no older than Paul and Jens, the two boys who had vanished in the Manawatu River back in July. He was dark-haired with intense brown eyes. A handsome fellow if he could just do something about the nasty sneer that had taken up permanent residence on his face. Something about him was familiar though. What was it? More than just the brief encounter at the hotel. Even then, although he'd not thought much about it, he'd felt a twinge of recognition.

The men were to have a photograph taken while there was still light, and as he watched the young man interacting coolly with the rest of the team he realized who the man resembled. Will, his own brother Will, murdered by the Hauhau many years ago.

His brother Will had belonged to the same regiment as Frank, the Die Hards, the 57th Regiment, when they saw action during the Taranaki Wars. Will had run into trouble with his corporal and rather than take the consequences had defected to the enemy. The result had been that the enemy had beheaded him and displayed the head on a pole across the river from where Frank and his men were bivouacked; Frank had spent some time obliterating the awful thing with shots from his Enfield rifle musket.

It was an awful memory and he was sorry to be reminded of it by this churlish young man. Like Mountjoy, Will had been a young man with a grudge against the world in which he found himself. But he directed his ire at those above him, rather than those beneath him on the social hierarchy. Of course, Will and Frank were lower status than Mountjoy, but that should no longer matter in New Zealand, a country where every man was equal to every other man and any citizen over the age of twenty-one had a vote. Recent immigrants were buying land and accumulating wealth regardless of where they came from; Pieter and Maren were good examples of that.

He was still thinking about his brother as the two teams of young men lined up three deep to pose for a photograph taken by Reverend Masterson, who apparently had more skills than simply Latin and cricket. Frank had never had his own image captured and he stood behind Masterton to watch. Some of the young men in the First Eleven struck a pose, cricket bats over their shoulders, and one lay down in front of the group, his bat propped up at right angles to the ground. Masterson held up one hand, and the men froze in those awkward positions for several seconds, while Masterson slide the plate into the back of the camera. Three or four seconds later it was done.

"Stand down," Masterson called cheerfully. "Now the Old Boys…take your places…" He said quietly to Frank, "This lot will be much more difficult. They're much more concerned about how they're going to appear to future generations."

The Old Boys sorted themselves into rows, laughing and jostling, each arranging himself in the most flattering position, some with thumbs hooked into vest pockets, others standing in profile to capture their good sides for eternity. Mountjoy had no such qualms, but stood with his shoulders squared, staring at the camera unsmiling, reminding Frank once more of Will when he was unhappy about something. He shook his head, wondering why some men could never be pleased with their lot in life, even when it was such an elevated one. This young man had even less reason than Will to be unhappy.

Frank and the reverend shared a bachelors' meal: some cold slices of mutton and a large chunk of three-day old bread, washed down with several glasses of ginger beer, which Frank was starting to enjoy almost as much as the real thing. It had been some time since he'd tasted anything quite so delicious. Nothing like abstinence to improve the taste of food.

He discovered a common background with the reverend, who had grown up near Farnham in Surrey and been schooled at Rugby. Frank had trained at the Aldershot Garrison, not far from Farnham, before being sent to Crimea as a lad. And his father's employer had sent his sons to Rugby, the public school made famous by Thomas Hughes in a book published shortly after the end of the Crimean War. Masterson had been there later than the two sons, but thought he'd heard of them. He and Frank also shared an interest in the use of force and how it contributed, or not, to the British role in the world. The reverend though religion was the key to change. Frank was not so sure.

Frank brought up the recruits he'd seen on the parade ground at Cook's Gardens earlier that day. "If Titokowaru or another Hauhau rebel were to return to Wanganui those men would be next to useless," he said.

"It's not likely to happen, though, is it?" asked the reverend. "Things have been quiet here for almost a decade. The volunteers are just for show, don't you think? To keep the natives on their toes?"

"Things are still shaky in some parts of the country," said Frank. "An old captain of mine who lives up in Gisborne wrote to me saying they'd recently had a scare with Te Kooti. They called in the volunteers and waited all night on the barricades, then discovered they'd been given false information. Te Kooti was still in the Ureweras and not on the way to slaughter them all in their beds. Just nervousness, I'd say."

"I hear that Titokowaru has turned to peace and preaches tolerance and the union of our two peoples," said Masterson. "That's a good thing, isn't it? They're a god-fearing people now, the Maori."

Frank nodded, thinking about Anahera. It was true that many warriors had turned to peaceful means, but not all of them. He'd seen Anahera praying, and couldn't believe that meant he'd turned away from revenge. It was more likely that he was using prayer to calm himself for the fight, or to ask for God's help in his battle. How he felt about Frank was another matter.

Masterson interrupted his reverie to ask if he'd like to watch him develop the photographs of the two teams, but Frank yawned and said he was tired. He was interested in photography, in any new inventions, but he didn't need to learn the minutiae. He couldn't imagine he'd ever have need of a photograph. Perhaps one of Mette…

He left Masterson in front of a small but ferocious fire, contentedly smoking his briar pipe. Everything was for the best in this best of all possible worlds for Masterson.

After a difficult night on a monastically hard bed that was several inches too short for him, Frank awakened early the next morning. He was up before the birds but not before his host, who was ready with strong tea, bread and marmalade, and a selection of boots and shoes laid out for Frank. He picked a dusty old pair of Blucher boots reinforced with hobnails in the soles, worn but serviceable. They were snug, but the toe caps of both had split, making room for his big toe.

He arrived at Market Square just as the town was rousing itself for a new day, shopkeepers sweeping off boardwalks and opening shutters, ready to display and sell their goods. As he'd hoped, a Cobb's Coach sat in Market Square about to leave for Bulls, Fielding and Palmerston. Cobb's was not an official mail carrier, but often carried mail, and Frank knew some of the drivers. Not this driver, however. He was a heavily built, surly looking chap dressed in a blue greatcoat not unlike the one Frank had left to the flames of his prison cell. Frank approached him tentatively and made himself known.

"Looking for a free ride to Palmerston then?" the coachman said shrewdly. "No money?"

Frank shook his head and showed the few coins he still had in his pocket. The coachman gave a barking laugh, throwing back his head and showing a mouth full of teeth whose rotting centres had been plugged with gold leaf. Frank reached into his pocket tentatively and took out the butterfly brooch. It was all he had left that was worth anything, and he hated to part with it, knowing he'd not get anything near what he'd paid for it. He'd been looking forward to giving it Mette.

"I picked this up in Wellington, at Te Aro House," he said. "Silver inlaid with indigo gemstones. Cost me five quid. You should be able to get at least three."

The coachman took it and turned it over in his hand. "Pretty thing, isn't it. For a lady friend, is it?" He looked back at Frank with eyes narrowed, assessing him. "Take you to Bulls then," he said, his hand closing over the brooch. "No further though. Picking up a group of ladies bound for a temperance meeting in Wellington, and can't be having a rough bloke like you on board. Best I can do."

Frank accepted reluctantly and watched the brooch disappear into the pocket of the coachman's greatcoat. One day he'd find another one just like it.

There were only two other passengers in the coach, a mature couple who sat not talking, even to each other, she in a poke bonnet and yellowed-lace shawl, sitting on one side of the coach, he with a dove grey coat and tall hat, which he held on his knee, on the other side. At Aramoho, a few miles along the Wanganui River, they heard a thundering of hooves approaching. Frank shrank back in his seat, making sure he could not be seen. However, the man rose and leaned out the window, dropping his hat on the floor of the coach in his excitement. A group of horsemen went by in a cloud of dust.

"Armed Constables," he said, as he sat back down. "In a hurry. Something must have happened. Don't see them in a group like that very often."

"He loves the sight of uniformed men on horses," said the woman. "He came to New Zealand twenty years ago to fight against the Maori. The army wouldn't take him though. Bad feet. Bumps on his heels made it hard for him to march. And he never did learn to ride."

"We've done well, though, haven't we?" said the man. "Didn't have two pence to rub together when we got here, and now we have a nice bit of land. I import whisky from Glasgow." He looked at Frank's boots, with the toes sticking out, and said encouragingly, "You'll do well eventually, just you wait and see."

The drive to Bulls took almost three hours, the coach stopping every few miles to pick up patrons or drop off mail. At the Whangaehu River they picked up an old Maori woman wrapped in a blanket with a woven flax basket she kept held to her chest. She sat on the top of the coach as it crossed the river on a ferry punt and said nothing, chewing at her lower lip, which was etched with blue lines of *moko* that ran from her lip down her chin. When she descended on the other side of the river, helped down by the coachman, her basket started to squawk and she stared ahead, ignoring the sound as if it was coming from someone else.

"Chooks," said the coachman, watching her hurry away. "Wonder where she got those then? They steal them from the settlers' farms on the other side of the river and bring them over here, these old Maori women. Then they sell the eggs to the settlers, who're wondering why their own chooks don't lay such good ones. Quite the business, I reckon. Supply and demand, like Adam Smith said."

At Bulls, Frank was once more on foot. A mere twenty-five miles from Palmerston, and he'd have to walk. Another night under the stars and he was tired of it. Wishing he'd demanded some cash for the brooch, he used his last few coins to buy a packet of ginger nuts and an apple at the grocers and set off towards Palmerston, munching away at his sparse meal.

He'd walked as far as Sanson, a good two-hour walk, when he was overtaken by a man in a pony trap. His clothes and general manner gave the impression that he might be a policeman, and Frank realized he would have to watch his words.

"I can give you a ride as far as the Ashhurst Road, just past Bunnythorpe," the man said. "I'm off through the Gorge. Will that suit you?" He held out his hand to Frank. "Constable Farmer from Woodville."

Frank shook hands then jumped up beside the man. "Woodville?"

"On t'other side of the Gorge," said Farmer. "And you are...?"

"Frank...Frank Smith," he said. "Heading south. Thought I might stop in Palmerston to pick up a bit of work. I hear there's work in the saw mills."

The constable looked at him sideways.

"Iffen you're a Scandi," he said. "That's all they hire in the sawmills in Palmy. Road work too. Take care of their own, they do, the Scandies."

"I'll find something," said Frank. "I can turn my hand to anything. What are you doing so far from home?"

"Been up to Wanganui," said the constable. "To report on a murder I investigated. The Ollandt murder. Heard about it, did you?"

Frank remembered Mette telling him about a recent murder when he had picked her up in Woodville two months ago. "Can't say as I have."

"Been all over the papers," said Farmer. "He was killed by his partner, Hans Thomsen, a Scandi. We took a search party out to look for Ollandt's body...he'd been missing for some hours...and Thomsen lead us right to it, and described it before he was close enough to see, unless he had eyesight like an eagle. Called out to us, he did, saying, 'What a horrible sight,' when even the sharpest of eyes couldn't see what he was looking at. He knew what we would find. Then we found blood on his pillow..."

"You got him right away, then," said Frank. "Easy bust..."

"Took a bit of smart detection," said Farmer, bristling. "Course it's not as bad as those murders in Palmerston, the ones by that Hauhau. Haven't heard of those either, I suppose. T'was in the papers as well."

Frank shook his head. Anahera, the Hauhau *rebel* who

had chased Mette from the bush, who had made three separate murderous attacks on Frank, and had killed his friend Sergeant Jack Jackson? No, he'd never heard of that Hauhau.

"They say he's escaped from prison again," said the constable. "Got a telegram about it at the division in Wanganui. Him and some other bad ones. There was a fire up the Wanganui River where he was being kept, and some of them escaped."

"How would anyone know?" asked Frank. "Wouldn't people have been burned? Could they tell who was missing?"

Constable Farmer glanced at him suspiciously. "There was a sergeant there, name of Wilson. With the Armed Constabulary. He said at least a couple of them escaped, and he thought the Hauhau was one of them. Don't know how he knew, but they're on the lookout for him, for them…two probably."

"You think they're dangerous, these men?" asked Frank. "I mean, are we likely to run into them?"

"No idea," said Constable Farmer. "But that Hauhau, if I was him I'd be heading up river to the King Country. Maybe find his way to Te Kooti in the Ureweras. Not this way. We're safe here I should think."

"And the other one?" asked Frank.

Constable Farmer shrugged. "Didn't say much about him. Just some European thug. No description or anything. Could be anyone." He looked sideways at Frank. "Could be you."

"Not likely," said Frank. "Never been in trouble with the law. Specially not with the Armed Constabulary. I wonder what he did?"

The constable shrugged. "No idea. Have to be something bad if he was in that prison though."

"It's for bad ones then, is it?" asked Frank.

"The worst of the worst," said the constable. "I wonder

why the constables didn't shoot them all before they left...not worth saving, any of them."

Frank had no answer for that.

Coming over a low hill they saw the shape of the new town of Bunnythorpe stretching out on the plains below them. New homes were going up, some of wood, and a few soddies – built with clods of earth reinforced with totara ridge poles, window frames stuffed with rags and dried grass to allow room for settling. Frank had seen soddies before up in Patea, and knew how well they worked in the New Zealand climate. Like so many places in this district, the homes were surrounded by swaths of burned tree stumps and scraggly bush, but the outlines of farms pegged out by surveyors for eager new landowners were visible.

As they came closer to the new town, he heard the echoing sound of hammering. A house with a floor, a section of roof and a rudimentary wall was going up on the left side of the road; a man he recognized was attaching planks to studs he'd already erected.

"My God," he said. "It's Pieter." He turned to his companion, hoping he hadn't heard him say a name, and said as casually as he could. "I'll get down here. Maybe I can get a bit of work and a bed for the night with that bloke over there. Looks like he could do with a hand."

Constable Farmer was preoccupied with the road and did not appear to hear what Frank had said, but he pulled back on the reins and let him down. Frank watched as he went on his way towards the Gorge. Farmer would have a lot on his mind, with the murder and the need to make the difficult journey through to Woodville. He'd not be likely to report that he'd seen a suspicious character on the road who claimed to be new to the district but recognized a local farmer.

8

A Trip to Bunnythorpe

Pieter and Maren were busy spending the inheritance that had not yet arrived from Denmark, and had purchased a small section of partly-cleared land in Bunnythorpe, on the Crown Lands that had been put up for auction two years earlier. The small 40-acre section was part of a larger holding purchased by an absentee landlord who was selling off pieces of it as they were cleared by Scandinavians, making a nice profit without the inconvenience of having to do physical work. Pieter had checked the soil, and been excited about the timber he would be able to sell to the Feilding sawmill to allow him to stock the land with dairy cows. He also liked the fact that it was at the junction from which railway lines radiated to Napier, Wanganui and Foxton. He could already picture himself selling milk and cheese to all those places.

Pieter no longer worked at the sawmill, but spent his days building a house for his growing family, often sleeping at the site to save the travel time. Maren visited Mette in the book shop and moaned about how she missed him. Mette found it hard not to remind her sister that she had reason to miss Frank even more, as no one had any idea where he had gone.

The Wanganui police had telegraphed saying they'd checked the SS Stormbird and found nothing, and that no important person had disembarked that they knew of. Karira had gone to Wanganui to do his own search. "I know Constable Crozier in Wanganui took it seriously," he told Mette. "But I prefer to see for myself, and talk to people up there. A telegraph doesn't allow me ask the questions I want, or to see how people respond."

He'd be gone for several days and all she could do was wait. Not having to go to work at the book shop made things worse, so she went in to help Mr. Robinson take inventory of his books and magazines, with the understanding that she could leave instantly if necessary. She was arranging a pile of her own little leaflets, entitled *Mette's Kitchen: Cooking in the Bush*, and working out how many of them had sold at a shilling apiece, when Pieter came through the door. He took off his hat and nodded at Mr. Robinson, avoiding the piles of books like they would jump at him and demand to be read, something he was not able to do.

"Mette." He said. "Maren says you should come to Bunnythorpe with me."

"Now?" she said. "I'm busy, Pieter, I have..."

"Nonsense," said Mr. Robinson. "Go, Mette. It will do you good to have an outing. You've been downcast all day. I insist, in fact."

She'd expected Mr. Robinson to back her up, and was a little annoyed when he forced her to go. Did her work mean nothing to him? But she did as she was told, and reluctantly fetched her bonnet and her light cotton shawl and climbed into Pieter's dray. The new dray was pulled by a slow-moving horse he'd picked up at the auctions. It was a step up from the shared bullock the Scandies from the clearing used, and he was proud of it.

Pieter certainly wasn't asking her to go to Bunnythorpe because it would be a nice outing for her, and she was curious as to his motives. She suspected he wanted her to fill out a form or read a paper. It was still difficult for the two of them to discuss his problem, partly because he didn't think it was a problem. He'd managed in life perfectly well to this point, and saw no reason to learn how to read now. But why would he not simply have her fill out the form in Palmerston?

Once they were out of town, and her annoyance with everyone had abated, she decided she may as well settle back and enjoy the scenery. The road followed the railway tracks and she watched with interest as the morning train passed them in a whoosh of energy. She'd never taken a train, just the tram to Foxton when it was still pulled by horses. The thought of hurtling through the countryside in a train terrified her. What if she got sucked from the window and thrown against the trees on the side? Or worse, into a river, as train tracks were often built alongside rivers. Recently, a horse had wandered across the track in front of a train near Feilding and been cut in two pieces. The driver had been forced to get out and scrape what was left of the front of the horse off the cow catcher.

"What's this you have in the back, Pieter?" she asked, noticing something covered by a large grey blanket in the back of the buggy.

"Oh, some pegs," he said, staring ahead. "And a few other things. It's just, well, I'll tell you about it when we get there."

"Pegs?"

"I have to keep replacing the surveyor's pegs," he said.

"Someone comes in the night and pulls them out."

"Why would anyone do that?"

He shifted awkwardly in his seat. "They say it's the Maori women," he said. "They don't like that we have their land – well, not their land as they sold it to the Crown. But they think it's their land and they're trying to stop us doing anything with it."

Mette thought about the Pa, and how Wiki and her brothers and grandmother were going to have to leave the home of their ancestors, and said nothing.

She was curious about what else he had under the grey blanket, and why he was being so mysterious about why she needed to go with him to Bunnythorpe. But he was a stubborn man and she knew better than to insist that he tell her what was up. She watched the slow plodding of his new horse, and thought of Copenhagen, Frank's horse, which made her sad again.

It was a half-hour ride to Bunnythorpe. Pieter became quieter and glummer as the time passed, his shoulders slumped. She knew that look. It was the one he got when Maren forced him to do something he didn't want to do. What could it be this time? She tried to start a conversation by asking him about the twins, but he answered with grunts, concentrating on the horse pulling the dray, his head turned away from her.

"Is something wrong, Pieter?" she asked finally, as the partly-built house came in sight.

He looked at her finally, and then looked away. He clearly felt guilty about something. "Nothing," he said. "But Maren…"

It was as she'd suspected. Maren had forced him into something against his will. She thought again of his problem with reading and writing. "Maren what?" she prompted.

Pieter stopped the dray and helped her down from the buggy; she stood looking out over the stretch of land. They would have a beautiful view, once all the trees had been cut down and the stumps burned away, giving the grass a chance to grow; she could live a happy life with a view like that. She turned and saw Pieter taking the blanket and the basket from the buggy. She took it from him, mystified.

"What...?"

He nodded towards the house, and climbed back on the buggy, giving the horse a little flick of his whip.

"Pieter?" she asked. "Where are you going?"

He looked at her helplessly. "Maren..." he said, and gestured with his head towards the house. She followed him for a few steps, saying his name again. "Pieter? Where are you going?"

Someone started hammering. The sound came from the house. She looked towards the sound, and then back at Pieter, puzzled.

"I have to put these pegs in," he said. "I'll be back soon. Maybe an hour. You wait here."

"Wait here? By myself? Stop Pieter. Where are you...? Why did you bring me out here? I thought..."

She heard hammering again, and looked towards the house again. And there, standing in the shadow of one of the half-built new walls, his back to them, stripped down to his trousers, was a figure she would recognize anywhere.

As Pieter drove away, she dropped the basket to the ground and said, "Frank?" Her throat was so constricted that she was sure he hadn't heard, but he turned. She said his name again, her voice stronger, "Frank?"

He stood, holding the hammer loosely beside his leg, looking at her, then dropped it slowly to the ground. He began to move towards her, but not fast enough for her. She raced towards him, laughing, her arms out, and reached him before he had taken more than three or four steps; with a bound she had her arms around his neck, kissing him all over his face.

"*Ah, min gud*, Frank, my Sergeant Frank. I thought I'd lost you forever."

He held her tightly, his face buried in her neck. "You kept me alive – thinking of you – or I would have given..."

"Where were you? We looked so hard for you, and Karira went to..."

"I was kidnapped," he said. "By the Armed Constabulary I think..."

"But why?"

"I wish I knew. They didn't tell me...just threw me in a cell and left me there...then there was a fire and I managed to escape into the river..."

She began to cry, the sobs changing to laughter and back to sobs. "I was thinking of a body in the river, and you..."

He stroked her head and said, "I'm here now and I'm never going to leave you again if I can help it...but how...where's Pieter?"

Mette released her grip on his neck but stayed close. "He gave me a basket and a blanket and went away. He didn't tell me you were here...I don't know why.... Ah, *min Gud*, I'm so happy to see you I can't hardly think...pegs I think..."

"Pegs? Surveyor pegs?"

"He said the Maori women have been pulling out his pegs. I wonder how it can make a difference, but..."

"The pegs mark the sections," said Frank. "When they're missing, the settlers argue about their land...and the police can't stop them...."

"Why not?"

"They can't catch them in the act," he said. "I heard Maori women are doing it, at night, and the Maori constables are letting them get away with it."

"That's very clever of the women," said Mette. "Frank, I think…"

"Do you have any food in that basket?" he asked. He sat down on the step and patted the spot beside him. "I haven't eaten all day and I'm famished."

She was beginning to wonder if Pieter was going to return at all. Clearly Maren had told him to leave her and Frank alone for a while. What did she expect would happen? She fetched the basket and looked inside.

"Yes, there's food in here. In fact, there is a lot of food. Maren wanted us to enjoy…a picnic I think, without Pieter here to ruin things."

The basket was a veritable feast of German sausage, bread, some large chunks of fine Taranaki cheese wrapped in cheese cloth, apples and pears and a large glass bottle of milk. A picnic would usually have made her very happy, especially such a delicious one as this. But at the bottom, wrapped in a napkin, she found a small carved bed, of the kind men whittled for dolls houses. She felt the blood rush to her face.

"Is something the matter?" asked Frank.

Mette wrapped the bed up in the napkin and thrust it back into the bottom of the basket. "Nothing."

"You've gone all pink. Not that it doesn't suit you, but…" Before she could stop him, he reached into the basked and took out the napkin. As he spread it across his knees, the bed fell out. "What's this? A toy? It looks like a bed."

She gave a deep sigh, looking down at her hands. "Maren

put it in there. She thinks it's a joke, I think."

"A joke about...? Oh, I see."

She looked up at him and risked a small smile. "It's not funny, is it?"

"Maren is trying to force you to..."

She nodded.

"She says I shouldn't make you wait until we're married. I didn't know it, but Hamlet was born just seven months after she and Pieter were married. He was...I'm not sure how you say it...*udtaenkt*...on the boat."

"Conceived?" he asked. "Look Mette, your sister has no right to force you into bed with me. And I wouldn't have thought Pieter..."

"He hated to go along," said Mette. "He was so strange while we were driving..."

"But what do you think?" asked Frank. "Surely that's what's important, not what your damn... what your family thinks."

She looked down at her hands, which were gripped in a tight knot. Should she tell him about the foredeck, and about the many nights she'd lain awake listening to Pieter and Maren through the thin walls of her lean to?

He put his hand over hers. "I can wait, you know, Mette. I don't want you to be compromised, if anything happens to me..."

She looked up sharply. "What might happen to you?"

"The Armed Constabulary could be looking for me..."

"Did you do something wrong? You wouldn't, I know you wouldn't..."

"Not that I can remember...." He put his arm around her shoulder. "Let's not worry about anything else now. We'll have the picnic and wait for Pieter...did he say how long he'll be?"

She hesitated. Maren had probably told him to give them plenty of time. "No, he…what's this on your shoulder? It looks like…"

"My tattoo?" he said. "I had it done in Patea years ago, when I was young and foolish. You see, it says Die Hard the 57th, for my regiment."

"I can't see any words. Just a pattern. It looks like moko," she said. "You look a little like a Maori, with your brown body and your dark eyes." She stroked his chest. "I like that."

He stood abruptly and walked away from the step. "I'd better put my shirt on. Where did I leave it?"

"Over here." She followed him, wondering why he was acting so strangely. "By the wood pile." She picked it up and held it out. "You must have been chopping…oh, here is Pieter coming back already." Pieter had crested the hill on the road from Bulls, and was driving his dray like a mad man, whipping at the horse as if he was trying to win the Wellington Cup. "Something must have happened."

"Frank, Frank," Pieter gasped as soon as he was within earshot. "You must hide. There are soldiers coming. They could be looking for you."

There was nowhere to hide close by. The house was half-built and full of gaps and openings. The surrounding land was, like most of the valley, a sea of tree stumps and dirt. But across the metalled road the bush was mostly intact; no one had purchased the land yet and just a few stumps showed where the surveyor had gone through and laid out the shape of a potential farm with his pegs. Close enough for Frank to reach in a minute or two.

"How far away are they?" asked Frank.

"I saw them from the top of the hill. They'll be here in five minutes, no more."

"I'll get into the bush across the road," he said. "And get down to Palmerston by the old Maori track that runs into Stoney Creek Road. I'll keep off the main road. Listen, Mette, find Karira and tell him I'll meet him at the tree where…"

"Go to the Pa," said Mette. "Find Wiki. She'll hide you…and I'll send Karira there…better than hiding in the bush…"

"Wiki?" he said. "Right. I'll look for her…" He sprinted towards the road and the bush beyond.

"Pieter," said Mette tentatively, "I should go with him." She had taken a a single step, when Pieter grabbed her arm and held it so tightly it hurt. "No. You must not. He can move faster by himself. You will stay here and talk to the soldiers."

She tried to pull herself loose, but he pulled her tighter, his fingers digging into her arms. "No Mette. We will talk to the soldiers. Slow them down. They can't be allowed to catch Frank."

She watched as Frank disappeared into the bush, her heart breaking. He was gone again. Would they ever be together?

The group of riders was on them in minutes. Five men, three in the formal blue uniforms of the Armed Constabulary, a young man in riding clothes and knee boots, and a large, dark-skinned man dressed oddly in a suit and a bowler hat. Mette had not seen any of them before, but she thought instantly of the man Agnete had seen talking to Frank on the Stormbird – a large Maori man in a bowler hat, although this man did not look like a Maori. The young man drew her attention. He looked familiar.

One of the constables touched his hat. "Were you here

yesterday?"

Pieter nodded mutely.

"Did you see a tall dark man pass by? A man in his late thirties, dressed like a tramp..."

Pieter could not speak. Mette put her arm though his, and she could feel him trembling. "Lots of people..." he said after a minute, his voice shaking.

The young man interrupted him. "What's your name?"

"Sorensen," said Pieter.

The young man thrust his horse forward. "Pieter Sorensen?" he asked.

Mette squeezed Pieter's arm. How did this man know his name? Best not to be truthful. But Pieter was unable to lie. He nodded slowly.

The young man dismounted and strode towards them. "This man knows something. His name came up..." He poked at Pieter with his whip handle. "Where is he? Where's Hardy?"

Pieter gaped at him without speaking, so Mette said, "We don't know anyone named Hardy. We're from Schleswig. Hardy is an English..."

The young man, who had not been paying attention to Mette, looked at her for the first time. "What's that you're holding?"

Mette put Frank's shirt behind her back. "Nothing. Just a shirt. It belongs to my husband and I was going to wash it." Her hands were shaking. Who was this young man? He was so familiar...

He jumped from his horse, yanked her arm forward and took the shirt from her hands. The large dark man had also dismounted. He stepped behind her, his very presence designed to scare her.

"I've seen this shirt before," said the young man. "Hardy was wearing it in Wanganui, when I had the misfortune to run into him there." He grabbed Mette by the shoulders and held her, his face inches from hers. "Now, where is he? Where's Hardy?"

"Easy there Mountjoy," said one of the constables. "We don't treat women like that."

Mountjoy glared at the constable. "I'll treat her how I damn well want," he said. "If it means finding out where Hardy is. And she's just a peasant anyway. Why should you care?"

"Listen," said the constable. "I'll take this man..." he pointed to Pieter, "back to camp, and we'll see if we can make him talk. A bit of gaol time will help, I'm sure. But leave the woman alone. She can help us make her husband talk..."

"You take him wherever you want," said Mountjoy. "I'll stay here and search for Hardy. He's probably not far away. He left in a hurry when he saw us coming – that's why his shirt's here." He looked at Mette. "And the woman stays with me. She had his shirt...she knows something."

The constable shrugged. "Very well. But I'm not responsible for whatever you do. Just remember that." He dismounted and took out a pair of handcuffs. "Put your hands behind your back," he said to Pieter. "Unless you talk to me this minute, I'm taking you back to our camp for a discussion. And you're not going to enjoy it."

Pieter complied, his face ashen. Mette watched in horror. Maren would never forgive her for this. There was nothing more terrible for a man from Schleswig than to be taken away by soldiers, and gaol was unthinkable. He was shoved aboard his dray beside a constable, who took the reins. The horse pulled the dray away slowly. Pieter looked back at Mette in despair as they moved off. "Maren," he said, "Maren..."

She nodded, understanding. Of course she would explain everything to Maren, once she was free of this angry young man and his ominous guard. To him she would say nothing, not even if he pointed his gun at her. Not even if he shot her.

Mountjoy took hold of Mette's arm. "Now you," he said. "If Hardy's still around, you're going to help me find him." He gestured to the man in the bowler hat. "Pulau, take her other arm. If Hardy's close by, he'll be in those woods across the road. I'm going to flush him out."

Mette refused to move her feet, but the two men dragged her across the road, her boots kicking up dust behind them.

"*Lad hende vaere,*" she heard Pieter call out. "*Jeg vil ikke sige noget,* Mette." He was trying to disguise what he had said, by starting with 'Let her go,' but adding 'I will say nothing Mette.' You never knew who might understand a bit of Danish.

"*Vaer modig,* Pieter," she called back. Be brave. And he was, she thought.

They paused at the edge of the bush. Mette pretended to faint, but the two men were having none of it, and dragged her back to her feet.

"Stand," ordered Mountjoy. "Or I'll toss you in the ditch and leave you there to rot." He turned towards the trees and yelled, "Hardy, if you're in there, come on out."

"He went that way, sir" said Pulau, pointing into the gloom. "See the track through the ferns…?"

"Right, thanks," said Mountjoy. Mette's arm was starting to feel numb, but the young man was making her heart numb as well. "Listen," he said to the guard, "you stay here with the horses. I'll…"

"Are you sure?"

"I can handle this myself...you," he dragged Mette forward. "Come with me, you whore. Hardy? Hardy? Don't make me hurt the woman..." He pulled a revolver from his belt and pressed it against Mette's forehead. "Move."

"Are you sure you don't want me with you?" asked the guard again. "She asked me..."

"Stay with the horses," said Mountjoy. "That's an order. Forget what she said. What does she know? I'm not a child."

Mette saw a faint look of contempt cross the guard's face. He pushed his hat down hard on his head and went back across the road to where the horses were grazing on Pieter's new farmland.

Mette could feel the nervousness of the young man through his grip. His hand was sweating, dampening her sleeve. "He's gone, I think," she said, as calmly as she could. "This Hardy. He was at our farm doing some work. My...my husband hired him, and when he saw you coming he ran off, he..."

He stabbed at her forehead with his gun. "Shut up and get in front of me. And don't do anything foolish."

She walked slowly forward. She could feel the gun as an almost physical presence, even though Mountjoy was several feet behind her. They moved like that along the trail of crushed ferns that Frank had left as he ran through the bush. She longed to run after him, to follow the tracks, to catch up to him. But she walked at a glacial pace, trying to give him more time to escape. The bush was eerily silent, as if all the birds and animals were holding their collective breath. Time stopped. She had no idea how this was would end. She could hear the young man breathing heavily, nervous despite his claim of being able to handle things.

They walked for several more minutes. She stumbled, and

he grabbed her by the arm and pulled her to her feet. "Don't try anything."

"I wasn't…"

He came up on them from behind. She felt a presence, then heard a loud thump; turning, she saw Mountjoy lying on the ground with Frank holding a gun against his head, the hammer cocked. The young man looked up at Frank and said nothing. But Mette saw fear in his eyes.

"Don't say a word," said Frank. "Mette, get his belt."

She ran forward and unbuckled the belt. Mountjoy resisted, but rolled to help her when Frank prodded him with his own gun.

"I'll get you for this Hardy," he said. "My family will hunt you down like the dog you are…"

Mette handed Frank the belt. "Who is he, Frank. Do you know him?"

"I've run into him before," said Frank, the gun not wavering. "Mountjoy, stand up slowly, and keep quiet. We both know you can summon your keeper if you want to, but we'll be gone and he'll find your body hanging from a tree…your father won't like that now, will he?"

Mountjoy found a small piece of courage and spat at Frank.

Frank wiped the spittle from his face. "I'd be more cooperative if I were you, son," he said. "I have nothing to lose at this point. Whereas you're a young man who probably values his future have. Now get against that tree."

Mountjoy did as he was told, his face twisted with hatred, while Frank looped the belt over a branch and around his neck, forcing him to his toes.

From the darkness of the bush they could see the guard puffing on a pipe a short distance from the horses. Frank whistled, and one of the horses moved towards them tentatively. He whistled again, and it started trotting. The guard followed him slowly, seemingly unworried, snapping his fingers to get the attention of the animal. "Get back here," they heard him say.

Mountjoy was clutching at the belt to stop it from choking him. "Pulau's going to kill you," he said, his voice raspy. "Both of you."

Frank ignored him. "Mette, when the horse gets here we're going to mount it really fast. His minder has a gun and he'll shoot, but at this distance he'll miss, especially if he's surprised. Stay calm and concentrate on what we're doing. Don't think about what might happen."

"What about the…about him?" she asked. "Won't Pulau help him first?"

"After he gets a couple of shots off at us," said Frank. "Ready?"

She took a deep breath. The horse had stopped trotting within a few feet of the bush. "Yes. Will you go first, or should I?"

"I will, and I'll drag you up after me. Have your arms up."

It was like the first time they met, and although she was terrified she was also excited.

He made a sudden move, running towards the horse and leaping astride it. She followed him, her arms in the air and he dragged her in front of him. Pulau, realizing what was happening, ran towards them, tossing his pipe aside and pulling his revolver from his belt. They were already a hundred yards away and moving quickly when they heard the first shot. She clutched Frank's arm and tried not to scream.

"Don't worry," he said. He leaned forward and spurred the horse faster, tucking Mette between his arms, sheltering her.

A bullet whizzed by them, not far away, and she screamed. Frank put his mouth near her ear and said quietly, "No one can shoot someone on a horse and score a hit at this distance. Perhaps with an Enfield, but not a revolver. He's just shooting wildly."

She did not find that comforting.

Twenty minutes later they reached the old Maori track where it crossed the metalled road. He rode along the track for a mile more then stopped where it split into two once more, one track going to Palmerston, the other towards the pa.

"Nice horse," he said as he dismounted and helped Mette down. "I'd love to keep it, but then they'll have me for horse theft. This isn't the wild west of America we're in here. I can't ride around shooting people and stealing horses. Pity."

"What are you going to do now?" she asked. "Won't they follow us…can they both ride on one horse?"

"That's why I'm stopping here," said Frank. He gave the horse a whack on its rump and it took off back in the direction from which they had come. "If Mountjoy's minder does come after us he'll assume we've returned to Palmerston and follow the track that way. We'd best get moving though. We may only have a thirty-minute start and he may be smarter than I think. He's a professional, I think."

"What will happen to you if they catch you?" asked Mette. "Will they send you back to gaol?"

"Worse, probably," said Frank. "A flogging, at least, maybe send me to the Chatham Islands."

"But why?" asked Mette. What did you do? Was it something to do with that man, the one called…"

"Mountjoy?" said Frank. He took Mette's hand and started

along the track. "I don't know. I met his father in Wellington and he reacted to me as if I'd done him harm somehow. I wish I knew what he thinks I've done…"

"Did he remind you of anyone?"

"How did you…? He did, as it happens…like my brother Will. What made you think that?"

"Well, your brother Will must have looked like you, because that young soldier looks like you. Perhaps you're related?"

He shook his head. "Not that I know of," he said. "A distant relative, perhaps."

Mette looked doubtful. "I suppose that's possible. But the resemblance is quite strong. I saw it immediately."

"Maybe he has some Spanish blood," said Frank. "Like me. Look, do you think you could manage double time for a while? We need to get some distance between us and…my cousin, or whatever he is."

They moved quickly along the track towards the pa, stopping to rest when they could hear the river in the distance. Mette finally had time to think, and to worry. "I hope Pieter will be all right," she said. "He's not used to soldiers, although he was very brave…"

"Won't Maren wonder where he is?" asked Frank.

"No. He often spends the night up at Bunnythorpe when the work is going well. She'll just assume…Frank, what are we going to do? How will you prove that you haven't done anything wrong when you don't know what it is someone thinks you've done."

He scratched his beard, thinking. "It's obviously something to do with Colonel Mountjoy. Seeing him in Wellington set this whole thing off…he's connected to the government, an adviser…although he'd need evidence to have me arrested. I can't imagine him having the authority to get me kidnapped, drugged and thrown in gaol. I wonder if there's someone more powerful behind him?"

"Could you ask the mayor, or Mr. Balance, the member of parliament…?"

"Snelson?" Frank shook his head. "No. There's nothing he could do. Balance maybe…I saved his life at the pa when Anahera attacked. But I could contact Captain Porter. He could find out…I'll tell you what. When we get to the pa, you go on to Palmerston and ask Karira to send him a telegram."

"I'm not staying with you at the pa?"

"Best you return to Palmerston," said Frank. "Staying with me isn't safe for you now."

9

Reunited

They reached the Manawatu River in the early afternoon, to the east of the town towards Ashhurst and the Gorge, moving in short bursts of running and fast walking. Mette had handled it better than Frank expected – better than he had, even, and she could probably have run the whole way. He'd needed to stop for a breath more often than she did, a testament to her youth. They were covered in scratches and sand fly bites, but there was no sign of anyone following them. Once they were at the river it was an easy walk downstream to the pa.

The business of removing the Maori village to make room for settlers' homes was underway, but two whare, the communal huts where families lived, were still standing alone at the edge of the river. Frank had not been to the pa since the chief, Hakopa, had sold the land to the government without consulting his people, and he was shocked by what he saw. The buildings had been destroyed and the people cast out like rats from a barn. He wondered where they'd gone. Not to Palmerston, for the most part. He knew Te Whiti was preaching that the Maori were one of the lost tribes of Israel, and had been condemned to wander the earth. Perhaps they had recommenced their wandering.

A young woman was harvesting potatoes on a patch of sandy land using an old surveyor's peg to dig the earth. "There's Wiki," said Mette, relieved. Wiki waved at them, and came over, surveying Frank with amusement.

"Wiki, this is the man I told you about, my fiancé Sergeant Frank Hardy."

"Will Karira's partner?" said Wiki. "Why aren't you wearing a shirt, Sergeant Hardy? Have you been in the river?"

"Frank, Sergeant Hardy, was gaoled by the Armed Constabulary," said Mette. "They took him to their prison up the Wanganui River and he escaped after a fire. And then they came after him in Bunnythorpe."

Wiki rolled her eyes in disgust. "Huh. The Armed Constabulary," she said. "What did you do to get in their sights?"

"Nothing that I can remember," said Frank. "I didn't have a chance to discuss it…"

"Well, you stay here," she said. "We'll look after you. Just like we did our cousin from Poverty Bay when he was here and the constables were chasing him."

"Your cousin…?" asked Frank. "You mean Anahera?"

"Some people call him that," agreed Wiki.

Mette stared at Wiki, shocked. "You knew about Anahera?"

"Course I did," said Wiki. "He's my cousin, well, sort of my cousin…"

"Anahera was in the Armed Constabulary gaol with me," said Frank to Mette. "Up the Wanganui River. He was locked in a cell in the path of an intense forest fire and they were going to leave him there to burn. I unlocked his cell and let him out."

"He escaped again?" asked Wiki. "I'm so happy to hear that. He was in prison for such a long time, and it was hard on him…"

"Hard on the rest of us when he escaped," said Frank. He'd been wondering if he'd done the right thing, turning Anahera loose again.

"Well, you're his friend now," said Wiki. "Lucky for you. He's a hard man and doesn't forgive people who hurt his family." She swung the surveyor's peg back and forward and smiled. "I liked him. He has good ideas and he's very strong. He's a warrior."

"But he killed…" said Mette. She stood abruptly, straightening her skirt. "I think I'd better return to town before it gets dark, I…" Frank could see that she was overwhelmed by the situation, and Wiki's sudden change of sides – at least from Mette's point of view – had not helped. She looked drained.

He took her hands in his. "Anahera has gone upriver," he said, not sure himself if it was true. "He'll be in the Ureweras by now. Don't worry."

She held his hand to her face and sniffed. "I'll try not to. But you seem to be in so much danger now, and if anything else happens…"

"I'll be fine," he said. "Tell Karira to send a telegram to Captain Porter, and you stay close to Karira and Hop Li. They'll take care of you if there's a problem. Tell Karira that Anahera's on the loose as well, and that he should keep an eye out for him."

"Never mind," said Wiki. She looked uncomfortable and Frank wondered if she knew something. "If he comes here I'll tell him not to kill you, or Sergeant Hardy. I'll get one of my brothers to take you home, Mette. He'll keep you safe." She whistled, and yelled, "Hemi, come here."

A slender Maori boy no taller than Mette's shoulder appeared from the reeds on the river bank. "Hemi, go into town with this lady. Make sure nothing happens to her please."

"Now?" asked Hemi. "I'm catching eels…"

"Now," said Wiki. "Right now."

Hemi rolled his eyes. "If I have to…"

He followed Wiki and Mette to the broken gate, dragging his feet, his whole body signalling reluctance. Wiki put her arm around Mette's waist as if they were old friends. It was difficult to see Mette leave; he felt as if they were attached by a long string and would always be pulled back together, no matter what happened. But the string was getting more and more tangled.

Wiki returned alone and said to Frank, "I played on those palisades when I was young. We used to pretend that we were still at war; we played Toa against Ingarangi. Of course, the Toa, which was us, always defeated the Ingarangi."

Frank nodded. "Ingarangi—English. I've been called that in my time. And Toa?"

"Warriors," she said. "Maori warriors of course. I'd love to be a warrior." She slashed at a weed with the surveyor's peg. "I want to fight for my land."

"The war wasn't that long ago," he said. "You don't remember it?"

She grinned. "I'm only seventeen, you know. I was born the year the war started and I was too young to know much about it."

"Now I feel like an old man," said Frank.

"Mette is younger than you," said Wiki, nodding in agreement. "Is she very much younger?"

"Many years," he said. "I'm not going to tell you how many. You've already made me feel much too old."

"My mother said they called her Hine Raumati when she was here with you," said Wiki. "Because she was interested in how we cook our food, and she seems to like food. Hine Raumati is the summer maid who causes the food to grow. My mother liked her, and so do I. I wish more...more Ingarangi were like her. Most of them don't care."

"Where's your mother now?" he asked, not correcting the mistake. Mette was Danish - Kanikani he thought -not English - Ingarangi. They were probably all English to her. "Why is she not here with you?"

She shrugged. "She went up to Poverty Bay with Moana. They're from the same family."

He met the other inhabitants of his new living quarters and thanked Wiki's second brother, Hohepa, a smaller version of Hemi, for allowing him to share his whare. Hohepa stared at him nervously without speaking. Wiki said something to the boy in a sharp tone, and the boy came forward and stuck out his hand cautiously to Frank.

"He's scared of you," said Wiki. "He's afraid of ghosts. Every time he sees a pakeha he thinks he's seeing a ghost."

"Turehu," said the boy quietly.

Wiki punched Frank lightly on the arm. "He's real, see Hohepa? Anyway, Turehu aren't as dark as Sergeant Hardy. They're pale, with red hair."

The boy stared at Frank, then punched his arm, grinning. Frank gave him an equally light punch in return, winking as he did so. Hohepa smiled and attempted a wink in return.

Wiki's grandmother, who had come out of the women's whare, watched them, smiling and nodding, stroking her moko-etched chin.

"No Turehu," she said. "Pakeha Maori."

A white Maori. Frank had heard people called that before, not usually in a complimentary manner, and he asked Wiki what her grandmother meant.

She said something to her grandmother in Maori, then translated for Frank.

"She saw the tattoo on your arm," said Wiki. "Back when my grandmother was young, there were white men – pakeha – who visited here and became like Maori. They lived with us and learned our language. They often had moko carved on their faces, all over their faces…"

"Like Kimball Bent," said Frank. "Ringiringi. He became a Maori." Wiki looked mystified and asked her grandmother a question. The old woman shook her head vigorously and made a sideways stroking gesture with her hand, indicating the more distant past.

"She says," said Wiki, "Kimball Bent, Ringiringi, was just a deserter and Titokowaru's slave. She knows about him. But she's talking about many years ago, before my mother was born. Before there were wars with the pakeha, and when Maori owned all the land of Aotearoa. She's told me these stories before. But I don't usually listen."

"Even before my time, as well," said Frank.

The old woman leaned towards him and poked her finger at him in short jabs. "Wake a field. Wake a field."

"Ah," said Frank, understanding. "Wakefield. The father or the son?"

"She says Journey," said Wiki. "Does that make sense?"

"Jerningham Wakefield," said Frank. "The son. He wrote a book about his adventures in New Zealand. I remember reading it when I was a boy. She met him?"

Wiki confirmed that was the case.

Frank smiled at the old woman, nodded, and said, "Wakefield."

She grinned back at him, revealing gums almost devoid of teeth, then reached forward and stroked the tattoo on his shoulder.

"*Ta moko.*"

"She likes your moko," said Wiki. "My grandmother is a Tohunga ta moko. Not many women can be moko artists, but she was because she's the daughter of a Tohunga. She still practices it when she can."

The other women now had a fire going, and had placed a large bird over the fire on a spit. One woman turned it by hand, close to the flames and in danger of burning herself. Frank moved forward and took the end of the spit from her, indicating that he would take over her job.

"Chicken…ah, *heihei?*" he asked as he turned the spit, remembering the old woman from the previous day with her bag of stolen chooks.

Wiki shook her head. "Huia. My brother Hemi caught it in the bush. We can't make the Hangi anymore, so we cook by a fire instead. My potatoes are in the fire as well, down in the ashes."

"It smells excellent," he said. "I've never eaten huia before, although I've heard them calling in the bush. I assumed they were smaller…more like a tui."

"No. Nice and big, but not many left," said Wiki. "Too easy to catch."

After they'd finished eating, the grandmother went inside the women's whare, and came out holding a rolled-up leather satchel that looked as if it had been well used, and a carved

carved box. When she was done, she sat back and tapped him lightly on the arm below the moko with the fixed chisel and said something that sounded like an incantation.

"Usually we would have to burn down the place where ta moko is done," remarked Wiki. "But we have only these two whare and they'll be burned down soon anyway, as soon as we leave. You'll be the last to receive ta moko in this whare." She put a damp flax cloth on Frank's arm. "Sleep with this on your arm. It has something in it that will dull the pain."

It took him some time to fall asleep on the woven flax mats in the boy's whare. The cuts throbbed relentlessly and he wondered how they could possibly have been worse without the cloth Wiki had given him. On top of that, the rich, fatty meal of huia sat in his gut and kept him awake. But eventually he drifted off into a dream of his own past, his life growing up in the stables of a huge estate, his love of adventure that had led to him joining the army. That had taken him to the Crimea, and then on to India.

In the late sixties, his company had made a forced march from Poona to Bombay through the jungles at night, listening to the roars of the man-eating tigers as they picked off any man who ventured away from the torches. Then they'd sailed from Bombay to Auckland —89 days aboard ship. He'd been sent to Taranaki after the Land Wars were over to help defeat Titokowaru. The vague figure of a woman lurked in his dreams...he chased her but she escaped. Mette? No. Someone darker, malevolent...wearing a silk dress that rustled as she moved.

box. She said something to Wiki, who shrugged, then said to Frank, "She'd like to carve a symbol on your other shoulder."

Frank knew he'd been offered a rare honour, and that he should accept. When he'd been tattooed by a rogue Maori tattoo artist in Patea, a week after the attack on Otapawa Pa, he had been drinking all day, and even drunk it had hurt like hell, but he said, looking directly at the grandmother, his hand on his heart, "I am most honoured."

She unrolled the leather satchel and laid it out to reveal her equipment. Frank's gut lurched slightly but he kept his face expressionless. The inside of the satchel revealed rows of pouches with bone chisel blades and a handle with a fixed blade for cutting.

"Albatross bones," said Wiki, pointing at the chisel blades. "It's going to hurt and it will leave a raised scar. Are you sure you don't mind?"

Frank shook his head firmly.

"Of course I don't. What will she carve? Something small?"

Wiki grinned at him. "You're scared, aren't you? I'll tell her to choose something little and it won't hurt as much—or as long."

She said something to her grandmother and they had a brief discussion.

"She says she'll do a koru, which is an unfurling fern leaf. It means new life, growth, and peace."

That's appropriate, he thought. He said, "I would like that. Thank your grandmother."

He spent the next hour with gritted teeth as the grandmother opened long circular cuts in his arm with her fixed chisel, and held open the cuts with the smaller blades and drew along them with a stick dipped in a sooty substance taken from the

10

V. Monrad, Esq. J.P.

Mette had just finished sharing a snack of Hop Li's pikelets, sitting on the sunny verandah of the Royal Hotel – Hop Li understood how distressed she was and what would help – when she saw Karira return. She'd talked to Maren, and reassured her that Pieter was fine and that there was nothing to worry about, downplaying his arrest, but he'd still not come home and Maren was in a panic. Remembering that Karira did not know that Frank had reappeared, she ran out to meet his horse, wanting to make sure he heard the full story from her before he talked to anyone else and said something he shouldn't.

He dismounted and led his horse into the paddock behind the hotel, waving to her as he passed. She followed him there, found him carrying his saddle across to the shed which served as a saddlery, and said quietly, "Frank is back. He's hiding at the pa with Wiki and her family."

"He's back? Where was he?" asked Karira.

"At the gaol where they took Anahera," said Mette. "On the Wanganui River. He said the Armed Constabulary had him, but he escaped when there was a fire…"

"Does he have any idea why he was taken up the river?" asked Karira. "I can't imagine…"

"No, no idea," she said. "But he went to Pieter's new farm up in Bunnythorpe. Pieter took me to Bunnythorpe, and while and I was there they came after him. He got away from…"

"The Armed Constabulary?"

"Yes. And a young man he'd met before," she said, and filled him in on the Mountjoy story, leaving out the scarier parts, which she preferred to forget. "What did you learn?"

"I spoke to the pilot who brought the Stormbird across the sand bar," he said. "He says there was dense fog and the boat sat outside the bar for four hours or more before he could bring the boat in through the narrows. While he was waiting he saw a row boat taking something – someone – off. He didn't think anything of it, because he's seen it before. Passengers get impatient and insist on being put ashore by jolly boat. But he says he thinks there were three men, and one of them appeared to be drunk, or at least having difficulty walking."

"The large Maori with the hat – the one you thought might be a constable, he was with the constables – the mysterious passenger and Frank," said Mette. "I don't think the man I saw was a constable. I'm not even sure he was a Maori. He was darker and different somehow. But tell me the rest. Did you find out who the mysterious passenger was?"

"All he saw was someone in a long cloak," said Karira. "I spoke to the local native constable and he asked around. He found nothing. And he doesn't know of anyone important who has recently arrived in Wanganui, which is odd. Wanganui is bigger than Palmerston, but not by much, and a new arrival, especially an important person, would have everyone talking."

"Anything else?"

"No, I don't think so. You said the man with Mountjoy, the younger one, might not be a Maori. What made you think that?"

"Just the way he acted," said Mette. He looked like a Maori, but he…I don't know…he sneered at Mountjoy when Mountjoy gave him an order. I don't see Maori behaving like that."

"Hmm," said Karira. "I think I can sneer with the best of them, but perhaps you're right. What I'm curious about is what would a father and son have against Frank?"

"I'm not sure," said Mette. "But there was something strange. The son, he looked…"

Before she could finish, the door opened and Constable Price entered.

"Karira," he said, "you're needed outside. The Armed Constabulary are here after Frank. They say he escaped from their gaol up the Wanganui River and is known to have headed this way. I don't believe they have the right person, but you'd better speak to them."

"That's not possible," said Mette, not sure how she should react or what she should say. "Frank wasn't in prison. Why would he be in prison. They must be mistaken."

Constable Price, his head thrust forward, regarded her through his heavy eyebrows. "Possibly," he said. "Although they seem quite sure. But Karira needs to come and reassure them that he has not seen Frank."

Outside in the Square a group of horsemen sat astride skittish horses; they were mostly Armed Constables, a different group than she had seen the day before, wearing the familiar blue serge uniforms rather than the informal shawl kilts, but one was not wearing a uniform: Mountjoy.

"That's him," she whispered to Karira. "Mountjoy. He's the young man who…"

She pulled her shawl over her head and face and mingled with the crowd that had formed. The big dark man with the hat, the man Frank called Mountjoy's minder, was behind Mountjoy, who had a red weal across his throat. She shivered, afraid he would recognize her. At least she'd changed her clothes since yesterday, and was wearing the brown dress she'd bought with her first pay, and the shawl made her look like all the other women, who had covered up at the sight of the soldiers. The horses moved apart slightly and she saw Pieter in their midst, sitting uncomfortably on his own horse, his hands tied behind his back, his normally ruddy face white and drawn. They must have kept him somewhere overnight. Pieter would have been terrified. Thank God Maren wasn't in town to see him…

The captain of the troop moved his horse forward in front of Karira, and looked down at him without dismounting. It was if he thought the advantage of height would give him more control of the situation, Mette thought.

"Constable Karira?" he asked.

Karira nodded; he was standing with his head back to give himself the advantage of some added height. "I was a constable, but no longer."

"You are the partner of Frank Hardy," said the captain. It was a statement, not a question.

"Sergeant Frank Hardy," said Karira. "Yes, I am."

"And have you seen him in the last forty-eight hours?"

"I have not."

"Do you have any idea where he is?"

Karira looked the captain directly in the eye. "No, I do not.

He left for Wellington several days ago and we haven't heard from him since. In fact, I just returned from Wanganui in a fruitless quest to discover where he might be." He looked over at Mountjoy and his minder, and added: "I discovered he was taken from a ship, the Stormbird, before it docked at the wharf in Wanganui. That's all I can tell you."

"He was in our custody," said the captain. "And he escaped. We need to find him. He's a dangerous man."

"Sergeant Hardy?" interrupted Constable Price. "A dangerous man? Surely you're not talking about our Sergeant Hardy? I've never met a more trustworthy or honest man in my life."

The captain glanced at Constable Price briefly, then looked again at Karira. "I understand you are no longer with the Native Police, Constable Karira," he said. "However, if you know where he is you are honour-bound to tell us. You swore an oath when you joined our ranks, and leaving the ranks does not negate..."

Mountjoy nudged his horse closer. "The last time I saw him he was heading this way," he said. He pointed at Pieter. "He had a woman with him, the wife of this man."

Constable Price glanced at Mette, puzzled. "His wife wouldn't be..."

The captain interrupted. "He was put down near Sorensen's farm by a constable from Woodville who gave him a ride in his trap. And he was heard by that same constable to say the name 'Pieter.' He also told the constable that he knew how he was going to get to Palmerston. We questioned Sorensen at our camp last evening and he refused to tell us anything. I left his wife in Mr. Mountjoy's care..."

"His wife?" Constable Price was confused. "His wife is..."

The captain ignored him, still looking a Karira. "The pair of them stole Mr. Mountjoy's horse at gunpoint and took off in this direction."

"Where do these peasants live?" asked Mountjoy, directing his question to Constable Price. Constable Price glanced apologetically at Karira and Mette and said, "There's a clearing a mile or so down the track. Go down to the church and you'll find the track. But I doubt you'll find him there. Why would..."

"Come," said Mountjoy to the captain, taking charge. "We'll search this clearing, and all the houses. I'll leave Sorensen in the custody of my man. He'll keep an eye him, on all of you."

"As soon as we've watered the horses," said the captain, re-asserting control. "And my troop will search this...clearing. You can remain here and wait until we return. Or come with us. Whichever you wish. But I am in charge. Are you clear on that Mr. Mountjoy?"

They left, Mountjoy opting to go with them and leave his guard with Pieter who sat on his horse, his hands still behind his back, his head down. Constable Price stood close by, but said a word or two to Pieter. He said nothing to Mette or Karira, apparently deciding the less he knew the better.

Mette sat on the steps to Frank's office and tried not to look at Pieter. She was afraid to see his despair, knowing that the Armed Constables and Mountjoy were headed towards Maren in the clearing. Maren was not used to dealing with any kind of authority and would no doubt be panicked and tearful if they pushed her. It was too much like the time the Prussians had come for their father, a peaceful, studious, man, telling him he must come and fight the French. Their mother had screamed as he was forced off with the soldiers, and the two girls, knowing that their brother Hamlet was probably dead already in the same fight, had to reassure their mother when everything had seemed – and was in the end – so terrible.

Someone came and sat beside Mette, and she looked up to see Mr. Robinson.

"My dear, what can I do to help?" He took her hand in his and gave it a squeeze.

"They took Frank for a reason that none of us understand," she said. "And now they've arrested Pieter for helping Frank, even though he didn't really. They say Frank was in their custody and escaped, but I don't understand why. And they're going to put Pieter in gaol, and it will be so difficult…"

He looked at the ground for several minutes, then rose resolutely.

"I have an idea," he said. "At least a way to help your brother-in-law. I believe Sergeant Hardy will be more than capable of taking care of himself."

She watched him leave, wondering what he might have in mind. He was heading towards the Lutheran church at the junction of the Square and the track to the clearing. The minister might want to help them, but she couldn't imagine him having any influence over the captain, or over Mountjoy.

Karira had gone to his office. "I sent a telegraph to Captain Porter, as you suggested" he said when he returned. "I'm not sure what he can do, but perhaps it will help. He may at least know what this is all about."

She sighed, and remembered what she had been going to say to Karira earlier.

"Did you have a good look at the young man?"

He looked at her, and she could tell he was thinking carefully before he replied.

"I did," he said finally.

A tear ran from one corner of her eye, and she brushed it

away.

"Why does he, why does he, look so much like…"

"Like Frank," he said, finishing her thought. "The resemblance is striking, isn't it?"

"Could it be his brother, the one who disappeared? Perhaps he was not beheaded after all. Perhaps he's been living with…"

"No," said Karira. "Frank would recognize his own brother, and he's too young anyway…no more than twenty. Frank's brother was murdered a decade ago, and he was already in the army."

"And he's too old to be a son of Frank's brother," she said. "If it's not just a coincidence, then perhaps he's Frank's…son."

"Would that upset you?" asked Karira.

She gave him a wan smile. "Twenty years ago, I was just learning to walk," she said. "I have no reason to be jealous if he has a son he doesn't know about. But…"

"I'm going to ride out to the Pa as soon as I can," he said. "I think Frank had better hide out somewhere in the bush for a few days. I'll press him about the resemblance. It will be better coming from me than from you, I would think."

They sat there for what seemed like an eternity, and eventually the sound of hoof beats presaged the return of the Armed Constabulary. Karira faced the constables, his shoulders back. "I hope you haven't caused any concern to the families in the clearing," he said. "Whatever you think anyone else has done, the families are blameless."

"They knew nothing," said Mountjoy. "Ignorant peasants. They were obviously too stupid to understand what we were asking. They just stared at us as if they couldn't understand English. They shouldn't have been allowed to come here…"

Mette caught Pieter's eye briefly and saw enormous relief

cross his face. Maren and the women had stood their ground, pretending ignorance. She hoped the soldiers hadn't scared the children.

"Constable Price, are there other places in the area where someone might hide?" the captain asked.

Mette held her breath. Please don't say the pa, she thought. Someone was sure to say it. If they went out to the pa, Frank would be trapped and certainly caught.

"There are men up at the logging camp," said Constable Price helpfully. "Some pretty rough types. You could check up there. Although I don't think..."

"Good," said the captain. "We'll do that. Constable Price, hold Sorensen in a cell until we return."

Mette heard a choked sound coming from Pieter. Being gaoled would be humiliating for him. "Does he need to be locked up in gaol?" she asked Karira. "He'll find it most upsetting."

"I don't think I can..."

The sound of a single horseman approaching interrupted him. She saw Mr. Robinson scurrying from the direction of the church, followed by an imposing figure of a man on a large black horse. Her heart leapt as she realized Mr. Robinson had brought Viggo Monrad to their help. Monrad was the son of Bishop Ditlev Monrad, who had come to New Zealand – to Palmerston – with his family after the war between Denmark and Germany over Schleswig. The bishop had been Prime Minister of Denmark, and after a few years in New Zealand had returned there, still a very important man. In New Zealand, he was also highly respected; his son Viggo had stayed behind and had become a leader in Palmerston. He ran the school board and was a Justice of the Peace, and everybody, especially in the Scandinavian community, both admired him and felt slightly nervous when they were in his presence.

Monrad rode up to the captain, looking down on him from his larger horse, and asked, "What's going on here. Why is this man in your custody?" His faint accent, along with his narrow face and well-trimmed moustache under a sharp pointed nose gave him an authoritarian tone that would be hard for anyone to argue with.

The captain was clearly not willing to take responsibility for any accusation this imposing man might have. He nodded towards Mountjoy. "This man brought me written instructions from HQ," he said. "I'm just following orders."

"Following orders?" asked Monrad, his voice underlining his disbelief. "The orders of this young *skjult*?"

"My father, sir, is Colonel Humphrey Mountjoy, late Commander of her Majesty's 64th Regiment in India, and British Consul in Samoa, and he has asked me..."

"And mine was once the Premier of Denmark," said Monrad coolly. "But I prefer to operate with my own credentials. I am Justice of the Peace for the district of Manawatu and I demand that you release my compatriot instantly unless you have something specific you are charging him with."

The captain made a signal to one of his men, who leaned over and slashed the rope binding Pieter's hands with his bowie knife.

"I will take full responsibility for this man," said Monrad. "Sorensen, return to your wife and children and don't leave your home for now."

Pieter nodded dumbly at Monrad, and slapped his horse on its rump. It ambled off towards the clearing, Pieter swaying awkwardly on its back. Mountjoy looked after him, frowning.

Had he had heard that Pieter was returning to a wife in the clearing, Mette wondered, and not the 'wife' he had seen with Pieter? And was he puzzled about why he had not seen that wife in the clearing?

The captain turned his horse, and he and the troop left towards the river and the track up towards the logging camp in the ranges. Mountjoy and his guard followed.

"Right," said Karira as soon as they's gone. "I'm off to the pa to get Frank before they decide to search there. I have an idea where he can hide for a day or two, until the constables are clear of town…the guard was Samoan, by the way. Not Maori. You were right."

"How could you tell?" asked Mette.

Karira shrugged. "I don't know…I just can…"

"Will you ask Frank about…?"

"I suppose I will," said Karira. "It will be tricky though…"

11

Hidden at the Pa

Frank awoke early and sat on a rock on the river's edge. A heavy dew had fallen during the night and the air was still damp and cold. The blanket around his shoulders didn't keep him warm, and he wondered how Maori men managed to withstand cold weather. Even in winter they were bare-chested, although some wore feathered cloaks. Many of them had adopted European clothing, at least partly. He supposed it was just a matter of becoming acclimatized to the weather. He remembered the dreary grey rains of England, and from India the intense heat that arrived with the rains. The British had taken to the hills when the heat during the rainy season became too much for them. He'd accompanied a group of women to the hills the first year he was in India. He had good memories of that trip. He'd been around the age that Wiki was now, perhaps a couple of years older, and everything had been new to him, including the scenery and the women.

He'd been sitting there for some time when Wiki came out of the women's whare, stretching and yawning.

"Good morning Sergeant Hardy," she said. "I hope you slept well."

He nodded. "Very well, thank you. I see your brothers were up with the tui this morning."

"They went looking for eels," she said. "They took the canoe down the river early this morning. I hope they didn't wake you. Are you hungry? There are still some potatoes in the fire if you'd like."

He ate a cold potato, ash-covered skin and all, while Wiki watched. After a few minutes her grandmother came out of the women's whare. She was holding a bag in her arms, and smiled at Frank. She wanted to show him something, it seemed. She gestured to him and he stood to meet her, glancing at Wiki who screwed up her nose and sighed.

"Sorry," she said. "I knew she'd bring out grandpa eventually."

He looked at her again, puzzled, then back at the old woman who stood cradling the sack in her arms. The way she stood reminded him of someone, or something, he'd seen before. He reached out his arms for the sack, but she shook her head, then gently, almost reverently, uncovered what she was holding.

Frank's stomach lurched and he was barely able to stop himself from regurgitating the potato he'd just eaten. An eyeless head with full moko and a shock of grey-black hair was staring at him from the old woman's tender grasp. He was unable to speak.

Wiki said something sharp in Maori to her grandmother, who covered the head slowly, frowning at Frank as she did so.

"I'm sorry, Sergeant Hardy," said Wiki. "I thought you would have seen one of these before."

"What is it?" he said.

"Mokomokai," she said. "A cured head. It's a very old Maori tradition. We preserve the heads of our chiefs and Tohunga after they die."

"How...?" he was not sure what he was asking, but she answered him anyway.

"Well, the eyes and brain are removed, and the head is boiled, then smoked, and left in the sun to dry. As you can see, it keeps the head in good condition, especially ta moko."

"The head is, must be, very old," said Frank. "One of your distant ancestors?"

"I told you," she said, getting annoyed with him. "It's my grandpa. My great grandpa I mean. My grandmother's father, who was a Tohunga."

"Your people still do this?" he asked, appalled at the casual way she had told him whose head the old woman had brought to show him.

"Not since I was young," she said. "The government banned it years ago. Grandpa died when I was five, so I don't remember him. That's why I like having his head. And we pray to him sometimes. It's like the gravestones you have in your cemeteries only more personal."

He shook his head. His heart had almost slowed to its normal pace.

"I knew Maori took the heads of their enemies, but..." He'd seen the decapitated head of one enemy, that of his brother Will, at the top of a pole.

She said something to her grandmother who was still glowering at Frank. Her grandmother spoke at great length, then turned and went back into the whare.

"I hope I haven't offended her," he said. "I didn't mean to." He explained as briefly as he could what had happened to his brother, and she nodded her understanding.

"I'll tell my grandmother about that," she said. "She'll

understand. Family...we always understand that."

"What was it she was saying to you just now," he asked.

"Mokomakai is an old tradition," she said. "And it's true we used to take the heads of enemies. But when my grandmother was a girl and the pakeha first came, they wanted the heads - the Mokomakai. They collected them and paid a lot of money for them. Then they gave our people muskets in exchange. My people had seen the pakeha using muskets and realized they could kill each other much faster. So they started making more heads to get more muskets in their battles, when iwi fought each other." She stopped and looked at Frank carefully. "We were always a warlike people," she said. "We fought each other before the pakeha came. But not with guns. The muskets meant more killing, lots more people dying. And some iwi began to kill their slaves to have more heads to sell. They would apply ta moko of important people to the heads of the slaves, and then kill the slaves and sell the heads..."

"The musket wars," he said, understanding. "I knew Europeans had provided the muskets, but I didn't know about the heads."

She went into the whare and came out several minutes later.

"My grandmother says to tell you she understands," she said. "Although I don't think you'll get another moko from her."

"Just as well," he said. "I don't think I could bear the pain. How does anyone stand having it done on the face?"

"She'll do ta moko on Hemi and Hohepa one day," she said. "They're used to the idea and know they must be brave. But for me, I could have the moko kauae, the chin moko, but I don't think I will. It's a very old-fashioned thing to do and I don't want to look like a grandmother."

He was silent for a while, then said, "Tell me about Anahera."

"Who?" she said. "Oh, my cousin from Poverty Bay...yes, of course. What do you want to know about him?"

"Who is he," he said. "What's his real name?"

She paused, obviously wondering how much to tell him. "We call him Tane Mahuta," she said eventually.

"Tane Mahuta," he said. "But I still don't understand where he comes from, who his family are. Why he was at the Pa? How is he your cousin?"

"He isn't really my cousin," she said. "I say that because we come from the same iwi, but not from the same hapu. You know the difference? A hapu is a family group and an iwi is a tribal group. I think he knew Moana. She came from Poverty Bay. Moana asked the boys from the Powhiri team if he could be added to the team, to lead them in the greeting...that time he almost killed the land agent. Did you know Moana?"

He nodded. "I met her once." She didn't know he had stopped the assassination of the agent, of Captain Porter. Just as well.

"She was very forceful," she said. "If she told you to do something, you did it. She made us all learn English, you know. The young people. My mother wouldn't, and of course my grandmother couldn't, she's too old, over sixty, but I've found it useful. But for the Powhiri, the boys didn't care who the leader would be anyway. They were sick of it. Every time an important pakeha came to the Pa they had to do one, and they hated it."

"Did her husband, did Hakopa know he – Tane Mahuta – was here?"

"I doubt it," she said, smiling slightly. "He had no idea what was going on, most of the...wait a minute. I remember you now. You were here that day, weren't you? You tackled him."

"That was me," he agreed. "He'd killed a lot of people. We

thought he intended to kill Captain Porter, the land agent. But I didn't expect him to be in the greeting party until I saw him with his spear raised."

"Who had he killed?" she asked.

"Several ex-soldiers," he said. "They were Die Hards, men from the 57th Regiment. My regiment. He thought we'd taken part in something that happened during the war with Titokowaru."

"And you hadn't?"

"Not exactly," he said carefully. "My officer - Captain Porter and I arrived just after it happened." He thought about the woman he had seen that day, holding the head of her husband. The woman he had discovered was Anahera – Tane Mahuta's– sister. That was who the grandmother had reminded him of, cradling the bag containing her father's head.

"He was just getting his revenge then," she said. "That's all right, isn't it? In war, people take revenge on one another."

"People don't like being on the wrong end of someone's revenge," he said. "I almost was myself, and I hadn't done anything wrong."

She put her head on her knee and thought about that for a moment, then raised it and said, "It isn't personal. But if a member of one group does something then they should pay for it as a group. Isn't that what war is about."

"You're very wise for your age," he said, smiling.

"Here's Willi Karira," she said, nodding towards the destroyed entrance to the Pa. "He must be looking for you."

He could see that her face had turned pink and she was twirling a strand of hair around her fingers. She had an open, expressive face that was easy to read.

Will was riding his own horse, pulling Copenhagen, Frank's

horse, behind him. Frank went to meet him. "Has something happened?" He patted Copenhagen's nose, and the horse nudged him, as if to say, where were you?

"We're going to have to get you away from here. The Armed Constabulary are searching Palmerston. They've been to the Scandi settlement and now they're headed for the logging camp. I suspect the Pa will be next. They know you were dropped off at Pieter's new place and they tried to arrest him."

"Arrest Pieter?" said Frank, shocked.

"Don't worry. He's fine. I'll tell you the details later, but we need to move before they come here. We'll hide you in the bush for a day or two, until they leave town. I telegraphed Captain Porter, to see if he knew anything…"

Frank vaulted onto Copenhagen, and turned to say goodbye to Wiki. She gestured to him to wait and ran back inside the whare, coming out after a moment holding a long, feathered cloak. "You'll need this to keep you warm at night," she said. "It belonged to my father."

"Thank you, Wiki," he said. "I hope your father won't mind me using it."

"He's dead," she said. "He died in the fight between the pakeha and Titokowaru. Up near Patea, at Turuturumokai."

"I'm sorry," he said. "I'm sure my people appreciated that he gave his life for us."

She shrugged. "Maybe," she said. "Except that he was fighting for Titokowaru and for my people."

He couldn't think of an appropriate reply, and followed Karira to the north side of the pa to a track he had not known existed.

"We won't take the usual route into town," explained Karira. "I don't want to run into the Armed Constabulary on the way to your hiding place. I used to play in the bush around here when I was growing up, so I can find my way there easily enough."

"Where are we heading?" asked Frank.

"Remember when we were searching for Anahera up behind the sawmill and we found his camp? And the place he made for himself on the branch of a totara tree? We'll go there. Even if they search in that area they won't think to look up in a tree."

"I might be able to pull myself onto the branch," said Frank, remembering how Karira had stood on his horse to boost himself up when they were searching for Anahera. "But how will I get down?"

"You'll jump if you have to," said Karira. "But the plan is that you'll stay up there for the next day or so. I'll come and get you when I think it's safe. I'll bring Copenhagen so you don't break an ankle jumping down."

"I don't suppose you brought my shirt with you," asked Frank.

Karira shook his head. "Where did you lose it?"

Frank shrugged. "In the bush, up near Bunnythorpe. Well, I've been in a hole and now I'll be in a tree, but at least I'll have time to think, and perhaps get us all out of trouble. And I'll be warm enough with this cloak."

"Mette and I think we might know part of what's going on," said Karira. "She says you met Colonel Mountjoy…"

"I met him in Wellington, at my hotel," said Frank. "And his son as well, or a man whom I believe is his son, at Wanganui Collegiate. Then he came looking for me – the son I mean – in Bunnythorpe. Why, I don't know."

"What did you think of the son?" asked Karira.

"An unpleasant fellow," said Frank. "Why?"

"Did he remind you of anyone?"

"He looked very much like Will, my brother Will," said Frank. "And for a minute I almost thought—or hoped—that it might be Will. It wasn't, of course. He was too young. If Will were alive he would be in his thirties by now."

"Where were you twenty years ago?" asked Karira.

"In India," said Frank. He stopped Copenhagen and turned in his saddle to look at Karira. "What are you saying, Karira?"

"He may look like your brother," said Karira. "I have no way of knowing if he does. But he looks very much like you. Very much."

Frank stared at him for a moment, puzzled, then his face cleared. "Are you saying that he's my…son?" he asked.

Karira nodded. "Is that possible?"

Frank scratched his chin through his beard. "I suppose so. There were women…"

"But you can't remember a particular instance…? I mean, someone who might have been married to Colonel Mountjoy, or married him soon after you…"

Karira was starting to look embarrassed, so Frank said, "I'll think about it while I'm marooned up the tree and let you know. But off hand…"

They rode in silence for a few minutes, then Frank said, "Does Mette know about this?"

"She saw him," said Karira, "and noticed how much he looked like you. She doesn't seem upset about it, but I can't always tell with women. She knows it would have happened many years ago…"

"She'll understand," said Frank. "I know her. What I'm curious about is why Colonel Mountjoy would think locking me away was an answer," said Frank. "You'd think he might call me out for a duel...I heard he's hoping to be given the governorship...perhaps that has something to do with it, although I can't think why..."

"I'll see what I can find out. Captain Porter might know something."

"Talking of Porter," said Frank. "I learned something from Wiki. She says all the young people at the pa knew about Anahera and his connection to Moana."

Karira raised one eyebrow. "Really?"

"She told me his name as well," said Frank. "She said his name is Tane Mahuta."

Karira's lip started to twitch, and within minutes he was crying with laughter. "She told you...she told you that?" he asked. "Frank, your leg has been stretched to twice its length."

"She seemed like an honest..."

"Tane..." said Karira, and started to laugh again. "Tane Mahuta means God of the Forest. It's the name given to a giant kauri tree, up in the far north. Hundreds of years old..."

"Oh," said Frank, chastened.

"I think I'm starting to like Wiki," said Karira. "Tane Mahuta indeed."

He was still chuckling when they reached the totara tree behind the saw mill. He handed Frank a bag of food and a flask of water, holding Copenhagen in place while Frank stood on her back and slowly dragged himself onto the broad branch. "If I'm not back in two days, jump down and run for the mill," he said, grinning up at Frank. "Or hobble to the mill. But don't worry. No one will think to look for you here. You'll be safe until I return. Tomorrow, probably, or the next day at the most."

"Make sure you come back," said Frank. "I don't want to

have the choice of dying up here or jumping and breaking both my legs." He settled back on the branch. "I suppose if Charles II could hide in an oak tree, I can manage a totara."

"Watch out for the Roundheads," said Karira. "And for giant walking trees. At least you'll be safe from crazed eels and killer kiwis."

Frank watched as Karira disappeared along the track. He felt as if he was back in his pit, with the trees as the bars. Once night closed in he would not be able to see anything. It would be worse than the pit, as he'd have to be careful not to fall in the intense darkness.

12

The English Periodicals

"Lady Debra Mountjoy," said Mette to Mr. Robinson. "Colonel Mountjoy's wife is named Lady Debra Mountjoy. She's the eldest daughter of a baronet. She married the colonel in July 1856 in India, and the son was born..." She stopped. Milo's date of birth was given as February 12. 1857, seven months after his parents married. "He was born in 1857," she said. She was reading from an old copy of *Burke's Peerage*, which Mr. Robinson had discovered on a shelf deep in the back of his shop. "And their only issue—does that mean son? —is the Hon. Milo Horatio Mountjoy. He was at Harrow when this was published...Frank said he... it sounds like the same family. What does Order of the Bath mean?"

"Who has that? And what level does he have?" asked Mr. Robinson.

"Lady Mountjoy's father..."

"Lady Debra," corrected Mr. Robinson, "If her father is a baronet..."

"Lady Debra," said Mette. "Yes, that's what it says. Her father is a Knight Commander of the Bath...that sounds very English. Does that mean he has to bathe the king?"

"He was probably a military officer then," said Mr. Robinson. "Or naval. High ranking. You think she — Lady Debra — may have something to do with Colonel Mountjoy and his son's vendetta against Frank?" He too had seen the young man, and Mette could tell her felt sorry for her, which did not do much to improve her mood.

"I'm not sure why," she said. "Could we find out where she is? Now, I mean? Or where she was nineteen or twenty years ago?" Mr. Robinson busied himself with a stack of books, and she realized she had given away her thoughts to him, or at least confirmed his suspicions.

"I have a large collection of magazines and newspapers I brought with me from London," he said. "Some *Illustrated London News*, *Cornhill Magazine* before it ceased publication, and the *Sunday Magazine*. They're old – but perhaps we can find her mentioned." He led Mette to magazines heaped up in an even darker corner of the shop. "Browse through them. You may find something."

Mette knelt and started through the pile. It should have been an arduous task, but she found herself entranced by what she read in the magazines. A most wonderful short story by a writer named Mr. Anthony Trollope—she'd have to see if he'd written anything else. And another by a man named George Eliot that looked interesting and well written. She had a lot to learn about English literature, she knew. After a while her knees ached and she stood and walked over to the window, stretching her arms. Mr. Robinson had made a pot of tea and he brought her some in a delicate china cup. Tea. It was the answer to everything for English people, and she had no idea why when coffee was so much more satisfying. Mr. Robinson liked his tea weak and scented, compared to most

New Zealanders, who like their tea boiled to a dark, tarry consistency. She'd read in the newspaper recently that tea might be the reason heart attacks were more prevalent in New Zealand, and was happy she was a coffee drinker.

She stood by the window sipping the weak tea slowly – it may as well have been water – staring out at the Square. A couple passed her shop, she plump, wearing a red dress and an odd hat, he tall with a floppy hat, neither seeming the type of people she usually saw through the shop window. Their arms were linked and they leaned together so closely that their heads touched. She put down her tea cup. Oh no. Did this mean that Gottlieb's brother and Pieter's sister were going to become one? Would that make her related to Gottlieb in some strange way? It felt very wrong. She couldn't imagine…but at least it would remove the responsibility for Agnete from Pieter. Of course it would also give Frederic Karlsen control over Agnete's inheritance. He seemed like a nice enough man … perhaps with some strange ideas…but Agnete might settle down under the steadying guidance of a husband, even one who had strange ideas and was willing to believe the oddest stories.

She returned to her task, and almost instantly found something interesting. An article entitled "A Lady's View of the British Raj." It was about India, and the anonymous author had apparently spent more time at dances, teas and musical afternoons than she had spent learning about the country itself and how it was governed. Mette ran her finger down the page, searching for a mention of a Lady Debra Mountjoy. She had passed it and was on the next page when she realized she'd seen something. Not Lady Debra Mountjoy, but Lady Debra Paget the daughter of a baronet who had just arrived in India.

She went back and read the paragraph. A young, recently arrived English woman who, the article implied, had come with her father in hopes of finding a husband in an India full of upper class military men and speculators looking to make their fortunes, but short of eligible women. Many women came on the same mission, but this one had succeeded. She had met and married an unnamed colonel soon after the Siege of Lucknow, where she had been trapped, briefly. The writer made some unkind comments about love's early blossoming, implying that Lady Debra had wasted no time in finding herself a spouse. He was a "fine upstanding man with a great future before him," the writer had said, implying that she had not chosen someone for his looks or money. The comment reminded Mette of something her mother used to say: if the baby is ugly say nice things about its clothing. Lady Debra was described as an English rose, with pale curls and deep blue eyes, like a tiny Meissen porcelain figurine.

Mette sat back, rubbing her aching back, and wondered what Colonel Mountjoy looked like. If he too was fair-haired and blue-eyed he must have wondered right from the moment of his birth why his son was tall with dark brown eyes and olive skin. Especially since – she looked at the dates again – especially since Lady Debra had given birth to her only son just eight months after arriving in India and seven months after marrying the colonel.

She showed the magazine to Mr. Robinson. "Do you mind if I keep this one?"

"You found something?" he asked.

She nodded. "I think I may have...." But she felt sad. She would have thought Frank was better than this, not someone who would impregnate a woman and leave her to find another father for the child.

13

Treed

After Karira left, Frank opened the bag of supplies Karira had given him, expecting more potatoes or bread, and was pleasantly surprised to find slabs of Hop Li's grainy-textured bread, some thick slices of baked ham, a jar of Morton's pickles, some Fry's chocolate, and best of all, two quart bottles of Blood's Stout. He ate half the feast and left the rest for later, although he was tempted by the second bottle of stout. Best if he stayed sober, he decided. He hadn't wanted to jump out of the tree, but falling from it in a drunken stupor was not something he wanted to do either.

He spent a somewhat comfortable night wrapped in Wiki's father's cloak, trying not to move. The broad branch had a natural indentation in the centre, making it easier to stay in place – Anahera had chosen this spot for a reason. Eventually he dozed off to the sounds of the forest at night: an owl hooting nearby, the panicked screech of a kiwi, and the who-are-you call of the huia. He awoke to a foggy, damp morning. A river mist had crept up and awaited the sun to disperse it. He could not see the ground from his perch in the tree. He was cold and his shoulders ached from trying to stay in place against the trunk. He hoped Karira would be along soon to rescue him from his self-imposed prison.

He ate the rest of the bread, cheese and pickles Karira had left, enjoying it despite the hardness of the bread and the warmth of the cheese. When he finished, he forced himself to think about the possibility that Milo Mountjoy could be his son. He couldn't imagine that Colonel Mountjoy had married someone who he – Frank – might have known in India. The English class system was at its worst there. There was very little chance of him even having a cup of tea with any woman who would then go on to marry Colonel Mountjoy. He'd had flings with camp followers, and women who'd come to visit his fellow non-commissioned officers – sisters and such – and the occasional lady's maid. But at eighteen, but appearing older, he was a mere corporal, the son of a coachman. His brown eyes and olive skin tended to make him a bad catch, even for the sisters of non-commissioned officers. He'd heard one describing him as having "a touch of the tar brush," a legacy from his mother, who his father had rescued during the Battle of Salamanca and later married and taken to England. She'd died giving birth to his younger brother Will, and he could barely remember her. But his father was still affected by the loss and kept a painting of her over the mantelpiece in his cottage. She'd been a striking woman, with a long neck, thick dark hair and an impressive Roman nose that neither of the boys had inherited.

He hugged the feathered cloak Wiki had given him around his shoulders, and thought of another option. His father. What if Milo was his brother and not his son? But surely not. His father lived on the estate of a wealthy man, where he'd been first a groom and then a coachman. The aristocracy of England spent weekends at his father's employer's estate; the men spent the time hunting, leaving their bored wives in the house. His father was a distinguished ex-soldier who might interest some aristocratic woman wanting a fling. But he'd been faithful to the memory of his wife for so long...

He sat on the broad branch of the totara tree, staring into the sun-speckled darkness of the forest, hoping for inspiration. He heard a slight noise below him and he pressed himself back into the trunk and pulled up his legs so he blended more into the huge tree.

"*Mach nicht so viel Lärm,*" said someone in a harsh, threatening voice. He was speaking German, which Frank understood somewhat. He understood that the man was asking someone not to be noisy. German. Could it be Gottfried Karlsen's brother Frederic? He peered down carefully, and saw the man was leaning against someone, a woman, his hand over her mouth.

"I promise, I won't, I promise, I promise, please..." said the woman in a muffled, panicked voice. Damn it, he thought. It's that woman. Agnete Madsen, Pieter's sister. He held on to a small branch and strained forward to see the tops of their heads. They were against the tree in which he now sat. As if there weren't enough trees in this forest, they had to pick the one where he was hiding. Karlsen was leaning against her heavily, his face just inches from hers, his hand pressed against her lips.

He was going to have to jump from this tree to save Agnete Madsen. He'd break both his legs and at best scare Karlsen off for a few minutes, but it had to be done. He edged out further, mentally preparing himself for a leap and an uncomfortable landing, remembering how it felt when Anahera had dropped on him from a tree not far from here. That had taken some determination, he realized now, especially for a large man.

Karlsen was fiddling with his trousers looking very much like his brother Gottlieb when Frank had surprised him by the river. A rape as well then. Yes, he would most definitely need to jump out of the tree onto Karlsen to save the honour of this despicable woman. But before he could, Agnete said, or rather moaned, something that stopped him from jumping.

"*Meine liebchen.*"

She began scrabbling at her red dress with one hand and hoisted it awkwardly above her waist. Her other arm snaked around Karlsen's neck, and Karlsen pressed against her, pinning her to the tree with his body while he used his hands to push his trousers down below his knees. She stood awkwardly on one leg, the other wrapped around Karlsen, as he began thrusting himself into her. Frank recoiled, repulsed, unable to escape the sounds as the two rutted and grunted below him. Eventually Agnete broke her promise and began to cry loudly with each thrust. When they finished—which seem to take forever—Karlsen said to her angrily, "You said you would not make a noise. How can we ever be in a house or a hotel if you cannot be quiet? We cannot always be in the woods to do this."

"Ah, my darling," said Agnete. "We will buy a very large house with thick walls, and I will scream all I want. You must like it when I do so. Does it not prove my love for you?"

Karlsen grunted and walked away from the tree, pushing himself back into his trousers, straightening the hat he had worn for the duration of the encounter. If he turned and looked up he would certainly see Frank. Agnete followed him into view and clutched at his trouser buttons, but he knocked her away angrily.

"When we are married..." she said.

He turned. "Have I asked you to marry me?" he said sharply.

Frank could not see her face, but he heard the sly coyness in her voice.

"Not yet, but I think you will," she said. "You have violated me, just as your brother did my sister-in-law, and I will go to the police if I am not given satisfaction. My brother will..."

Frank did not hear what Agnete thought Pieter would do, as Karlsen stormed off towards the sawmill, Agnete following him close behind. He could see her hands waving as she walked. She had found someone to replace Mads Madsen and Mr. Williams and was using her powers of persuasion and her skills to rope him in. She was incorrigible.

He felt like he needed a cold bath with lots of carbolic soap. These two deserved each other. He just hoped he would not be forced to share Sunday tea with them. But despite his disgust, he felt somewhat aroused, and he started thinking of his own history with women.

There was the woman who had thrown herself at him aboard the boat on the way to India. She was older than him, a tall blonde with pale blue eyes who spoke very little but knew what she wanted, which was a quick encounter in her cabin, with as little conversation as possible, followed by a quick exit on his part. He couldn't remember her name, if he'd even known what it was. Then there was the sister of a British Parliamentarian, in India to oversee the start of the dissolution of the East India Company – he'd been quite fond of her. They'd talked of marriage, he remembered, although she was as young as him and didn't understand that he would be an inappropriate match for her. The brother had stepped in to separate them and she went without an argument. But with her he hadn't…and he'd had a brief fling with a maid after the relief of Cawnpore. He'd been with the East India Company rescue force sent to escort them back to Allahabad after the release was negotiated. And then the unthinkable. Rebels turned on them, and most of the men in the force were killed.

When Cawnpore was eventually back in Company control, they'd discovered that 120 English women and children had been massacred, their dismembered bodies thrown down a well. He'd been put in charge of rescuing two women, one the daughter of someone with influence, and her maid. The pair had been captured and taken to Nana's harem, and he'd gone with a captain to negotiate their release for a large ransom. The daughter was distressed but calm, almost too calm, reminding him of the way soldiers were after battle. However, the maid was stronger and had endured her capture stoically, with a sense of acceptance. He'd accompanied them back to Agra and had never seen them again.

He heard hoof beats approaching from the direction of the sawmill and pushed himself back against the tree trunk. He couldn't see the track, but heard at least six horsemen pass beneath him at equal intervals. It could only be the Armed Constabulary. No one else rode in formation like that. He stayed where he was without moving, and a short time later they returned. They stopped fifty yards past the tree and he heard them talking, although not what they were saying.

He leaned forward carefully. Five constables, not six; one man addressed the rest - probably in charge - but one was twisted in his saddle looking straight at Frank. He stayed where he was, realizing it would be worse to move back than it would be to keep still. If he had been seen, there was nothing he could do. A minute later a sixth constable caught up with the others, shaking his head, and the man at the rear nodded and turned. With a signal from the lead horseman they departed.

He'd not seen the last man to arrive clearly – just his profile as he spoke. But he knew who it was. Wilson was back in Palmerston, no doubt helping the search for Frank.

With the troop gone, the quiet of the bush closed in again. He contemplated climbing down from his perch and making a run for it. He could jump a ship heading to Melbourne and start again in Australia. Change his name. Work as a jackaroo on a sheep station in Queensland, or head up to Darwin and work on the prawn boats. But there was Mette. She was holding him here. His life had improved dramatically since he'd met her. He was happier; he felt better when he was taking care of her, not thinking of himself.

But then something dark exploded into his memory.

Agnete had said, "You have violated me like your brother violated my sister-in-law." Unless Gottfried had attacked Maren, which he was sure he had not, then Agnete knew about what Gottfried had done, or almost done, to Mette, her only other sister-in-law. If Karlsen was still searching for the man who had killed his brother, this knowledge would be a first step towards the answer. Frank had beaten Gottfried Karlsen after he discovered what he'd tried to do to Mette, and for that reason Karlsen had ambushed Frank and Mette in the Manawatu Gorge; Frank had been forced to kill him with the tomahawk he'd taken from Anahera. How did she know about the rape attempt? It must be Maren again, not knowing enough to keep quiet. Would Agnete tell Karlsen about it again and again until he heard what she was saying?

The day stretched on, as he huddled in the cloak hoping Karira would come, and thought about his problems. Was Colonel Mountjoy obsessed with his son's parentage? Had he already believed he wasn't the father, and had therefore reacted to Frank in such a strange way at the hotel in Wellington? And why would having Frank sent to the secret Armed Constabulary prison up the Wanganui River solve anything? Then there was his other problem: how long before Frederic Karlsen found out that Frank had killed his brother?

The sun rose higher and at what he judged to be midday he heard the beat of horses approaching. He stayed motionless until he heard, "Hardy? You there?"

He leaned out and looked down at Karira. "Can I come down now?"

Karira was grinning up at him. "I remembered that you might need to perform your ablutions," he said. "That part slipped my mind. I decided I should come now, and not leave you for another day…"

Karira had brought Copenhagen with him, and he nudged the horse up to the tree, his own horse beside her to keep her in place. "Lower your legs and I'll guide you to the saddle."

Frank found a sturdy branch that protruded from the one where he had spent the night, gripped hold of it and lowered himself backwards into space, while Karira directed his feet. In a short time, he was clutching the trunk of the tree as he balanced on Copenhagen's back, gradually lowering himself to a seated position, his hands sliding over the bark of the tree as he did so, his arms reaching barely half way around the trunk.

"You came earlier than I expected," he said. "Thank God. I couldn't have stood it much longer."

"The iwi are massing in the Square," said Karira. "I saw the Armed Constabulary leaving on the road to the Gorge. I was thinking I could take you to my uncle's new house." He looked Frank up and down. "You'll fit right in. Although I can't say you look all that much like a Maori. More like a *pakeha* Maori, but that will do. And I heard Ringiringi is in town. You can hang about with him and exchange stories about being light skinned in a dark-skinned world."

"Did the Armed Constabulary look for me at the pa?" asked Frank.

Karira nodded. "Yes, and they had a hard time with young Wiki. She told them stories about seeing white ghosts—*Turehu*—in the bush, and how our people believed that the pakeha were reincarnations of their ancestors, come back to haunt us and punish us. She has a future as a kaikōrero paki– a teller of funny stories."

"How did Mountjoy react?"

"She said he totally dismissed her as some kind of naïve fool," said Karira. "She saw the resemblance to you, by the way. It's going to be hard for them to keep that from surfacing." He paused and looked at Frank from the corner of his eye. "Any idea who the mother might have been, if he is in fact your son?"

"I've thought about it," said Frank. "I have a couple of possibilities."

"Just a couple?" said Karira. "Hmm. Well Mette found the name of Colonel Mountjoy's wife. Lady Debra, born Lady Debra Paget."

"The name doesn't sound familiar," said Frank. "Although…"

"She arrived in India by ship," said Karira, "and married the colonel within a month. The son was born seven months after the wedding."

The woman on the ship, then? She'd been the most unlikely of the candidates. He could imagine her being Milo Mountjoy's mother, however. A self-absorbed personality with no warmth.

"I think I know the mother," he said. "Or knew her, at least. Can we find out if the woman I remember is the same woman who married Mountjoy?"

"The best thing to do is find a way to see her," said Karira.

14

The Desirable Corner Half-Acre

By Order of the Public Trustee. . .For Sale. The desirable Corner Half-acre, with two-roomed house, situated in New Chum's Town, Palmerston North, late the property of Charles Henry Trim; deceased. For further particulars, apply to Eliot Warburton, Solicitor; Palmerston North.
Manawatu Times, 20 June 1877

Mette was captivated.
"Such a beautiful house, Hop Li," she said. "And close to the Square, and Mr. Robinson's, and all the shops." She spun around in the centre of the kitchen, trying to take everything in. "A Leamington range with hot plates, and a closed oven." She fingered the dampers on the top of the stove. "What are these for?"
"Keeps the fire going," said Hop Li. "You keep it open, the fire goes quickly, keep it closed, the fire goes for long time, and keeps the top hot. Food boils slowly."
She ran her hand along the edge of the kitchen table. "And this beautiful table for a family to sit around. Who carved it? It's very beautiful. The legs are like the carvings on the

meeting house at the pa. They look like snakes…or giant eels."

"A man from the pa," he said. "He lives in town now, does nice work with an adze – he uses heart of kauri wood. I would hire him again. That's not yours…the table. That sits there to make the kitchen good when I show people the house. I'll move it to another house later."

She went through a wide doorway into the next room. "And this is the parlour?"

He followed her in. "You put a Chesterfield couch there with nice cushions, or two chairs beside the fireplace. Put up some curtains…red curtains for luck. Have a big fire in the grate…little bits of apple tree wood to make it smell good. Make it seem like home." He was obviously thinking of how he could sell the house. If she ever bought one of her own she would ask him for suggestions on how to make it look nice. He gestured with his head towards the third of the four rooms. "Big bedroom in there, for mum and dad. Then two other bedrooms, one for boys and one for girls."

Mette went into the bedroom for mum and dad. "There's already a bed here," she said. "Is it just for display as well?" It was a large bed with a striped cotton spring mattress. She pushed on the mattress, watching how springy it was, and thought how wonderful it would be for two people to live in a house like this, sharing such a bed, with – eventually – two fair-haired children in the other rooms…

"Your sister bought it," he said.

"Maren?" said Mette. "Maren bought this house?"

"No, no," said Hop Li. "Your sister bought this <u>bed</u>. For you and Frank."

"I don't understand," said Mette. Her heart was pounding. Why would Maren buy them a bed? She had threatened to do so of course, when they were married, but why follow up on her threat and leave the bed in this wonderful house?

"This is your house," said Hop Li. "I told your sister it was your house."

Mette sat down abruptly on the bed and stared at Hop Li. "This is my house? Hop Li, I would like more than anything in the world for this to be my house. But how is it possible?"

"I have a lotta money," he said, confusing her. "Mostly in China though. I need more here to build more houses. I make a good profit that way. Frank goes to the manager at the Bank of New Zealand and says he needs money, and the manager gives him money. There you go sergeant, he says. I go to the Bank of New Zealand, the manager says, no, why do you need money, Chinaman?" He looked at Mette, with his eyes narrowed and contemptuous, imitating how the manager at the bank would react if he asked for money.

"Frank borrowed money for you?" she asked.

He nodded. "And then I built five very nice houses. Lots of Chinamen here work for nothing. I feed them, pay a little, let them sleep in old house by river. Works good. No more gold for them now, the diggings are finished, most of them."

Mette thought about that. "But Frank didn't give you any of his own money," she said. "He has only small savings, and his army pension. He told me so."

"No," said Hop Li. "But I give him interest for borrowing the money for me. Not real interest. But this house, which I build for very cheap. Cheap, but the best one. On a corner with a very big section. Lots of room for a garden. Good for you and Frank"

"Then this is really going to be my house," she said. She threw her arms around Hop Li. "Thank you Hop Li, thank you. I can never repay you."

"No need, no need," he said, his body arching backwards, trying to escape her grasp. She could tell he was embarrassed and let him go.

"What will you do with the other four houses?" she asked. "Will you rent them to people, or sell them?"

"Rent," he said firmly. "Fifteen shillings a week. I make three pounds a week and pay for the houses in two years. Then I build more houses. You know someone who wants a house to rent?"

She considered his question. "Yes, I do." She told him about Wiki and her grandmother and two younger brothers, who would soon be forced to leave the pa.

"If a Maori family moves in here, no one else moves in next door," he said. "Not a good idea."

"Then where can they move?" asked Mette. She imagined living next door to the lively young Maori girl, and thought how nice it would be to have her next door, getting to know her. But she knew she wouldn't change Hop Li's mind.

"She want some work?" he asked.

"Perhaps," said Mette. "She might like to work and help out her family, once she's in town. They'll need to find money somewhere."

"I have an idea," he said. "I'll think about it and then tell you later."

"Who would you like to rent these houses to?" asked Mette. Whoever moved in, they would be her neighbours. Hers and Franks. Their children would grow up together, and play together in the street while their parents played cards together. She would drink coffee – or tea – with the women while the men were away at work, and they would knit and sew and talk about their children together. And later she would sit in the sun in the parlour window and write down her recipes that she created from the vegetables in her very own garden, out the...

"The English," he said firmly. "They come now. No more Scandies, but lots of the English. I see them coming into town every day, the new chums. They know nothing about anything, but they think they can come here and be the masters of us all. I would like to take some money off the English. I call these the Hardy Heritage Homes. They think an Englishman built them so they must be good. They don't believe they were made by Chinese."

"It's a pity no more Scandies are coming," said Mette. "I'd like to see more people from my country in Palmerston. But I'm surprised that you're so negative about English people. Frank is an Englishman, and you like him."

He nodded. "Frank is my friend. I owe him lots of things, not just the money help."

"How did you meet?" she asked. "Was it a long time ago?"

"We met in the Gorge," said Hop Li. "When Scandies were building the road through there, three, four years ago. I took food from Palmerston to sell, and he was driving his coach from Napier to Woodville. The coach wasn't coming through the Gorge to Palmerston yet, but sometimes he rode his horse up through the Gorge to see how the road was going. I got in some trouble. They said I stole something."

"You stole something?" said Mette, shocked.

Hop Li avoided her eyes.

"No. They SAID I stole something. One Scandi saw a Chinaman taking a hammer, and he says it was me. I say, I did not take the hammer. The Scandi says, I saw you take the hammer. Not me I say."

"He confused you with someone else," said Mette. "You know, you all look very much alike, Chinese people. Although I know sometimes people think all Scandies look alike."

Hop Li looked her up and down. "That's because you DO all look alike," he said. "I think your sister is you, all the time."

Mette laughed. How could someone confuse her with Maren? They had different hair and different coloured eyes. Maren was round and plump, and she was tall and too thin. And Maren was much prettier.

"I just remember she's the pretty one, you're the clever one," said Hop Li. "When you say something, I know it's you."

"How did Frank come into this," said Mette, blushing. She preferred to be the clever one, although she wished she was as pretty as Maren.

"Frank gets me and four other Chinamen lined up, and he says to the men, 'Which one did you see take the hammer?' And the man says, 'I can't tell. They all have the same face, like sheep.' And then he points to the wrong one and says 'Maybe this one?' But that one just arrived on the coach, and Frank tells them that."

"And they let you go?" said Mette.

Hop Li nodded. "And then Frank says to me after, 'Where did you put hammer?' And I gave it to him and he put it in the grass for the men to find."

"But I thought you said you didn't steal the hammer," said Mette.

"Just borrow," said Hop Li. "But I can't tell the men that. They wanted to throw me off the cliff into the river. I can't swim, even if I survived the fall."

Mette smiled, and walked into the kitchen. "This is such a

lovely house. Frank will love it as well, I know he will. But we can't move in until we're married. And that may not happen for a while now. Frank will have to clear his name first. Did the Armed Constabulary leave town?"

"The man with Frank's face left," said Hop Li. "Karira says he went back to Wanganui. And some of the troopers. But I saw one of the constables here. One we played cards with, me and Frank. The rest left town. Maybe he came back to watch the Maori meeting."

"There's a meeting?" asked Mette. "I wondered who all those people were coming in to town."

"Big hui," said Hop Li. "Be careful when you go outside today. Men racing up and down on horses; you'll get run over if you're not careful."

Despite Hop Li's warning, Mette crossed the Square looking for Karira, pushing her way through the throngs of Maori. She had to see Frank, to reassure herself that he still loved her, and even, a little bit, to make sure she still loved him after what she'd found in the English magazines. Karira would tell her where Frank was, and when he'd be back. If Mountjoy and most of the Armed Constabulary were gone, she hoped that meant Frank could have a brief respite in town.

The mood was lively, with men standing in circles talking, and woman seated in groups with legs crossed and shawls wrapped around their shoulders. In one group, Wiki sat with some younger women. Mette waved to her, but Wiki did not return the wave. Perhaps for Wiki, too, all the Scandies looked the same. It was an odd thought.

In the centre of the Square someone had left a trap, the harness empty. An older man stood on top looking at the crowd, ready to speak. Interested, Mette made her way towards him. He wore a cloak that she knew meant he was a chief, and his face, long and distinguished, was heavily covered with moko over every part. A long white object hung around his neck – it looked like a horn, or a tooth of some large animal. She hoped he would speak in English, but even if he didn't she wanted to see the reaction of the people watching. She pushed closer and waited.

Someone beside her said a name – Peete te Awe Awe. Unlike English, the vowels in the Maori language were consistent, and she was learning to hear it, if not to understand it. That was the first step. She could still remember the day when she could suddenly hear English. A woman had bumped into her and said, "Pardon me," and she'd heard and understood the words separately: *"Undskyld mig."*

The man on the trap raised his arms. The crowd was instantly silent, and those who were further away began to move towards him, jostling her forward with them and hemming her in. She felt suffocated, unable to move in the dense crowd.

Peete te Awe Awe began to speak. In Maori, as she'd expected. She watched him, enjoying the rhythm of the language and the rapt expressions on the faces of the listeners. He must be saying something very special. A tall, broad-shouldered man stepped between her and the speaker, and she leaned left to get a better view. He moved again. *"Af vejen,"* she said loudly, assuming no one near her would understand. "Get out of my way."

Although the tall man was more than ten feet away, he turned slowly in her direction, as if he'd heard her and understood.

And she found herself face-to-face once more with Anahera.

There was no doubt in her mind. The size, the stance, the unforgettable tattoo on his face ... it was him. She pushed away from through the crowd, holding the eyes of the man who had killed so many people, and who had tried so hard to kill Frank. He would kill her now, when Frank was not here to save her.

He stared at her for what seemed like several minutes, his eyes half-closed, expression unreadable as she put as much distance between them as she could. Then a slight, very slight smile, so slight that she was unsure if she was seeing it, lifted his lips, and he dropped his head in a nod. As she watched, he moved away into the crowd, his head remaining visible for several seconds.

Surprised, she started to push forward in the direction he'd gone, but bumped into someone and stumbled, stepping on her own skirt, and falling to her knees. Hands reached out, lifted her to her feet and helped brush dirt from her skirt. She stood on her toes, searching for a glimpse of Anahera. But he had gone. She had to find Karira, let him know that Anahera was in Palmerston, so he could warn Frank. She could not stand the thought of his enemy killing Frank, who she once again was sure she loved, and did not want killed. That would kill her as well. She would die of sadness.

15

Gathering in the Square

Frank and Karira saw Mette as she came from a group of new-built homes and headed across the Square, which was filled with tents and people bustling around setting up cooking fires, chatting, and selling goods. In front of the telegraph office a group of elders sat in a circle in a deep discussion.

"There's my uncle," said Karira. "We'd better talk to him first. We'll find Mette later…"

Hakopa gave them a small nod of greeting as they dismounted, but continued speaking in Maori to the men in the group.

"They're talking about land confiscations," said Karira. "The government confiscated the land of any iwi involved in the wars between Maori and Europeans, and they want to test the legality and ask the government to do so by the law and not by the sword."

"But your uncle sold his land," said Frank. "It wasn't confiscated."

"He's firmly on both sides of the argument," said Karira, smiling wryly. "Depending on who he's with. This group wants to take their case before the Supreme Court – they're formulating a letter, because the government has just delayed doing anything one more time."

"What do you think? Will that work?" asked Frank, curious.

Karira shrugged. "They have to try, I suppose. I think those who fought against the Crown can't expect to have it their way now. That's why they've brought in Hakopa. They know what he's done, but he has good standing with the government, and can talk to them."

Frank and Karira sat outside the circle of men as the discussion went on, each man speaking at length. Eventually the talking stopped, and the men stood, nodded to each other, and moved off towards their tents.

Hakopa came towards them and greeted Frank warmly.

"Sergeant Hardy," he said in slow and cautious English. "I must thank you once more for saving us when the rebel Anahera attacked Captain Porter. He brought disgrace on my *hapu*."

"Sergeant Hardy needs our help," said Karira. "The Armed Constabulary troopers are looking for him. We need to hide him for a few days. He's done nothing illegal…wrong…but…"

Hakopa avoided Frank's eyes, not inspiring much confidence. "*Haere mai ki toku whare*," he said, having run out of English words. "*Ka nga te ra*."

"He says, go to his house at sunset," said Karira. "For now, just lose yourself in the crowd. There'll be food over in the centre of the Square all evening. Lots of good food. Roast pig, smoked eel, dried fish, potted birds…and potatoes of course."

"Are you sure we can trust him?" asked Frank. "I know he's your uncle, but…"

"You could be right," said Karira. "I wonder if we should head up to Wanganui…"

"To investigate the Mountjoys?" asked Frank. "That seems like a good first step. We could go now. Why wait until tomorrow? I'd just need to have a word with Mette, get some fresh clothes, and then..."

Karira nodded his agreement.

The crowd in The Square started to increase in size, and there was a sense of celebration. Frank and Karira led their horses through the melee, watching the reaction of the Maori to Frank's disguise. He was sure he was fooling no one, but then there were no Europeans here, other than Constable Price who could be seen in the distance outside the police station, watching and waiting for trouble, Jimi by his side.

A cluster had formed in the centre of the Square, and Frank saw a chief mounting a trap, ready to make a speech. The chief stood there like a statue of a Greek philosopher, one hand under the fold of his short, feathered cloak, the other at his side, and began to speak. The people in The Square moved towards him, mesmerized.

"Who's that?" asked Frank, feeling himself pulled to the centre as well.

"Peete te Awe Awe," said Karira. "Chief of the Rangitane iwi. He was instrumental in selling the Manawatu block to the government more than ten years ago. If it weren't for him, Palmerston wouldn't be here."

"You don't sound happy about that," said Frank.

Karira shrugged. "I used to think we were doing the right thing," he said. "Moving forward, becoming like you – the British – but now I'm not so sure."

The crowd was starting to respond to Peete te Awe Awe's speech with shouts and movement. Over in front of the police station an altercation had broken out, and they could see

Constable Price and Jimi struggling with a man.

"We'd better help Price," said Frank. "I think he's in trouble."

"I'll go," said Karira. "He knows you and probably trusts you, but he'd feel bound to turn you in if he knew the troopers were after you. Take the horses to the paddock and I'll give Price a hand."

Once in the paddock, Frank removed the saddles and brought the animals water and bags of oats, stroking Copenhagen's mane affectionately. "Haven't seen you much lately, have I?" Copenhagen butted Frank gently on the shoulder with her head and snickered softly. He'd had her for almost three years, one of the best mounts he'd ever owned.

Hop Li came from his kitchen carrying a billy can. "You're back boss," he said happily. "You see Mette yet? She's been pretty sad I think."

"I saw her in the distance," said Frank. "But I haven't spoken with her. I will as soon as Copenhagen is settled and I change my clothes. Don't mention to anyone that I'm here. Have you seen any troopers about?"

"They were here earlier," said Hop Li. "But they left for Ashhurst." He waved the billy can at Frank. "I'm going to pick pea pods in my garden. Just coming in. Good taste. I'll give you some later."

Frank picked up a curry comb from a box by the kitchen steps and started brushing down the horses. He was happy Hop Li was out in the garden, acting like an early alert. It was in this paddock that Anahera had attacked Frank, almost killing him with hard slaps to his face. Hop Li had saved him with his unexpected skill with a push dagger, plunging it into Anahera's belly. It had slowed him down, but not killed him.

He was almost finished when Karira arrived, more ruffled

and upset than Frank had ever seen him.

"What happened to you? Did you have trouble helping Constable Price to subdue his prisoner?"

Karira looked despondent. "Not really. Jimi and I got him under control, but then the women came at us."

"The women?"

"The Maori women. They threw themselves at us, and Warena – the man Price was trying to arrest – escaped. He ran into a hotel and smashed the glass in the door. Then he disappeared."

Frank grinned. "You were beaten back by women? Shame on you man."

"That wasn't the worst part," said Karira. "One of the women was Wiki, from the pa."

"Hmm," said Frank. "I'm not surprised. She's a rebellious young woman."

"She called me a traitor," said Karira. "And slapped me across the face. That was the hardest part, because I'm afraid that she's…"

"You think you're a traitor?" asked Frank. "That's nonsense. You're one of the most honest, loyal men I've ever met."

"Loyal to the Crown, you mean," said Karira. "Sometimes I think I should… here's Mette."

Mette came through the paddock gate, looking distraught. Frank dropped his curry comb and took hold of her hands. "What's happened? You look like you've seen a ghost."

"I think I did," said Mette. "I saw Anahera. He was over by the trap in the centre of the Square listening to Peete te Awe Awe. He looked right at me and smiled."

"That doesn't sound like Anahera," said Frank. "I don't think he's smiled in his entire life. Are you sure?"

"It was Anahera," said Mette. "I know it was. And he recognized me. That's why he smiled...it was almost not a smile. His lips just moved the tiniest bit. It almost seemed he was trying to tell me something, but I don't know what."

"I'll finish with Copenhagen and we can go to the office," said Frank. "We need to talk in private, and think things through, about Anahera, and about Wiki as well."

"Wiki?" asked Mette. "What has Wiki got to do with anything? I saw her sitting with a group of women earlier, but she ignored me."

Frank and Karira exchanged glances.

"We'll talk about it inside," said Karira.

"Wiki slapped him," said Frank quietly to Mette. "She was one of a group of women who got in the way of Constable Price while he was arresting a Maori for furious riding."

"She's rebellious," said Mette. "You know when we were out at Pieter's farm, and he went out to replace the pegs ... he told me that groups of Maori women had been out there pulling them up. And at the pa when Constable Price found Gottlieb's body, I saw a pile of pegs. I thought nothing of it until we were at Pieter's farm, and then I realized..."

Frank shook his head. "I hope she isn't doing that. She'll get herself in trouble."

"I think it's very brave of her," said Mette. "She's living at a pa that used to be a wonderful place, and now it's in ruins, and the land is going to people like us who've come from other countries."

"That's the way the world works," said Frank. "Although I agree it's unfortunate."

"More than unfortunate," said Mette. "It's unfair. Oh, and I forgot. The telegraph boy gave me this for Will. I said I'd leave it at the office..."

Karira reached for the envelope, but Frank took it and tore it open. "It's a reply from Captain Porter."

"What does he say?"

Frank scanned the contents. "Constable Karira. In Feilding on Thursday for land sale. Stop. Meet me there. Stop. Arrest came from highest level. Stop. Captain Porter. That's tomorrow...I should be there when he arrives."

"He's expecting me," said Karira. "I think it would be best if I...something's up with Hop Li."

Hop Li had come out of his pea garden waving frantically.

"What's happened?" said Frank.

Hop Li waved his hand towards the garden. "Something to show you, boss. Something not good."

He hurried ahead of them through the garden to the edge of the bush. His billy can was lying in the dirt, the contents spilled across a pair of scuffed Blucher boots. The boots were lying beside a blossom-covered manuka shrub, which was alive with honey bees.

"Someone left his boots...?" said Frank.

"No, no," said Hop Li. He picked up one of the boots and dropped let it go. It fell heavily. "Someone is inside the boots. He's dead."

Frank pulled aside the branches of the manuka to reveal a bare leg above the boot. "My God. There's a man here. How the hell...?" He turned to Karira. "Help me pull him out."

Karira and Frank each took hold of a leg and pulled the body from its hiding place. It appeared slowly from beneath the bush, face down, the head flopping loosely from one side to the other.

"This is not good," said Frank. "He's a trooper. Help me turn him over and …my God. It's Wilson."

Sergeant Wilson of the Armed Constabulary lay with his head at an uncomfortable angle, his face bright red, eyes popping. He'd died with terror in his heart.

"What happened to him?" asked Mette. "And who is he? How do you know him?"

"He was here in September, searching for Anahera," said Frank grimly. "Hop Li and I played cards with him. And I ran into him again at the prison. He shot at prisoners trying to escape a bush fire. Killed most of them. And he took a shot at me and Anahera as we stood beside the river."

"Should I fetch Constable Price?" asked Karira.

"No, not yet. Mette was right. Anahera is back and he's killed Wilson. See those red marks on the cheeks, the lines? They're hand prints. Anahera tried to kill me by slapping me on the face, and he came close to finishing the job." He patted Hop Li on the shoulder. "I'd be dead if Hop Li hadn't come to my rescue."

"No problem, boss," said Hop Li. "And I can be a witness this time if you need …"

"Witness? Why does there need to be a witness," asked Mette. "Frank…will they think…?"

"You're right, Hop Li. I could be blamed for this murder," said Frank. "They're searching for me because I left a trail – stupidly – and if they know I'm here they'll blame me for this."

"You need to get away from Palmerston right now," said Karira. "Before too many people know you were here."

"You can't leave again," said Mette. "I can't have you leave again. Please Frank, can't you stay in hiding until…"

"I saw him in the bush with a troop," said Frank. "I wonder why they left him behind?"

"They'll be back," said Karira. "They don't travel alone. When he doesn't catch them up they'll come looking for him. Sorry Mette, but Frank had better get as far away from here as he can..."

Frank put his arm around Mette's shoulders and gave her a squeeze. "I'm sorry my darling, but Karira is right. Hop Li, could you give us a couple of hours start before you talk to Constable Price?"

Mette shook Frank's arm away and faced him. "I'm coming with you."

Frank and Karira exchanged glances. "No, I think not..." said Frank hesitantly. He was conflicted. He hated leaving her again, but she taking her to Wanganui would be foolish.

"I don't care what you think. I'm not waiting at home again. And won't you want to go to Wanganui next, to see what you can find out what you can about the Mountjoy family? I could help you with that."

Frank scratched his chin. He could see Karira behind Mette shaking his head and frowning.

"If I stay here, Anahera might kill me as well," she said. "I'll be safer with you..."

It was a weak reason, as clearly Anahera had come to take his revenge on the man who had tried to kill him. But he gave in to his own needs and said, "I suppose you have a point with that. And having you with me will be a disguise. We'll look like a regular married couple...maybe you could even talk to the Mountjoys..."

"I can talk to the Mountjoys," said Karira stiffly. "Do you think they won't speak with me for some reason?"

"You represent the law...," said Frank. "They might see you, but they won't tell you anything."

"I could go to the Mountjoy's house and ask if they needed a maid," said Mette. "Or, no, I have a better idea. Wait here for a minute." She started towards the gate, then turned back towards them. "Promise me you won't leave before I get back."

Frank shook his head. "We can ride up to Feilding together," he said to Karira, watching Mette pass through the gate and into the crowd beyond. "We'll take the track up to the Kimbolton Road where there isn't much traffic. Then we can take the coach up to Wanganui from there. The coach passes through from Ashhurst and no one in Feilding will have heard anything. We'll have to make sure the troopers aren't there of course…"

"Can she ride?" asked Karira. He was clearly not happy with the thought that Mette was coming with them. "Is there even a horse available for her?"

"She can ride with me, on Copenhagen," said Frank. He walked away before Karira could protest.

They still hadn't spoken when Mette returned thirty minutes later. Frank was examining the body again, while Karira paced back and forth at the steps to the hotel kitchen where Hop Li was frantically pounding bread dough into submission.

Mette was carrying a small, battered carpet bag. "I asked Mr. Robinson if he minded me going away for a few days," she said. "I told him I was going to visit a relative in Napier, so if anyone asks he'll put them off the scent without lying. I don't think he could tell a lie."

"What do you have in your bag?" asked Frank.

She smiled. "Oh, just some clothes and…other things. Now, am I going to ride with you Frank?"

"Of course," he said, smiling down at her. "How else would we go? I'll change into my normal clothes first though. Then we'll be on our way." As he passed Karira he slapped him on the shoulder. Karira stared back at him gloomily.

* * *

Karira was still annoyed with Frank as they neared Feilding, galloping on ahead and stopping occasionally to wait impatiently as Copenhagen caught up to him with her heavier load.

Mette didn't care. She clutched her carpet bag and leaned back against Frank, wishing the ride would never end. Frank held her with one arm around her waist, squeezing her occasionally. She could feel him smiling with his whole body. He was in danger, they were riding on the most uncomfortable horse she could imagine, and her bottom was numb, but it was bliss.

The track wound through bush, much of it burned or cut down, with intermittent farm fields planted with oats or corn. Once or twice a man stopped working and raised his hand to them, but no one paid much attention. By late afternoon they were on the outskirts of Feilding. Karira reined in and pointed towards a small stony river that briefly abutted the track before turning east.

"Let's water the horse," he said. "And then I'll go into town alone to make sure it's safe."

Frank dismounted and held out his arms to Mette. She slid down, her face close to his, while waves of disapproval came from Karira. "Hide yourselves further downstream," he said. "I'll take both horses and look for stabling. Make sure you can't be seen from the track."

"Is something the matter with Karira?" asked Mette as he left.

"He seems angry at us." She hated seeing Karira disapproving of her. He had become like a brother to her, someone she could talk to about anything. She had been wanting to talk to Frank about Milo Mountjoy, to ask if he could possibly have a son, but it was so much harder with him than it was with Karira, who could read her thoughts.

"He doesn't like seeing us being… affectionate to each other," said Frank. "Perhaps we shouldn't be so obvious when he's around. I forget he's not my brother sometimes." He took Mette's hand and drew her towards the river, and found a fallen tree trunk to sit on. "He's not here now though."

She rested her head against his chest. "Thank you for letting me come with you," she said. "I feel much safer when I'm with…"

"We'll have to be careful in Wanganui," he said. "We'll know more once we've talked to Captain Porter."

She decided to ease into the topic. "When we find out what's going on, we'll be able to go back to Palmerston and start our lives properly. I can't wait…"

She was cut off by the sound of horses. They were far enough away from the track that whoever was coming would not see them unless they were actively searching. But Frank pulled Mette down behind the fallen tree trunk, covering her with his body as the horses approached, and then thundered past.

"Armed Constables," said Frank. "Lucky we were off the track. Looks like they're heading towards Palmerston. It won't be long before they find out Wilson has been murdered. Price will know by now."

They stayed low, waiting to see if any more constables would ride by. After thirty minutes, Karira arrived on foot, scrambling along the side of the stream, looking rattled.

"It's a trap," he said. "We're walking into a trap."

"You mean it wasn't Captain Porter who telegraphed you?"

Karira shook his head. "I think it was," he said. "Captain Porter's in Feilding with a dozen Armed Constables. They're guarding all the exits. I was at the Denbigh Hotel to see if they could stable the horses, and they told me the stables were full because of all the constables in town. I left our horses tied to a post outside the railway station and came back along the stream."

"Captain Porter set a trap for me?" asked Frank. "That can't be true. I've known him for years...surely..."

"It's for you, alright" said Karira. "I saw your...I saw Mountjoy there. Captain Porter was on the verandah of the hotel, but I saw Mountjoy inside."

"Damn," said Frank. "Of all the people, I'd never have thought Porter...some constables just rode by. I thought they were on their way to Palmerston, but they're probably only going half a mile or so. If they station themselves on the rise they'd see anyone approaching and block them in once they passed."

"Then we're trapped?" asked Mette, her voice quivering. "We can't get out?"

Frank squeezed her hand. "They don't know we're already inside the perimeter. We'll find a way out, I promise..."

"The smart thing to do would be to go into town," said Karira. "They'll be looking outward, waiting for you to ride in. Then if you can find a way to get onto the coach going north to Wanganui...or to hide until they give up and leave..."

"Couldn't we go in by the river?" asked Mette.

Karira gave Frank a sideways look. "Perhaps Mette should return to Palmerston. Mountjoy knows her, and..."

"You want to send me home?" asked Mette.

"That would be the best…" said Karira.

"No," said Frank. "I'd like Mette to stay with me. We'll circle town by the river and see if we can bypass the town…maybe catch the Wanganui coach on the other side somewhere. Karira, you get the horses and head back to Palmerston."

Karira looked annoyed. "You trust Mette to discover something in Wanganui that I could not?"

"She has innocence on her side," said Frank. "No one would suspect her of anything. She can be part of my disguise."

Mette set her carpet bag on the ground and knelt beside it. "I have a plan," she said, opening the bag and pushing her clothing aside. "I didn't want to show you before, but I brought some of my booklets with me…my recipe booklets. I could go door to door and ask to talk to the cooks. Perhaps even to the cook at the Mountjoy home…"

Frank smiled. "You see, Karira? A perfect way to investigate. And if you return to Palmerston you can see what's happening with the Wilson murder. Make sure no one thinks it was me. And tell Price Anahera is in town. Remind him of the time he tried to kill me with the face-slapping…the same *modus operandi*."

Karira agreed sullenly, mounting his horse. "Take care of her then," he said as Frank walked with him to the track. "If you get blamed for murder, she mustn't be implicated. They haven't ever hanged a woman for murder in New Zealand, but that doesn't mean they won't."

It occurred to Frank for the first time that Karira might have feelings for Mette. He wondered if Mette knew. Probably not. "Of course, I'll take care of her," he said, feeling a surge of annoyance. "I'll always take care of her. Why would you say that…?"

"You don't exactly have the best record," said Karira. "I saw evidence of that no more than an hour ago. A man who is obviously your son…"

"That was twenty years ago," said Frank. "I was hardly a man myself. And I'm not sure he is my son. I know he resembles me, but…"

"More than a resemblance," said Karira. "He looks exactly like you, only younger."

"And is trying to make me disappear, for some reason," said Frank. "Look, Karira, I intend to do the best I can for Mette. Please don't concern yourself."

"Someone went to a lot of trouble to make you disappear," said Karira. "And it can't just be Mountjoy. He's not much more than a boy. It must be something – or someone with something to lose. A lot to lose. And with some influence." He kicked his horse and set off back to Palmerston.

Frank watched him until only the dust thrown up by the hooves remained. "Someone with something to lose," he said. "And we'll find out who that person is in Wanganui. Mette and I together."

16

Taking the Train

Mette felt like she was being torn apart by Cossacks on horses. On the one hand, she was relieved and happy to be with Frank again. But on the other, the thought that he'd fathered a son, and such an awful one, saddened her. She'd once heard someone described as being a chip off the old block, and had asked what that meant – she was always trying to improve her English, and they had such strange expressions – and had learned it meant a child was like its father. How could Milo Mountjoy be such an awful person and Frank be a good person if Milo was his son?

She watched Frank talking to Karira, her mind in turmoil. He came back smiling, and her doubts dissipated once more, at least for the moment.

He held out his hand. "Give me your bag. We're going to get around the town using the river. Karina says it comes out near the train station, and from there we can walk along the tracks until we're outside town."

"What about Captain Porter? Aren't you…"

"I don't know what he's up to," said Frank. "I can't believe he wants me sent back to gaol. But I can't take any chances.

We're going to Wanganui…to survey the Mountjoys in their natural habitat."

She knew he meant to make her laugh, but barely managed a smile. "Walking?"

"Not the whole way," said Frank. "We'll head towards Sanson and catch the coach there, if we can't pick it up earlier. Or we could hire another horse in Sanson at the stables."

Feilding was a large but thinly-populated town, with hundreds of small huts, each on its own acre of land, giving the place the feel of a military camp. The first part of the walk beside the river was through heavy bush, and at times they were stepping from rock to rock. But once they neared the centre of town they were on what was clearly a popular walkway. Mette took Frank's arm, and they strolled along like a couple of town stalwarts out enjoying the late afternoon sun.

The town was quiet, but in the distance, they could see a man sitting on the balcony of what must be the Denbigh Hotel.

"There's Porter," said Frank. "Karira was right."

Mette could see a man of around fifty, with greying hair that had receded from his forehead, and grey whiskers around his jaw. He wasn't wearing a uniform, but rather an expensive charcoal serge suit with a maroon-coloured vest. He was smoking a pipe and staring into the street. "I don't see Mountjoy," she said. "But Karira said he was inside…oh no. He came out."

Frank put his head down. "Keep moving," he said. "We're about a hundred yards away from the station."

Mette continued to look as she walked. "He's getting on his horse…"

"Let's hope he doesn't suddenly feel like a ride along the river…" said Frank.

"He's angry about something," said Mette. "I can tell by the way he's throwing himself on his...what's that?"

"What's what?" asked Frank risking a quick glance at the town.

All along the street in front of the hotel, dark-clad townspeople, the men in broad-brimmed hats and the women in shovel-shaped bonnets, were pouring from their homes.

"I know who they are," said Mette. "I've seen them before in Haderslev, and in Palmerston. They're Brethren. They're on their way to church. They go there every night to await the end of the world...we have a few Brethren in Palmerston, but they don't have their own church so they come to the Lutheran Church with the Scandies."

"Good timing on their part," said Frank. "They'll help to prevent the end of our world."

Milo Mountjoy rode into the middle of the throng, yelling at them to get out of his way. When they ignored him, he whipped his horse, spurring it through the crowd to create an opening; blocked by the crowd, the horse reared up and threw him to the ground.

"Here's trouble," said Frank. "He won't like being shown up in front of that lot...what the hell?"

Mountjoy was on his feet and had picked up his riding crop. He began applying it to the rump of the startled horse, which reared up, shrieking in pain.

"The bastard," said Frank. He pulled away from Mette towards Mountjoy, but she held him back. The crowd had surrounded the scene and an elderly man stepped forward to remonstrate with Mountjoy. She saw Captain Porter lean out from his balcony and say something, which Mountjoy ignored.

"No, Frank. Leave him," she said. "You won't stop him. All

you'll do is let them see you..."

He stopped, but was breathing heavily. "A horse," he said. "My God, a horse, for something that was his own stupid fault...I..."

"Come, Frank," she said. "We're almost at the station. Let's hurry past while everyone is upset." She put his arm through his. "Please Frank."

He put his hand over hers. "I can't bear to see a horse beaten," he said. "I grew up with horses. My father was head groom when I was a boy...he'd kill anyone who did something like that to a horse. And so would I."

Not a chip off the old block then.

In the street, the townspeople were moving on towards the church. It was almost sunset, and they needed to be at the church before the sun went down, to be ready to meet their maker. What must it be like to think every single day that you were going to die that night? The Brethren began to sing, and she felt an instant calmness that carried her the rest of the way to the station.

"Abide with me, fast falls the evening sun..."

They reached the station, a small wooden building with a tin roof, and entered the rear door; the platform was immediately in front of them, with a steam locomotive beside it and an engineer working at something inside, his back to them; steam belched quietly out the side of the engine.

"Perhaps we could take the train," said Frank. "I didn't realize one was running from Feilding..."

The engineer popped his head out from the cab. He was a man of about forty, so bald his head shone, a ginger coloured handlebar moustache providing his only hair. "Sorry sir. The train isn't running yet," he said. "Another month or two...the tracks aren't complete..."

"That's a Fairlie's Patent, isn't it?" said Frank. "My God, what a beauty. If we'd had machines like that at Sebastopol..."

"You were at Sebastopol?" asked the engineer. He wiped his hands on an oily rag, grabbed hold of a pole and swung down from the cab, ignoring the wooden steps someone had placed there.

Frank nodded. "I began my career in Crimea," he said. "We didn't know much about trains for war back then – at least I didn't, although the Turks did. But the Americans used of them later..."

"During the Civil War," said the engineer. "Exactly. That's where I learned my trade as a fireman...became a driver later. I drove an iron-plated flatcar with a forward-facing Brooke banded 32-pounder gun... and two hundred rounds of ammunition. An amazing thing it was...could have changed the whole war if we'd had... I wasn't on the Union side, however, and they had the right of it. You can't enslave people, I know that now. Robert E. Lee commissioned the flatcar, you know. They say he had a train full of gold bullion..."

"You're an American?"

"British originally," he said, holding out his hand. "Charles Cartwright—Red they call me, from Manchester. And you are...?"

Why was he called Red, Mette wondered, as Frank reached out his hand to the engineer? Was it because the top of his head was so red and shiny?

"Frank Hardy," said Frank. "Sergeant Frank Hardy, late of Her Majesty's 57th Regiment of Foot...working as a private investigator now..."

"Would you like to take a ride in Old Merry?" asked

TAKING THE TRAIN

Cartwright. "I named her after the Merrimack...although some call her the Pelican..."

"How far are you going?" asked Frank. "We were heading to Wanganui on the coach, but stopped in here in case there was a train..."

"Not all the way to Wanganui," said Cartwright. He looked Frank up and down. "About three miles short of town. The tracks aren't completed, but I've been doing some trial runs on the finished part. I could do with a man to shovel the coal...thought I'd have to do it all myself, but I'd prefer to keep watch on the instruments. What do you say? Give it a go?"

"Will you be alright with that my dear?" Frank said to Mette, as if they were an old married couple. She nodded. Her knees had turned to water. She would climb on this giant beast, and they would roar away down the track, and if she was lucky she wouldn't get sucked out of – well, she couldn't get sucked out of the windows because there weren't any – off the floor of the engine and into the scrub beside the track.

Frank clambered onto the engine and reached down to help her up. Her hand was quivering. "Are you nervous?" he asked.

"No," she lied. "Just a little, because it's so high up...is there somewhere I can hold on?"

"I detect a Scandi if I'm not mistaken," said Cartwright. He was twiddling with the dials while Frank watched intently. "A decent, hard-working people."

Mette was distracted for a few seconds. "That's kind of you to say. Yes, we do work hard, especially the men..."

"You women don't exactly sit around doing nothing," said Charlie. "Now the English...hand me that wrench please Frank..."

"We work hard," said Frank. He'd taken off his coat and

rolled up his sleeves.

"But complain a lot," said Charlie. "These new chums who are arriving from Home, especially the ones coming to Feilding - they're leaving as fast as the next lot arrives...did you see those Brethren?"

Mette was back to feeling nervous. "Ah...yes..."

"They've come in and taken some of the empty houses," said Charlie. "From the folks who left."

"What do they have to complain about?" asked Frank. "The...folks who've left. Why would they leave?"

"Say they were promised a higher remuneration than they've been offered."

"How much would that be?" asked Frank.

"Seven shillings a day. Two shillings more than the five the emigration form – which they signed — promised. They wanted ten shillings a day — more than they'd get from any employer in the Manchester Block." He shook his head to show what a terrible thing it was for a man to want a living wage. "The colonial rate is generally a very fair seven shillings a day. Ten shillings is a journeyman's wage, not a labourers. I can't find help, because I offer only seven shillings..."

"Four days a week, seven shillings per day. That's what my brother-in-law was promised," said Mette, forgetting her nervousness for a moment. "He works — or used to work — at the sawmill four days a week, and the other two days he found work for himself on the road crews. But he just bought himself a cleared section." Talking about Pieter made her think about the farm he'd bought himself, and the bed Maren...She clutched on to a pole beside the steps to the engine and tried not to look at Frank or think of the bed. That would only make her more nervous.

"The Scandinavians are better workers than the British," said Cartwright. "You come here with your axes and expect to work hard clearing the land. The British come here from their shops and their farms and expect that suddenly everything will be laid out for them on a platter and they won't have to do hard physical labour." He put his hands on his hips and looked back at Frank. "Talking of which — time to start shovelling that coal. Get yourself stripped off and grab that shovel."

Frank complied, scooping coal from the hopper behind the cab and throwing it into the firebox.

Mette found something more substantial than the pole to hang on to — she had no idea what, but it seemed solid — and they were off in a thunder of moving machinery, clouds of steam and smoke, and a general feeling that they were on their way to hell…or Wanganui, whichever might be reached first.

17

The Rutland

By the time they reached the end of the rails, Frank's back was ached and his arm muscles begged for mercy. He'd shovelled coal for over an hour, and was dripping with sweat. He couldn't imagine how anyone could do this job for an extended period. It was worse than General Chute's forced march across Taranaki, when they'd trudged up and down hills until they'd run out of food, and had been forced to eat the horses. For seven shillings a day he would have preferred being shot at by the Turks, or the Indian Sepoys, or even the Hauhau.

When the train finally slowed – after Red Cartwright pulled back hard on the hand brake for several minutes – Frank stepped back from the job and checked to see how Mette was managing.

She was holding on to the corner of the cab with her eyes closed. He reached over and touched her arm, and saw her jump. "We're slowing down," he said. "Time to get down soon, I think."

"Are you sure you don't want to return to Feilding with me?" asked Cartwright. "You did well. I'd pay you eight shillings for the day…"

"Kind of you to offer," said Frank. "But I think Met...my wife has had all she can take. If you could put us down here we'll walk the rest of the way to Wanganui."

Cartwright pulled a watch from his vest. "It's ten o'clock," he said. "Are you sure you want to walk to town this late at night?"

"I believe we can make it," said Frank. If they got to Wanganui in an hour, the hotels would still be open. Some had night clerks who could be awoken. There was no use resting now. Mette clearly needed a bed for the night.

They climbed down from the cab, Frank first. Mette leaned down and collapsed into his arms. "I'm tired."

"We have to keep moving," he said. He hated to admit it, but Karira was probably right. He shouldn't have brought her with him. It wasn't that she slowed him down, but that he was asking too much of her and felt guilty about it. She'd jogged from Bunnythorpe down to Palmerston, or most of the way, and had done better than he had, her youth and her daily outdoor walks standing her in good stead. But he was more used to the long slog. "We'll stay on the tracks as much as we can. There'll be a few places without tracks, but the cuttings are all done. Cartwright said if we stay near the tracks they'll lead us right to the Wanganui River...to the bridge."

Much more than an hour had passed before they reached Wanganui - nearer to an hour and a half. By then he was half carrying her, his arm around her waist, her arm over his shoulder.

"Almost there," he said, as the river came into view around a bend in the tracks. The lamplights of Wanganui flickered in the distance. "Once we're over the bridge we'll be in town and you'll be able to rest."

She straightened up and looked towards the town. She was still clutching on to her valise, and not for the first time he wondered why they hadn't simply left it somewhere, but she'd refused the suggestion. her pamphlets were not the only way to open doors; tramps and beggars were common and cooks often generous.

"Here?" she asked. "Where? Wanganui? I think I can get there... but what if we see someone who knows..."

He'd been thinking of that. "No one is about in the middle of the night. We'll get to the Rutland Hotel - it's just over the bridge. A few more steps..."

He managed to rouse a sleepy night clerk at the Rutland. The clerk, a wizened little man in his sixties, came to the door carrying a flickering candle, and wearing his nightdress and nightcap. He eyed Frank and Mette incuriously...used to people turning up in the middle of the night needing a place to sleep.

"Would you have a room for the night?" asked Frank. "We just arrived from...by train from New Plymouth..."

"Doesn't the New Plymouth train get here at nine?" said the clerk, yawning.

"It was delayed," said Frank. "A cow on the line. Dead unfortunately. But..."

"Well, come on in then," said the night clerk. "You won't be wanting a meal I hope? The cook has gone to bed long since."

"Some bread?" asked Frank hopefully.

The night clerk nodded. "I can rustle up some bread and butter," he said. "You can have the casement room at the end of the upstairs hall. It's small, but if you're desperate...ten shillings for the night."

It was highway robbery, and the owner would not see a penny of it, but Frank forked over a ten shilling note anyway. There were times when the money didn't matter, and this was one of them.

"Follow me," said the clerk. He started up the stairs, with Frank behind him in the pool of light thrown out by the candle. But Mette had lost the last bit of spark she'd used to get across the bridge. She sat on the bottom stair and leaned against the wall, her eyes closed.

"She's finished," said Frank to the night clerk. "Sorry, but I'm going to have to carry her." He hoisted her in his arms and started up the stairs. He'd thought he would never be able to use his arms again, after shovelling all the coal into the firebox, but he made it to the door of the room before she slipped from his grasp.

The night clerk unlocked the door and put the candle on a small wooden Duchess dresser beside the washstand. Frank picked Mette up and dumped her on the bed.

"I'll just pop down and get you some bread and butter," said the night clerk. Leave the door ajar to give me some light."

Frank sat down beside Mette, pulled the bedclothes around her, and watched her sleep until the night clerk returned. She was flushed, and slept with one hand clutching the blanket, like a child seeking comfort. He stroked her head and told her she would feel better tomorrow, but wasn't sure he believed it himself. What an idiot he was. Tomorrow he would put her on the coach and send her back to Palmerston.

The night clerk returned with a plate of buttered bread. He'd found some apricots as well. Frank ate half of the bread and left the rest, with the apricots, on the dresser where she would be able to see it if she awoke during the night. When he blew out the candle, she stirred, and murmured, "Maren...bed..."

"Don't worry about Maren now," he said softly. "Get some sleep. I'll be right outside the door. Open the door and call me if you need anything..."

He left her and went down to the end of the hall where a small alcove led to the fire escape. A faded old embroidered arm chair blocked the window to the fire escape, and he sat down and made himself comfortable. The chair would have been perfect for anyone the size of the night clerk. But for him, it was only slightly better than sleeping in the totara tree.

The sun pouring through the window of the alcove woke him the next morning. He stretched, feeling as if he'd been in a battle, and massaged his neck.

"Oy, what are you doing there?"

A maid with a bucket and mop stared at him suspiciously.

"Sorry. My wife is in the casement room..."

"What're you doing out here then?" asked the maid, frowning. She was an older woman with grey hair tied back in a bun, probably the wife of the night clerk.

"I was..." said Frank, lost for words. What was he doing? He wasn't sure himself.

"Tossed you out, did she? I 'spect you were snoring. My husband snores something terrible. I wish I could make 'im sleep in the hall." She left to do her cleaning, swinging the bucket happily, having taken indirect revenge on her husband.

Frank knocked on the door to the casement room. Mette opened it immediately, as if she had been standing there waiting for him. "Where were you? I was worried. I thought you'd gone off without me."

"I was here," he said. "I found myself a comfortable place to sleep down at the end of the hallway. Did you sleep well?"

"Yes, and I ate the bread and apricots when I woke this morning. What are we going to do now?"

"We're going to find out where the Mountjoys live, and pay them a visit," said Frank. "At least I am."

"No," she protested. "I've come all this way with my pamphlets and I want to talk to the cook before I do anything else."

His resolve weakened. "I intended to send you back to Palmerston…"

"After I talk to the cook," she said. "When we see what she has to say about the Mountjoys I'll go home, I promise."

He didn't believe her, but found it hard to say no.

18

The Cook and the Lady

The cook at the Mountjoy home eyed Mette with a calculated expression, rubbing her hands on her apron. Mette had interrupted her doing her baking. A plate of jam tarts sat on the window sill, and the cook had been rolling out a batch of shortbread when Mette knocked on the door. Mette could barely keep her eyes off the tarts.

"A shilling," said the cook. "That's all I have in the cash box."

Mette held out a copy of her pamphlet and nodded. "A shilling would be…"

"Are you hungry?" said the cook. "Would you like to come in for a cup of tea?"

"I would like that, thank you," said Mette, wondering if the cook had any coffee but afraid to ask.

"You look as if you've been pulled through a bush backwards," commented the cook, as Mette took a seat at the kitchen table. "Help yourself to a tart and I'll put on the kettle."

Mette bit into the tart - a flat, round thing with sweet pastry on the bottom, jam in the middle and almonds sprinkled on the top of something buttery and nutty. "That was the most delicious thing I've ever tasted," she said. She licked her fingers and eyed the plate, wondering if she dared help herself to a second.

"Thank you," said the cook. "It's a Bakewell tart, from my home town in Derbyshire. The receipt has been passed from mother to daughter for centuries, I believe. Have another." She held out the plate to Mette. "But that had better be all. I have a young man living here who loves my tarts. He'd be most upset if he didn't have at least five waiting for him at tea time."

Mette took a second tart, but held it. She would wait for the tea to be ready, so she could wash it down with the hot drink. Pity it wasn't coffee… "Children live here?" It seemed like a natural thing to ask.

"Well, he's not a child any longer," said the cook. "Although the way he behaves, you'd think…"

"Just one then," said Mette. "A young man?"

"Young, yes," said the cook. "Twenty next month. But he has a terrible temper, and sometimes I think he might as well be a two-year-old." The kettle started to whistle; she picked it up with a cloth around the handle and poured it into a massive, battered silver tea pot, standing away from the steam.

"Are his parents here as well, or just the two of you?"

"His father's back and forward to Wellington frequently," said the cook. "Does something for the government. What I don't know. He's home today, but leaving again tomorrow. But his mother, well…she never leaves home."

"Is she ill?"

The cook poured her a cup of tea and Mette blew on it to cool it, trying not to snatch up a piece of the Bakewell tart which could taste on her tongue…she wanted to eat it so much.

"Ill?" said the cook. "Not ill exactly…but not well…"

Mette was unable to see the difference, so she pretended to understand, nodding slowly. "Are you alone here? Do you have other help?"

"A girl comes in to clean," said the cook. "And Elizabeth takes care of Lady Debra. She's been with her for years — her companion, really. Then there's Pulau…"

"That sounds like a Maori name," said Mette. "What does he do?"

The cook paused. Had Mette gone too far with her questioning? But then she answered. "Hard to say, really. Takes care of everything for the family. He isn't Maori though. He's Samoan. He's been with them since they were in Samoa. Colonel Mountjoy was the British Consul there for many years…"

"Samoa?" asked Mette. "That's in the Pacific Ocean somewhere I suppose…and he left his home to be with them?"

"There was some trouble there…" said the cook. She stood abruptly. "Well, I'd better get back to work. Can you find your way out?"

The temperature of the room had changed.

"My shilling?" asked Mette.

"Oh, of course. Sorry." The cook opened a drawer and took out two sixpenny pieces. "Here." She picked up Mette's pamphlet. "This is interesting. We have some plants in the wild part of our garden…"

"I spend a lot of time in the bush, hunting for…" said Mette.

"Where?" said the cook, without looking up from the pamphlet. "Which bush? The Seventy Mile Bush somewhere? You're a Scandi, aren't you?"

Mette kicked herself mentally. "Oh, I live in…"

"Palmerston, it says on the pamphlet," said the cook.

"Yes, yes, Palmerston," agreed Mette. "Thank you for buying my... I'll be off now..."

She hurried outside, afraid she'd said too much. Was the cook suspicious of her, or was it just that she knew she shouldn't be talking to strangers about the family situation?

The house was at the end of a long metalled driveway and Frank was waiting along the road above. The house was situated close to Wanganui Collegiate, and he had walked towards the school, saying he would wait for her there and watch the cricket, if a game was in progress. He'd be happy watching the empty field if he knew it was used for cricket. Why were men like that? She could never understand Frank's love of cricket – something she would have to learn, she supposed.

She was half way up the tree-lined driveway when she heard a door slam. She ran back down the driveway and concealed herself behind a tree. Pulau had come out the door carrying something — or someone. A woman she thought. Another woman followed them out pushing a bath chair. The Samoan placed his bundle carefully in the chair, and appeared to pull something over her lap...a blanket probably, although it was a warm day. The trio moved between the flower beds – beautiful flower beds Mette could not help noticing - pointing at the flowers, the two walkers pointing and chatting. They did not seem to be paying attention to the woman in the chair, who sat stiffly, her head erect and unmoving. An older woman? Or could it be the "not well" Lady Debra?

Wanting a better view, Mette left the safety of the tree and moved closer to the house. The kitchen windows were on the same side as the door the trio had just exited, and the cook wouldn't know she was there if she was quiet. She had to see Lady Debra and find out was wrong with her.

She reached the house and moved towards the corner, staying as much out of sight as she could, ducking below window sills. Through one window she saw a man sitting at his desk, working on something. Colonel Mountjoy. He glanced in her direction and she drew back. He was a plain man, with a typical English face, and if Frank was Milo's father she could understand why.

At the corner of the house she stood with her back to the wall and peered around at the garden. She was within fifty feet of the woman in the chair and her caregivers, but could not hear what they were saying. Pulau stood with his arms crossed, nodding, as the companion, a tall stern woman in a grey silk dress that matched her hair, spoke to him. Mette could not see Lady Debra, who had been left to stare at a bed of yellow roses. She was dressed in a deep indigo blue dress, silk probably, and her blond ringlets had been tied back in a blue bow. Her shoulders were covered in a white lacy shawl. The whole effect was very pretty, but Mette wanted to see her face. She edged closer...

"Hey, you, what do you think you're doing?"

The cook was leaning out a window directly behind her, about to shake the cloth that had been wrapped around the Bakewell tart.

"I...I was admiring your roses," said Mette. "I'm sorry...I'll leave..."

"I think you'd better," said the cook.

She saw Lady Debra's head start to turn. "Bethy?" she said, her voice quivering with fear. "Bethy? What's happening?"

Red-faced, Mette ran up the long laneway. She had nothing

to report to Frank — almost nothing — except for…an idea popped into her head. Could that be the answer? Surely not…

As she reached the top of the long driveway, a carriage followed by four men on horseback swept past her. Armed Constables. They must be there to collect Colonel Mountjoy, although the cook had distinctly said he was leaving tomorrow.

19

An Overdose of Chloroform

A cricket game was underway on the Wanganui Collegiate playing fields. Frank stood in the shade of the school chapel and watched as he waited for Mette to return from the Mountjoys. He was feeling worse about bringing her to Wanganui. Had he been more concerned with keeping her by his side than keeping her safe? What a fool he was.

"Sergeant Hardy?"

Frank turned to see a recent acquaintance closing the chapel door behind him.

"It is Sergeant Hardy," said the Reverend Masterson. "And looking considerably better than when I last saw him." He swung a cricket bat in his left hand but was not wearing his cricket whites.

Frank shook his hand. "I'm back to normal," he said. "You aren't playing today?"

"No, not today," said Masterson. He looked quite downcast at the thought. "But as I said when last I saw you, I play for the Old Boys when they need me, which is not often, unfortunately. The first and second elevens are up today, getting ready for a match with Wellington Boy's Collegiate next week. More of a practice than a game...so there's no point..."

Frank looked out at the players. He thought he could see Mountjoy on the field, but wasn't sure. He was a house tutor, and shouldn't be playing for either of the two school teams, but this was a practice, and if they were short-handed...

"I'm awaiting my fiancée," he said. "She's going from house to house selling her cookbook."

"And you'd just be in the way," said Masterson. "I understand. Would you like to go into the chapel while you wait? It's cool there. Unless you want to watch the cricket, of course..."

Frank glanced out at the field again. That was Mountjoy, he was sure of it. He'd best get out of sight. "I would, of course, but then my fiancée, Miss Jensen, wouldn't be able to find me."

"I'll be out here pruning the roses," said Masterson. "I was just on my way to do that...why not go inside in the cool — perhaps for some quiet prayer and contemplation?"

"How will you recognize...?"

Masterson smiled and hazarded a guess. "Young, beautiful, fair-haired..."

"That's true," said Frank. "But aren't there many...?"

"Not in Wanganui," said Masterson. "Not that I've seen. And anyway, few women come past this chapel; I'll just ask everyone who does if she's looking for a tall, dark, handsome man."

"Thanks for the compliment," said Frank. "But isn't every woman looking for a tall handsome man?"

"If they nod too eagerly I'll simply ask if they would take a medium-sized pleasant-looking man instead," said Masterson. "And I'll settle for not so beautiful as well, even a red-head. As long as she's virtuous...for her price is far above rubies."

Frank assumed he was quoting from the Bible. He thought briefly of Agnete, whose price was closer to coal, and who was almost the exact opposite of the woman Masterson was looking for. No, Agnete would not do for John Masterson. He would need to find himself a woman like Mette, if another such woman existed. "Thank you, John," he said. "I'll explain what's going on later, when Mette gets here."

He went through the vestry door into the church and sat in one of the front pews. Beyond the pulpit, a small stained glass window pictured the Virgin Mary holding Christ across her lap. the walls on either side depicted the Stations of the Cross on painted ceramic salvers. He felt as if he'd made his way along those stations, and wondered when he was going to reach Calvary. He sat slumped, staring at the baptismal font, drained of emotion, wondering when he was going to be able to get on with his life, his life with Mette that had offered such promise. He wanted a son…had always wanted a son. But he'd imagined a full life with that son, not some changeling who was suddenly identified as his. How could that have happened to him?

A click awoke him from his reverie. The vestibule door opened and Milo Mountjoy peered inside. He was wearing his cricket whites and still wore the batting pads he'd donned for his turn at bat. He saw Frank and came through the door slowly, staring. "I thought I saw you…"

"Mountjoy…" Frank said wearily. "You've come to kill me, have you?"

Mountjoy shook his head and sat down on the pew, as far away from Frank as he could get. "They told me…," he said. "They told me…"

"What did they tell you?"

"That I was your son...yesterday..."

"Did you not know before that?"

Mountjoy shook his head and started to sniff. He'd lost all his bravado.

"Then why...?

"They told me what you did to my mother, how she changed..."

"What I...? What do you mean?"

"You attacked her. They said that you tried to rape her, but Elizabeth stopped you from..."

Frank sighed. "That's not true, you know."

Mountjoy wiped his dripping nose with the back of his hand. "It can't be, can it? If you're my father, Elizabeth didn't stop you, so..."

Frank shook his head. "None of that happened. I met her on the boat on the passage to India. She asked me to her cabin...." He considered telling Mountjoy that she'd asked half the young men on board to her cabin, but that wasn't something a son should hear about his mother.

Mountjoy looked at Frank, a spark of life in his eyes. "You're telling me my mother was a whore?" he said. He took a step towards Frank, his fists raised. "How dare you..."

"I'm not saying that," said Frank, although he had been. How else to describe a woman who acted that way with young men? "And Elizabeth, your mother's companion, wasn't even on the boat, not that I remember."

Mountjoy's anger boiled up again, and he began walking back and forward along the first row of pews, punching his fist against his hand. "Everyone will know..." he said.

Frank stood and took a step towards him. "Look, it's not

your fault you're in this difficult situation," he said. "If your father found me an embarrassment he could have spoken to me. And I will say the same to you. I'm not trying to ruin your life. I'll move to the South Island, or up north to Auckland. We'll never cross paths…"

Mountjoy lunged at him. "No one will know," he said. "But I'll know. I'm a nobody…what kind of family do you have? Servants, I suppose…or worse…"

"My father is a decent, brave man, and you're lucky to have his blood in your veins," said Frank, fending off Mountjoy easily with his forearm.

Mountjoy looked past him at something or someone over his shoulder, and Frank had a few seconds to realize he should have been more alert; two large arms pinned him from behind, one around his chest, the other around his neck. He was lifted from his feet, unable to move as he pulled desperately at the arm around his throat. He kicked backwards, his heel connecting with a shin bone, but that made his captor squeeze him harder, pushing the air from his lungs.

A woman came from behind, a tall, grey-haired woman who looked familiar. She reached into her purse, and pulled something out. He smelled the faint sweet scent of chloroform. Christ. Not again. He kicked back at whoever was holding him, and tried desperately to move his face away from the oncoming hand.

As the chloroform-soaked cloth came towards his face, accompanied by the rustle of a silk dress, the whole sordid story became clear to him. "Be…Be…" But his throat was constricted by his captor and a dark shade covered his eyes. He thought he heard Mette call his name, and fought to say something, to warn her…

20

A Cricket Lesson

Mette reached the end of the Mountjoy's tree-lined lane and looked around. There was no sign of Frank, so she walked in the direction he'd told her he would be, and still could not see him. She stood outside the Wanganui Collegiate chapel, worried. Where could he have gone? Could they have followed her from the Mountjoy home, and even now be taking him away to prison again?

"Miss Jensen?"

Mette turned towards the speaker, a sturdy, fair-haired young man carrying a cricket bat over his shoulder. She was frozen with indecision. Was this a fellow conspirator of the Mountjoys? If she said yes, she was Miss Jensen, would she immediately find herself carried away to the same prison as Frank? But he looked like a nice man, not someone who…

She took a deep breath and replied. "Yes, I am Miss Jensen."

"Jolly good," he said. "I'm John Masterson, Reverend John Masterson. Frank asked me to look out for you. He's in the chapel."

Mette put her hand on her heart. "Thank goodness. I was worried he'd been taken…"

"Taken?" asked Masterson. He looked puzzled. Had Frank not told him the whole story?

"Taken...ill," she improvised. "How do I get into the chapel?"

"Through the garden gate," said Masterson, pointing. "I'll let you in." He started singing to himself softly. "Come into the garden, Maud, for the black bat...I say, that's appropriate." He swung his bat at one of the rose bushes.

She passed through an arched entranceway hung with tiny yellow rosebuds into the most astonishing rose garden she had ever seen. The scent was overpowering and the beauty of it stopped her in her tracks. "Ah, *min gud*," she said. "I've never seen anything so very beautiful..."

"Thank you," he said. "This is my garden, I'm happy to say. The Lord gave me the talent and I do the best with what he gave me. I keep my tools - he held up his cricket bat - in the vestry - it's through the door at the back of the church."

Unsure what he meant, she bent and touched a large, deep crimson tea rose. "Look at this, how beautiful..."

"The Lady Debra," he said. "I named it after one of our most generous benefactors. It's a hybrid, not unlike the Rosa Mr. Lincoln, named for the late, well...I suppose it's more than similar, if I'm to be honest. I actually used the same two..."

"Lady Debra?" Mette leaned down and sniffed the rose appreciatively. "Would the benefactor be Lady Debra Mountjoy?"

"Actually, yes. Although her husband, the colonel, made the donation in her name. She isn't really able...well, never mind."

"I saw Lady Debra earlier," said Mette. "In her garden. She was in a bath chair, assisted by her companion and a large Samoan man. Is she not well?"

Masterson apparently did not notice that Mette knew the birthplace of the servant. "She's been unwell for many years," he said. "Since India. I believe she and her companion were at Cawnpore. She was carried out with a broken ankle, or so I heard, and the ankle has never properly healed. It's taken a toll on her body. On her mind as well, unfortunately. And Cawnpore traumatized her, of course, as it did everyone who was there."

"Her mind?" asked Mette. "Is she able to speak, or…" give orders, she thought.

Masterson shook his head. "Very little. They say she has the vocabulary of a child. The colonel has been very patient and loving…he could have sent her to an asylum, but has refused to do so. He's a distant cousin, of course, so there's some family feeling as well."

Mette's mind was starting to spin with all the information. India was the key to all this trouble that Frank was in. Had he done something to bring on Lady Debra's condition? Did her pregnancy send her off the rails? Despite herself, she could not help thinking about Gottlieb, and what he had almost done to her. Surely Frank would not…but no. Impossible. She was sure she knew the answer now, and that wasn't it. Not that it was an answer she was happy about, and she was not in a hurry to see Frank, knowing what she knew.

"What are you doing to the roses?" she asked, desperate to change the subject.

He held up his cricket bat. "Deadheading them," he said. "Not much cause for that yet, but there are a few…" He put both hands on the cricket bat, eyed the Lady Debra carefully, and took a swing. A wilted head arced towards the grass.

"That's an unusual way to deadhead," said Mette. "I've never grown roses, but I do have a nice summer garden outside my book shop."

"Would you like to give it a go?" he asked. "Frank can wait a few minutes..."

Mette took the bat and swung at another dead rose, but missed it by several inches and spun around, laughing.

He took the bat from her. "Not like that. Look," he showed her his hands, which were clasped around the top of the bat. "See how I'm holding it? One hand slightly overlapping the other, the thumb like so..."

She took the bat again and placed her hands in the same position. "Like this?"

"Move your thumbs very slightly...yes, that's the way. Now try again with that pink one. Keep your arms straight."

She swung the bat back, in the way she had seen him do, then swiped at the rose he indicated. The bat connected with the rose, but also with the bough it hung from and showered them both in rose petals. "I'm so sorry..."

"Never mind," he said. "Ah. Speak of the devil..."

Mette turned. Lady Debra's companion and Pulau, her servant, still pushing Lady Debra in her bath chair, were entering the chapel through the vestibule door, which faced away from the street towards the school building. Mette could see now that Lady Debra was not fully in control of her senses. Her head was slumped forward, no longer erect as it had been in her own garden. She looked as if she was asleep. The companion, Elizabeth, reached down and wrenched her back into position as they passed into the vestibule, pushing her head roughly into place against the back of the bath chair.

Cricket bat in hand, Mette ran for the vestry door.

The scene before her in the chapel terrified her. Milo

A CRICKET LESSON

Mountjoy stood in front of Frank, enraged, striking at him, while Frank fended him off with his arm. Pulau and Lady Debra's companion were immediately behind Frank, the companion clutching a purse like a weapon. Was she going to hit Frank with it? Did she have a gun in her purse? "Frank, look out, they..." she said.

Pulau threw down his hat and put his arms around Frank, lifting him from the ground. The companion thrust Lady Debra's bath chair to one side, causing Lady Debra to cry out; then she tore open her bag and pulled out an embroidered handkerchief and a small vial, which she emptied on the cloth. While Frank struggled in Pulau's bear hug, the companion moved towards Frank with the cloth raised. She was going to chloroform him again!

Mette stood still for two seconds, then ran forward, the cricket bat raised over one shoulder, and took aim at Pulau's head. "I knew it was the companion."

"Overlap your hands, overlap your hands," yelled Masterson. "Careful now..."

Mette moved her thumbs slightly, balanced herself carefully, then swung as hard as she could, putting all her weight behind the move. She was going to save Frank, even though, in that moment, she would have liked to hit him on the head with the cricket bat instead of Pulau.

The bat connected with the side of Pulau's head with a satisfying thwack, and she heard Masterson exclaim, "Well played," as Pulau let go of Frank and slid to the ground in an awkward heap, taking Frank to the ground with him.

Masterson ran forward and jumped astride Pulau's prone form. "I have him, I have him." Together, he and Frank rolled Pulau on his front, and Masterson sat astride his back, close to the neck. When Pulau came to, he would find it difficult to remove the bulky reverend.

Frank rose groggily to his feet, staring at the companion, stunned. "Betty?"

She glared at Frank, still clutching the chloroform-soaked rag in her hand. "Yes Frank. Betty. And now you've ruined everything."

Milo Mountjoy, who had been standing there swaying, watching the events uncomprehendingly, lunged at Frank. "You bastard. I'm going to kill you. You said you didn't know Elizabeth, you said she wasn't there, and now…"

Frank took a swipe at Mountjoy with his closed fist, but Mountjoy dodged out of his way, sneering. "I can outlast you," he said. "I'm younger than you, and…"

He was stopped in mid-sentence by a punch from Frank that hit him full on his mouth; he fell back, holding his jaw, then spat out blood. "You broke my bloody tooth, you…"

Frank followed Mountjoy, fists up, ready to hit him again if he moved, but Betty threw herself between them. "Stop Frank, stop. Don't hit him, don't hit him. He's our son Frank. He's our son."

Milo Mountjoy let out a howl. "Noooo."

They stood as if in a tableau, like the one performed by partygoers at Christmas gatherings, of the Death of Admiral Nelson, no one knowing what to say. The impasse was broken when the chapel door opened and Captain Porter strode in, an Armed Constable on either side of him.

Mountjoy tottered to his feet, blood still streaming from his chin. "Thank God you're here, Captain Porter," he said.

A CRICKET LESSON

"Arrest that man."

Captain Porter looked at him coolly. "I think not, Mr. Mountjoy. In fact, I think you and your father have some explaining to do. I've been talking to him for the last half hour and he's admitted enough to have him sent home in disgrace."

Lady Debra stirred in her bath chair. "Not mine…not mine…" she whispered.

Mette thought she saw a glimmer of something in Lady Debra's eyes, a glimmer of knowledge and understanding

21

Colonel Whitmore

"Colonel Whitmore, the Colonial Secretary, would like to see you," said Captain Porter. "He was led to believe you had raped someone's daughter when you were in India, and that you were still a threat to the woman. He gave permission for Colonel Mountjoy to have you picked up and incarcerated." He scratched his cheek and looked thoughtfully at Frank. "I didn't believe a word of it of course, but he asked me to round you up..."

"You didn't argue in my favour?"

"Of course," said Porter, not entirely convincingly. "But one does what one is ordered to do...I would have listened to your side, naturally, if you had talked to me in Feilding..."

"You think the colonel was the one...?" asked Frank, thinking of the chloroform, and the woman who had used it on him. She and Milo had been left in the custody of the Armed Constables, who were to sort everything out. "And I didn't rape anyone, by the way. They told Milo that I'd attacked his mother, or at least the woman he thought was his mother. But of course she isn't; the companion, Elizabeth - I knew her as Betty - is his mother. I was barely twenty when I met her, and she was ten year's older...we'd been drinking...she seduced..."

Captain Porter waved his hand at Frank. "Twenty year olds are quite capable of making decisions about who they get into bed with."

"Well, I wasn't exactly unwilling," admitted Frank. "But we were caught up in a terrible event - the butcheries of Cawnpore, the escape - and emotions were high. I barely remembered what happened afterwards. I had another woman entirely in mind when I realized Milo Mountjoy might be my son."

Captain Porter looked at him sideways. "Hmph. I suppose she seduced you as well."

They'd taken Mette back to Palmerston and were on the way to Wellington on the down coach, where the captain intended to make a case for Frank with the government. The recent revelations would help, he thought.

"Are you sure it was the colonel who was responsible for drugging me and taking me to the prison?" Frank asked. He'd delayed talking about the whole thing until Mette had been safely deposited at her sister's house. Her sister would be another problem, as she was ready to kill Frank when she heard the truncated story Mette and Frank had told her. But he would take things one at a time.

"You think otherwise?" said Porter.

"I think it was Betty - Elizabeth," said Frank. "She was the one with the chloroform. And Mette says she's been with Lady Debra since the massacre, according to the cook. Karira learned I was taken off the Stormbird by a mysterious passenger in a long cloak who kept to his — or her, I believe — cabin, and a large man. A man answering to Pulau's description was seen on the boat. I have a vague memory of a woman being with me on the jolly boat, and the two of them seem to work as a team. Both are loyal to the Mountjoy family.."

"Perforce," said Captain Porter. "Pulau is wanted for murder in Samoa. Colonel Mountjoy also had some contretemps in Samoa...reprimanded for supplying brandy to a local...but he had some pull, of course...his father-in-law...and got out under odd circumstances, taking Pulau with him. The constables have hold of Pulau now and will put him on a boat back to his homeland where no doubt the police will be waiting for him. Good work on Miss Jensen's part, by the way, taking him down like that. A striking woman." He smirked at his own pun. "You two make a splendid team."

Frank smiled. "I realize that," he said. "I've been treating her as a precious flower, thinking she needed me to protect her. But she proved otherwise. And she discovered some excellent information about the Mountjoys when she bearded them in their ...in their very comfortable den."

"You know Colonel Mountjoy was penniless before he married Lady Debra?" asked Porter. "And he's a distant cousin of Lady Debra. She's the only child of a very wealthy man. He took her to India to look for a husband, and the colonel, with his inside knowledge, scooped her up as soon as she got there."

"Do you think he knew...?"

"That you were his son's father?" said Porter. "I believe he thought he was the father, but he understood Betty was the mother...knew Lady Debra wasn't up to it, even before the massacre. Betty was probably on the scene before Lady Debra arrived. The pair of them colluded to pass off the young cuckoo as the grandson of Lady Debra's father. Then the colonel saw you in Wellington and his world fell apart. Betty must have decided to fix it for him, and for herself. Young Mountjoy didn't know initially, of course, although he was told that you had attempted to rape his mother, causing her to become an imbecile."

"A baronet," said Frank, ignoring the comment about Lady Debra. He wasn't completely sure Lady Debra's mind was gone. Not entirely. "A man high up in the Admiralty." Mette had filled him in on all her information during the trip to Palmerston, although she'd been uncharacteristically morose the whole time, huddled in the corner of the coach by herself. Tired, no doubt.

"He was an Admiral of the Blue," said Porter. "During the Napoleonic Wars. And he became immensely wealthy during that time. Brought back spices and tea from the East, gold coins from Spain...plunder, mostly..."

"And my father brought back my mother," said Frank. "And got the best of the bargain, I think." He stared out the window of the coach through heavy grey sheets of rain. They were approaching the Otaki River, which was swollen from a recent fresh. The coachman had informed them that he may have to wait on this side until the river subsided.

The coach stopped and the coachman leaned down, water dripping from his hat. "Sorry sirs, but this is as far as I can go. We'll get you across on the ferry and aboard the up coach, which will become the down coach, if you get my meaning. The up coach will return to Wellington and I'll go back to Wanganui."

Captain Porter and Frank climbed down from the coach, pulling their collars up in a futile attempt to keep dry.

"Reminds me of being on the campaign," said Porter. "Remember how much it rained, and all the mud?"

"I remember that day after the raid," said Frank. "When we stopped the sergeant who had taken the head of the chief...because Whitfield had asked for ears as proof...and the sergeant thought a head would be better..."

"Yes," said Porter. "And that woman staring at us, holding her husband's head. What an image that left on my eyeballs."

"Anahera's back," said Frank. He'd discovered that Anahera was the brother of the woman who held the head, whose two sons had also been beheaded, giving Anahera good cause for his vengeful rampage. "In Palmerston. Mette saw him in the Square, during the meeting last week."

"Constable Karira told me about that," said Porter. "But we believe he's gone... he's heading back to the King Country, to the protection of the Maori King. He'll hide out up there and make forays out, I would think."

"Did Karira also mention the body?" asked Frank cautiously. "The body in the paddock behind the Royal Hotel? An Armed Constable..."

"Wilson?" said Porter. "Yes, he took us to where you found the body, but it was gone...here's someone offering a ride across the river..." He gestured towards a young Maori in a canoe, who waited in the rain for customers from the coach. "Let's take a canoe across. No point in waiting for a ferry."

As they climbed into the canoe and gave the man sixpence each — ridiculous, according to Porter, but they had no choice — he added, "Not that we don't believe that Sergeant Wilson has been murdered, or that Anahera was responsible. But we can't do anything without the body. There are still natives with rebel inclinations in Palmerston, and they must have got to the body first. It'll be in the Manawatu River and heading out to sea by now. Could wash up on the beach I suppose. Too bad. He was a good sergeant."

"He shot at Anahera," said Frank. "Wilson did. And at me. He killed most of the prisoners as they ran from the fire. A brutal act..."

"Couldn't let them get away," said Porter. "Have them roaming around the countryside. Fortunate that he didn't get you, of course...."

"What will you do about Anahera?"

"We'll have to send a party up after him," said Porter. "Into the King Country. Could be tricky...maybe we'll have you along on that..."

They boarded the newly reclassified down coach on the other side of the Otaki and settled back down into the comfort of the buttoned-velvet seats. Frank was soaked through to his skin. He tried to squeeze water from his jacket, but it clung to his body anyway. "I'm not going to be able to see Whitmore like this," he said. "And I didn't bring a change of clothing with me."

Porter sized him up. "We can get you fitted up at the regimental headquarters in Wellington," he said. "Not as a Die Hard, however. You may have to settle for the 63rd. You'll keep the uniform of course. Come in handy...we'll put you in charge of training recruits when you're back in Palmerston, and you'll be there when we need you to go after Anahera."

"Mette will like that," said Frank. He had no intention of heading off up the Wanganui River looking for Anahera in the King Country. And he and Mette probably wouldn't be anywhere near Palmerston, if he had anything to say about it. "She'll like the uniform, I mean, not the training part, or..."

"Most women do," said Captain Porter. "Which is why I don't wear mine any more. Mrs. Porter doesn't like it."

"I didn't know there was a Mrs. Porter," said Frank. "Is this a recent occurrence?"

"Mrs. Porter and I have been together for twenty years," said Porter. "Well before the Land Wars. Nothing like having a good woman by your side."

Frank nodded. "I know I've found myself the right woman, although..."

"She seemed upset," said Porter. "Understandable, really, I suppose."

"I hope she can forgive me," said Frank. "I realize now how hard it must have been for her. I assumed she would understand how long ago it was, and how..."

"The past is not important," said Porter. "What you should be thinking about is your future together. She'll forget the past eventually."

"I thought we might move to the South Island," said Frank. "Buy a small farm, or I could find work in Christchurch..."

"Too many earthquakes," said Porter dismissively. "And the South Island? Away from her friends and family?"

"But her friends and family are..."

"In Palmerston," said Porter. "Where you should also be. Some of Mrs. Porter's family are in Gisborne. Scots, who as you know are..."

"Difficult," said Frank gloomily. "Like the Scandies, some of them."

Captain Porter slapped him on the shoulder. "It's something you have to live with — the family. It's part of the bargain."

The rain stopped and eventually they came down from the

ranges to the flat land beside the Hutt River. From there it was a straight run to Wellington. Frank and Captain Porter had by then both fallen asleep, Frank with his arms crossed, head down, unmoved by Porter's snores echoing through the night like the guns of Inkerman.

Porter woke with a start as the coach bumped along the Hutt Road and rubbed his eyes. "I needed that," he said. "We have to see Whitmore tonight for some reason. He's in a hurry. We can get a hotel later." He smiled to himself, as if he knew something that Frank did not. "The contemptible little brute will want to see you wearing a uniform of course, so we'll stop for that as well."

"Contemptible little...?"

"The inflated imbecile, the diminutive beast...a few of the many names Whitmore has been called. A magnificent military man, however."

"And the man responsible for asking for the ears of Maori rebels," said Frank. "Which led to all our troubles with Anahera."

"You can't judge a man by what he says, or what he's called by others" said Porter. "Judge him by his success."

22

The Consciousness of Plumpness

A writer in the Australasian says: "If anyone wishes to grow fleshy, a pint of milk taken before retiring at night will soon cover the scrawniest bones. Nothing is more coveted by thin women than a full figure; and nothing will so rouse the ire, and provoke the scandal of the 'clipper builds' as the consciousness of plumpness in a rival. In cases of fever and summer complaints, milk is now given with excellent results. The idea that milk is feverish has exploded, and it is now the physician's great reliance in bringing through typhoid patients, or those in too low a state to be nourished by solid food. It is a mistake to scrimp the milk pitcher. Manawatu Times, January 30, 1878

Back in Palmerston and staying temporarily with her sister, Mette still felt sad. Everything had been explained. Frank had met Lady Debra and Elizabeth, the companion, then known as Betty, a common nickname for Elizabeth, when he escorted them from Cawnpore. Lady Debra had broken her ankle, and after he'd helped carry her out, he and Betty had shared a few beers together, and one thing had led to another...perfectly explainable, but it made her cry every time she thought of it, especially now she had seen the companion.

All the Scandies in Palmerston were unhappy about Gottlieb's death. Few of them had known him, and no one knew that he had attacked Mette in the night, or that he had tried to throw her off the cliff into the Gorge. But they were sorry to discover he'd been murdered and were ready to attend his funeral and lament his passing, dressed in their best mourning clothes while they did so.

The ladies at the Lutheran church had decorated it with pine branches, and the woman from the clearing arrived for the funeral in dark clothing and shawls, kept in boxes for just such an occasion. Many of them carried handkerchiefs to dab at their eyes, crying over a man they had never met and probably would not have liked.

"Poor Gottlieb," said Johanna Nissen to Mette. "Imagine being murdered by that terrible savage. Gottlieb must have been terrified...a tomahawk. I wonder how he felt when he saw that axe coming towards him..."

Mette had a fairly good idea how Gottlieb felt when the tomahawk came toward him. She had been there. She had watched as Frank threw it at him, and had fainted with fear, worried that if Frank missed they would both be doomed. But he had not missed, and Gottlieb had plunged into the Gorge and been swept away in the Manawatu River, the tomahawk stuck in his head. And then Frank had pulled her back up from the brink of the Gorge, with help from his horses. He was so brave and strong...

The service was conducted by the Reverend George Sass, the first Danish Lutheran minister in New Zealand, who had come down from Norsewood for the occasion. He was a distinguished gentleman with a pointed beard and a carefully-curled moustache, and having him at your funeral was considered an honour.

Agnete arrived at the church with Pieter and Maren. She wore a demure pearl grey dress, her head covered in a lace shawl, and walked behind Pieter with her hands clasped in front of her, looking down. She almost resembled a nice person. She and Pieter and Maren sat at the back of the church next to Mette, Mette feeling like a terrible hypocrite. Frank had still not returned from Wellington, and Mette was finding it difficult not to worry about what they had discovered in Wanganui and how it would affect their lives. She did not think at all about Gottlieb, or Frederic, or Agnete.

The Reverend Sass entered the church, followed by the coffin, which was carried by Karira and some of the men from the road crew. Karira made a face at Mette as they passed, raising his eyebrows as if to underline the strangeness of him carrying the coffin of a man who had been killed by his partner. He'd spent time getting Frederic to believe that the whole case was over, now that they could bury his brother. Mette had asked him if he knew what had happened to Wilson's body, and he had not seemed interested. She wondered if that was because Wiki had been involved. Or even Will himself. She would probably never know.

Frederic followed the coffin and the procession moved to the front of the church. He did not look at Agnete, who glanced at him and started to cry, sniffing softly into a linen handkerchief.

"Did something happen between Agnete and Frederic?" Mette asked Maren. "I thought they were together..."

Maren shook her head without looking at Mette. "Agnete

was sure she had him on the hook, but he had a different opinion. He's going back to Melbourne as soon as his brother is buried."

"Poor Agnete," said Mette. "What will she do?"

"She's living in a hotel," said Maren. "We're going to have to find a place for her. It's very difficult for a single woman to rent a house, especially if she has children."

"Is she sad that Frederic is going to Melbourne without her?"

"A little. She was hoping she'd found someone to care for her, with Mads gone - someone who would stay here in Palmerston, and make a life with her."

Mette shook her head angrily. "It isn't right," she said.

Maren looked at her questioningly.

"It isn't right that we women have to find a man to take care of us...why can't we take care of ourselves?"

Maren laughed. "The next thing you'll be saying is we should be allowed to vote in the elections," she said. "Like that crazy woman in the newspaper the other day. Imagine what Pieter would have to say about that?"

Mette knew exactly what Pieter would have to say about that. But she said nothing. She knew that Maren would always honour and obey Pieter. Would she do the same for Frank? She wasn't sure any longer.

The funeral over, and everyone having dispersed, Mette sat in the sun outside the church and wondered what she would do with herself if Frank didn't return from Wellington. What if he decided he'd had enough of her and her family. She'd have a place to live - Hop Li would let her stay in her beautiful new house. And she could probably continue working at the book shop. But a life like that stretched in front of her with no joy.

Pieter came through the gate from the church cemetery with Frederic Karlsen. He'd been helping Frederic lower Gottlieb's coffin into the ground, undertakers being scarce in Palmerston. Frederic now believed his brother had been killed by Anahera, and no longer wanted to pursue the killer. She thought he was probably afraid of him, with all the stories he must have heard while he was in Palmerston.

"Ah, Miss Jensen," said Karlsen, leering at Mette, his face more than ever resembling his brother's. "I wanted to speak with you..."

Assuming Frederic wanted to talk about her translation work, she moved over to make room for him on the bench.

Karlsen sat down and took off his hat, holding it on his lap. "I know that you were a comfort to my brother, before he died so tragically," he said. Mette and Pieter exchanged horrified glances.

"Agnete told me that you and he were..."

Mette's throat constricted and she stared at Karlsen, unable to speak. He assumed that she had done for his brother what Agnete had done for him. That she had 'comforted' him.

"I didn't..." she said.

He patted her arm. "I understand," he said. "Gottfried was lucky to have someone like you to take care of his needs...the needs every man has." He stood up. "Now I must leave and return to Melbourne." He turned to Pieter. "Tell your sister that I enjoyed our time together. I hope she will like living in Palmerston. Myself, I can't see what anyone would...well, *ganz gleich*."

Pieter sat down beside Mette and they stared at each other. Mette finally broke the silence. "I feel sick," she said. "I think

I'm going to vomit..."

Pieter put his hand on her arm. "No one else thinks that about you," he said. "No one. I promise. Agnete, yes. She has always been a luder, and she lets every man she meets know it. I can't do anything about that. But you...you are a decent, god-fearing woman. Why else would a man like Sergeant Hardy choose you to be his wife?"

Mette was unable to stop herself. "Maren told me about the boat...about how..."

Pieter blushed. She'd never seen him do that before, and it made her like him more - a little more.

"We were very young," he said. "Both of us. I'm sorry I allowed myself to...my only excuse is that I didn't know any better..."

"And everything has turned out very well," said Mette. "Maren is lucky to have you, and now you have a dairy farm, and a new house, and three babies with another one on the way." It all sounded excellent as she said it.

"You will also have such a life," said Pieter. "With Sergeant Hardy...Frank."

"I hope so," said Mette. "But you know, of course, about his son...the terrible young man who came to find him at your farm." She assumed Maren had told Pieter all the details, and of course she had.

"Frank was also a young man," said Pieter. "And caught up in a terrible war. He would not have left the woman with his son if he'd known. Sergeant Hardy is an honourable man..."

He was right, of course, and Mette finally felt her heart opening to Frank again. Then Pieter spoiled it, because he couldn't help himself. "You're lucky to find such a man as Sergeant Hardy," he said. "Considering you're not as pretty as your sister - you're too tall and thin, and as well you think and talk far too much, and do not keep your opinions to yourself."

23

The Diminutive Beast

The Hon. Colonel Whitmore was the tallest short man Frank had ever seen. Whitmore, like Frank, had served in the Crimean campaign; he'd also fought in the Kaffir Wars in South Africa; and he'd served as aide-de-camp to General William Eyre who commanded the forces in Canada. In 1861, he'd been appointed military secretary to Lieutenant General Duncan Cameron, who was on his way to take over command of forces in New Zealand. Whitmore had led several military campaigns in New Zealand, and was now Colonial Secretary in Sir George Grey's government. But although he barely came up to Frank's shoulder, he still managed to make Frank feel small, even when they were sitting.

Frank and Captain Porter had stopped at the regimental headquarters to find a uniform. Miraculously, one had been available in his size, and they had carried on in a hack to the Masonic Hall to meet the colonel, who was a member of the Pacific Lodge of the Grand Order of Freemasons and was dining at the hall that night. They joined him after dinner in the drawing room.

"Fought in India, I hear?" said Whitmore to Frank, managing

to look down on him from below. "And in the Crimean campaign?" They were sitting in a pool of light in one corner of the room, on comfortable royal blue velvet wing chairs.

The room was otherwise empty, except for one chair immediately behind the colonel. Frank could see the top of a grey head - a bewigged head by the look of it - and hoped the occupant of the chair wasn't someone who would be interested in their discussion, as he'd certainly be able to overhear what was said. "And in Taranaki, under your own command," he said. "And later, on the pursuit of Titokowaru…although I was with the Armed Constabulary by then…"

"So Captain Porter tells me," said Whitmore. "And now you've been in a spot of bother."

"I was taken up the Wanganui River, to the Armed Constabulary prison" said Frank. He'd been wondering if Whitmore knew about the secret prison. But Whitmore nodded, indicating that he did and that Frank should continue.

"I managed to escape - there was an earthquake and a fire. I had no idea why I was there. I discovered later that I was there because of something that happened in India twenty years ago."

"And what was that?" asked Whitmore. He took out his pocket watch and glanced at it. "Parliament has a sitting tonight, and I…"

"I fathered a child," said Frank, cutting to the chase. "And that child has grown up believing he was the son of Colonel Mountjoy. I believe the colonel had me sent up the Wanganui River because he saw me as an embarrassment."

"Ah," said Whitmore. "Well, these things happen. What do you want me to do about it?"

"I'd like an assurance I won't be sent to prison again without a reason," said Frank.

"I can ensure that won't happen," said Whitfield. He stood and clicked his fingers. A servant came running forward with his coat. "I wouldn't worry about it if I were you." He glanced at the chair behind which the grey head was still evident. "However, someone would like to speak with you. Alone. Captain Porter?"

Porter jumped to his feet and looked at Frank apologetically. "I'll see you at the hotel," he said. "The Old Identities on Lambton Quay..."

The two men left and Frank rose to his feet and looked at the grey head. A hand was raised, with one finger moving slightly, beckoning him. He walked around to the other seating area, unsure about what or who he would see there. The gloom deepened, but a faint light showed him the occupant of the chair.

An elderly man in a faded green cutaway frock coat of the sort popular in the early years of Victoria's reign watched as Frank sat cautiously on the chair opposite him. "The resemblance is striking," he said. "I see now why my son-in-law felt the need..."

Even seated, the man sat erect, his shoulders back, his posture assisted by a black ebony cane with the head of a silver bulldog serving as a hand grip. His hand was thin, the knuckles enlarged, but it held the dog's head firmly. His little finger was weighed down by a large ruby ring, the cost of which would cover the purchase of hundreds of small farms.

"Sir George...?" asked Frank. Lady Debra's father, in the flesh and in New Zealand. The baronet inclined his head slightly towards Frank.

"You heard what was said...you understand..."

"I do," said the baronet. "You and my daughter, in India..."

Frank drew in his breath. Sir George may have heard, but he had not understood.

"I accept that my daughter had a momentary transgression," said the baronet. "I see why...you're a fine-looking man, and Mountjoy is, well..."

Frank wondered if he should tell the truth about Milo Mountjoy's mother, but the baronet was looking at him, his dark eyes glittering with knowledge. He knew. He just preferred not to acknowledge it, even to himself. "What will you do?" he asked.

"Send you away," said the baronet. "Australia, perhaps? South Africa would be even better."

"I have no intention of going to either Australia or South Africa," said Frank, standing up. "I can't see how you think you can force me to leave."

Behind him, the baronet murmured something.

Frank turned. "What was that you said?"

"Ten thousand pounds," said the baronet. "If you leave New Zealand and promise never to return."

Frank looked down at the baronet, a slow-burning rage building inside him. "I won't be bought off," he said. "I don't intend to leave New Zealand for any reason..."

The baronet tapped his cane on the floor, a nervous habit, contemplating his options. Eventually he said, "He – your son – stands to gain a large property, you know. I'm in New Zealand to expedite the purchase...no point in waiting until I'm dead. Seven thousand acres in the Seventy Mile Bush, another thirty thousand near Queenstown in Otago...good sheep farming land, the best..."

"And you think Milo will be able to handle that responsibility?" asked Frank.

"He has my blood," said the baronet. "And blood will out..."

"You should hope it does," said Frank shortly, thinking of his own father - Milo's real grandfather - who had fought with Sir William Beresford at Albuera, and afterwards had carried his mother by coach all the way to Calais, to save her from the marauding Portuguese troops.

"Perhaps Auckland then," said the baronet. "Far enough away that you won't be seen by anyone who matters. My son-in-law will have to give up his aspirations for the governorship, I suppose, but..."

"And how much should I expect to be paid for going to Auckland?"

"Two thousand pounds," suggested the baronet, then, seeing Frank's face, he added, "You don't want the money, do you?" he asked.

"No," said Frank. "I don't. As far as I'm concerned you can take your...your grandson and set him up in Otago. I doubt I'll ever go there. In fact, I'm willing to give you my word that I'll never set foot on the South Island, as long as he and his family never set foot in the North Island. That will solve your problem."

The baronet sighed. "I suppose that's one solution." he looked at Frank for several minutes before saying anything. "I have a feeling that Milo has the right father at least," he said. "Perhaps that will prove to be an advantage for him, in the end."

"I'd worry about your daughter, if I were you," said Frank. "Don't leave her alone with those two."

The baronet nodded slowly. "I hear she isn't well," he said. "If that's the case, I'll take her back to England with me. I'll find a good doctor and we'll get her back in good form. A good Swiss or German doctor. You were close, you two?"

Frank struggled with himself for a few minutes. Should he tell the baronet the full truth about Milo's parentage? That he had none of the baronet's blood at all, but the blood of a servant and a sergeant in Her Majesty's Imperial Army? In the end, he said nothing. If Lady Debra was safe, he no longer cared about any of the rest of them, unholy trinity that they were.

He left the Masonic Hall, thrust his hands into his coat pocket, and walked quickly down Boulcott Street to Lambton Quay, along Cable Street to Oriental Parade. He had did not know where he was headed, but needed to work off his anger.

Colonel Mountjoy and Betty had connived to bring up her son as the grandson of the wealthy baronet, whether or not they believed Colonel Mountjoy was the father. Perhaps initially they had not intended to profit from the situation, thinking they could live together as man and wife while offering minimal care to poor Lady Debra. Milo Mountjoy was another matter. It was hard to deny his own responsibility. Perhaps one day…

It was a full moon, and as he walked around Oriental Bay he could see the reflection of it in the harbour. Two ships were anchored out by the heads, and another half dozen at the docks. The dark shadow of Somes Island, where diseased immigrants were quarantined or left to die, crouched inside the darkness in the distance. Wellington was a thriving town, and the beauty of the town in the moonlight was enchanting. But it did nothing for him. It may as well have been a blood moon.

By taking the position as British Consul in Samoa, Mountjoy had ensured they were far enough away from Lady Debra's father to avoid suspicion. But after he ran into trouble, they had come to New Zealand to start fresh. And then the baronet had let them know he was on his way at the very time that the colonel had seen a man whom he wondered might be his son's real father. Betty, concealed in the coach, did not need to wonder - she knew. The question was, did the colonel know about Milo's parentage, or did he believe until then that he was the father of Betty's child?

He reached the foot of Mount Victoria, where he'd seen the twenty-six pounder being dragged to the top when he was in Wellington looking for Agnete. He climbed the long slope and found the gun placed on a parapet looking out over the harbour. It was dark, but lights glimmered along Oriental Bay and the water looked deceptively calm.

A soldier huddled in a small hut near the canon came out and hailed him. "Who goes there?" But his heart wasn't in it, and when he saw Frank in his uniform he gave a half-salute and retreated to his hut. He'd been left there to signal the hour, not to defend the city.

Near the cannon, he found a seat built into the stone parapet, facing the harbour. He sat and looked out at the moonlit water. Thirty thousand acres in Otago, on prime sheep farming land. That's what bothered him more than anything. And there were the Scandies, up in the Seventy Mile Bush, burning trees, pulling out stumps, building roads, working themselves to death, for what? To earn enough to pay for a forty-acre lot. It was obscene.

Eventually he fell asleep, awaking to the voice of the soldier in charge of the timing gun. "Mind, sir. I'm setting off the cannon."

The sun was just starting to appear over the hills on the other side the harbour. The retort echoed around the ranges and came back to the top of Mount Victoria three times. He stood and stretched, and watched as the full sun burst into view, breaking the harbour into light and shadow, his mind made up.

He knew now what he wanted to – had to – do.

24

Scandinavian Glee

The entertainment given in aid of the Palmerston Sunday School came off on last Wednesday night, and proved to be both pecuniarily and otherwise a most unqualified success. The bill of fare presented was a most enticing one, embracing instrumental and vocal solos, duets, part songs and glees, with a dash of the comic element thrown in by way of savor.... In the song "Tenting," Mr. Snelson, though evidently nervous, acquitted himself very creditably, and the manner in which the choir joined in the magnificent chorus was beyond all praise and made the item the choicest on the programme. And no small feature in the entertainment was the introduction of a Scandinavian Glee, which on conclusion was heartily applauded, and an encore demanded.
The Manawatu Times, May 18, 1878

Mr. Snelson, the mayor of Palmerston, had found the perfect way to raise money for the Indian Famine Relief. More than three million souls were known to have lost their lives in the famine, and the entire Empire was attempting to stop that number from getting any larger. The British Government alone had amassed almost three hundred thousand pounds for the relief.

After the mayor of Feilding had successfully presented a concert, raising seventy-five pounds, Mayor Snelson had determined that he could do better. He would raise a hundred pounds in one fell swoop for the poor survivors who were still in desperate circumstances. Palmerston would have a concert followed by a ball at the Forester's Hall. And to tempt residents even more, everyone would be in fancy dress. New Zealanders loved nothing better than a fancy-dress ball. The mayor had commandeered the Palmerston Bachelors to sponsor the event.

Mette and Maren attended the fancy dress ball dressed as Swiss peasant girls - not so very far from their actual way of dressing – wearing embroidered aprons they had brought from Denmark, with the addition of white Swiss linen caps lined with bobbin lace that Maren had stitched. Pieter and his friend Hans Christian Nissen had been more ambitious, and were dressed as Jolly British Tars, swaggering around with arms folded across their chests and large grins on their faces. Maren had added flares to their trousers below the knee, and they wore white shirts with sleeves rolled up to their elbows and flat pieces of cardboard on their heads that were supposed to look like sailors' caps. They were part of the Scandinavian men's glee group who were going to sing later in the evening.

"You look charming," the mayor said to Mette. He was dressed as a ferocious-looking bearded Turk. "Is Sergeant

Hardy going to join us?"

"He's in Wellington on...on business," said Mette. "I'm hoping he'll be back tomorrow, or the next day."

"I have no idea when he'll be back," she said to Maren when the mayor had wandered off with Brudder Bones, a Minstrel with black cork smeared across his face, to find something to quench their thirst. Mrs. Snelson had been insistent that no alcohol should be sold in the Hall, and Mette's cousin Knud was doing a brisk business out among the traps and drays tethered outside the schoolhouse.

Maren squeezed her arm. "He will come back, won't he?"

Mette said nothing. It had been three days now, and she was terrified that Frank had decided not to return. Pieter's words had made her realize how much she loved him and wanted him and needed him to come back.

A ripple ran through the room, and Mette noticed that all the women from the Scandi clearing were staring at the door of Foresters Hall where the bachelors had gathered. Mrs. Hansen, the midwife, had gone pink and was giggling, and Johanna Nissen, dressed as Little Bo Peep complete with bonnet and crook, was looking back and forward between the door and Mette, her face a picture of envy.

"He's here, isn't he?" she said to Maren.

Maren turned carefully and then looked back at Mette, her eyes wide. "He's a very handsome man, Mette," she said, putting her hand on her stomach. She was pregnant again, with the twins barely three months old. "I hope you…"

Mette frowned at her sister. "Don't mention the bed again," she said. "I think you've caused me enough worry already."

She stood waiting. After a few minutes she felt his presence behind her. Apart from anything else, the Scandi women were now staring just at her, and Maren was smiling broadly at someone over her shoulder.

She turned to face him. He was wearing a uniform she had never seen before, blue with gold epaulettes on the shoulders and gold buttons down the front. On his arm, in the place where she knew his tattoo was situated, three parallel gold lines indicated that he was a sergeant. Which of course he was.

"Are you supposed to be a little Dutch girl?" he asked, smiling.

Mette slapped him lightly on his chest. "Of course not. We're Swiss," she said.

"I think you'd look better as a Daughter of the Regiment," he said. "But I see Mrs. Snelson has taken that role."

"I wanted Mette to dress as a houri," said Maren. "But...ouch. Mette...!"

She had expected Frank to be annoyed with Maren's comments, but he looked at her sister and smiled. "She can dress as a houri for me," he said. "But not for the whole of Palmerston."

That sent Maren off into hysterics, half laughing, half crying. Frank held out his elbow to Mette, and she took his arm.

"May I escort you home, Miss Jensen," he said.

She took him to the new house, which she had wanted to do ever since she had first seen it with Hop Li. She had dreamed of them living there together. And now it was about to come true...unless Frank had come to take her back to Wellington, or to Wanganui or Patea. He seemed to have rejoined the army, with his handsome new uniform.

She unlocked the door and stepped aside as he walked into

the house. She could not read his expression. "Our house," she said. "Hop Li built it for us…"

She followed him into the kitchen and started to babble, annoyed with herself as she did so. "Look at this…a new, modern stove that is so easy to use, and lots of cupboards…" She opened one of the cupboards… "This one opens to the outside with netting at the back, to keep milk and cheese cold but not let rats and possums in."

He said nothing, so she stood by the table and stroked it lovingly. "This beautiful carved table isn't ours…Hop Li uses it to show people how nice a house can look if…"

He took a few more paces and she turned to see where he was going. He had walked into the parlour and was staring through the bedroom door. "This is the bed that Maren bought for you, I imagine," he said.

"How did you…?"

"Pieter," he said. "Look Mette…" Her heart sank. "It's a wonderful house, and Hop Li will have no problem renting it to someone. But I can't take it."

"But why…?"

"I know you love it," he said. "And we could have a very good life in Palmerston, living here." He took her by the shoulders and looked into her eyes. "But it isn't my place. I didn't build it."

A faint hope was growing in her heart. He didn't want to leave Palmerston, just this house.

"And you didn't build it either, or choose the furnishings. We have to build somewhere together."

"But where…?"

"I bought a small piece of land outside Fielding," he said. "Not far from Bunnythorpe. You'll be able to walk over to your sister's place. And you'll have room for a very large garden. As large as you want. And fruit trees..."

"You're going to be a farmer?" she asked. It was the last thing she expected from him. "But you'll hate being a farmer. Are you sure...?

"Not a farmer," he said. "I'm going to start a stud farm, to breed horses. You know how I love working with horses. It was Captain Porter's suggestion, and he helped me find a section with exactly the right conditions. Good grass, a stream running right through the middle, trees blocking the prevailing winds...and there are horse races taking place all over the district now. Fielding, Marton, up in Hunterville. And on the other side of the Gorge...Woodville, and Pahiatua..."

"Why are you wearing a uniform then?" she asked. "I thought you must have rejoined..."

"I've been appointed to lead the reserves," he said. "Under Captain Viggo Monrad. I won't have much to do, but if I'm called on I'll have to go. Things are settled now, and Porter has assured me I won't be sent to the Front. It will mean extra money coming in while we build our farm..."

She was still not quite ready to throw her arms around him. "Maren says Agnete needs a place to live. Frederic went back to Melbourne and she's very upset. Perhaps she could have this place."

"Of course, if we're not using it and if Hop Li agrees. She'll have to buy herself some furniture."

"I was thinking..."

"About the bed?" he asked. "We can take it with us, if you like. We may not have such a modern place as this...we may even have to live in a soddy for a while, but..."

"No. I was going to say, I hate to think of Agnete sleeping

SCANDINAVIAN GLEE

in…in our bed, especially as she will… but we don't need it as much as she does. I have a little money saved, you know. From my books, and Mr. Robinson says he wants to print more and sell them in book shops all through the Manawatu and Wairarapa. If I buy us another bedstead, perhaps one with a feather tick, we can leave this one for Agnete. And…"

"A good solution," he said. "And…?"

"John Masterson is coming to Palmerston tomorrow," said Mette. She could see Frank was wondering why she had changed the subject, so added. "We're getting married."

"I know," he said hesitantly. "And we have to decide when…"

"Tomorrow," she said firmly. "We're getting married tomorrow. John has said he'll marry us. He'll be in Palmerston tomorrow. And about that bed…"

25

Epilogue: Old Identities

She awoke suddenly with a memory drifting around in her mind. She lay there for a few minutes trying to capture it; something that had happened in the past two or three months that needed solving. What was it? It came to her with a full, horrible force. The Turehu. The boys at the *Pa*, back when she and Frank had been searching for Paul and Jens, had said they had seen a Turehu, and they had pointed across the river.

The Turehu was a white spirit with red hair that lingered in the woods like a ghost. She had learned that quite recently. What if it was Jens they had seen? Jens with his pale skin and his red hair? What if he had pulled himself from the river and climbed onto the other bank, and died there before they could find him? What if his body lay there at the edge of the river, on the side where few ventured because of the denseness of the bush?

She rolled towards Frank, put her arm around him, and shook him.

"Frank, Frank. I just realized something very important."

He grunted, kissed her hand and held it against his cheek.

"The Turehu," she whispered in his ear. "What if it was Jens?"

EPILOGUE: OLD IDENTITIES

"Wha...?"

"The boys at the pa said they saw a Turehu across the river. It could have been Jens."

He was half-awake now, and had caught up with her thoughts. But not enough to say anything that made sense. "We'll look for him...in the morn...," he said. She heard him start to snore softly.

We're in Wellington, she thought, we can't look for him in the morning. He's a hundred miles away. Well, at least she knew now, and they could look for him as soon as they returned to Palmerston. Nothing would make her forget. Nothing. And she knew that finding him would give everyone so much comfort. They would be able to bury him in the small graveyard of the Lutheran church, beside his friend and cousin Paul. Jens been declared dead, but without a body it was hard to completely let go the possibility that somewhere he existed, alive. Finding his body would end that feeling.

She lay there, pressed against the warmth of Frank's naked back, and stared into the darkness, a darkness broken only by the window of the hotel, with its heavy curtains, through which some small slivers of light managed to filter. She remembered now how the boys in the clearing, the Scandi boys, had told her that there was a troll in the woods, and she had laughed at them. Then the Hauhau had tried to steal her piglet and she had realized what—or who—it was who they had been talking about. Not a troll, but Anahera. A real person, not a figment of their imaginations. Later, at the pa, the same kind of boys, but Maori boys, including Wiki's brother Hemi, still young enough to believe in ghosts and fairies, had told her they had seen a Turehu and she had not made the connection.

She drifted off to sleep, happy. At last they were going to

find Jens.

An hour later she awoke, thinking now of Frank. The memory of Jens had brought back their first meeting. It was a memory she treasured, and she enjoyed reliving the experience. That sent her mind to the memory of their wedding, just a few days ago. John Masterson had married them in the Lutheran church. Captain Potter had offered up his men as a guard, to hold swords over their heads as they left the church. But Frank had a different plan, and she had agreed. A guard of Scandi men with squared axes had lined the path from the church, holding their axes crossed. It had been a strange experience, but they had loved it, and laughed about it for days.

She woke early next morning, with the vague memory she had dreamed something important. Something to do with trolls. No. Just a nightmare. She'd dreamed of trolls when she was a little girl. She snuggled up to Frank and fell back to sleep. Their lives together so far had been exciting. What would the next years bring? More adventures she was sure.

If you would like to read more of Frank and Mette's adventures, please sign up for my newsletter on my website: www.wendymwilson.com. You can read the first three chapters of the previous book on my website as well.

Also, I would appreciate if you could take some time to write a brief review. Reviews make a huge difference to an author, as they allow us to promote our books on various promotional sites, most of which require a minimum number of reviews; even a short review will be helpful.

EPILOGUE: OLD IDENTITIES

Finally, if you are interested in the lives of these people, follow me on Instagram - @profwendy and on Twitter @profwendy.

26

An Excerpt from Dead Shot

The next book in the series is **Dead Shot**, set in the horse racing world of 1880 New Zealand. Mette and Frank are married but have not yet had children. Below are the opening chapters. I expect Dead Shot to go on sale later this year.

Patea: This morning a Dead Shot filly belonging to Mr. John Milroy was found dead within a few yards of the Institute. The skull was fractured and a small hole led to the brain. Experts examined the wound, and there seems a diversity of opinion as to whether it was made by a bullet, some sharp instrument, or a kick from another horse... there is room for doubt. Wanganui Herald, 3 December 1880

AN EXCERPT FROM DEAD SHOT

Chapter One: Room for Doubt

Patea, West Coast of North Island, 2 December 1880

Paddy Williams, groom and man-of-all-work was awakened from a delicious dream about Bridget O'Reilly, his true love back in Ireland, by a bang that set all the horses in the stables off. He was sleeping in one of the empty stalls at Mr. Milroy's, charged with keeping an eye on things, but mostly on Mr. Milroy's prize stud horse Dead Shot who was worth his weight in oats.

He sat up in alarm. "Who da fook's dere?"

A door creaked. Someone or something left the stable. He pulled out a match and struck it against his trouser leg, his hand trembling slightly. With the flickering light of the match casting shadows on the walls, he peered over the door of the stall at the one directly opposite. Dead Shot stared back at him, his eyes dark and unfathomable. Alive and unharmed. Not in trouble for that, then, letting one of the most valuable sires in New Zealand get slaughtered a few feet from him while he fantasized about Bridget O'Reilly.

He lit another match, lifted his blackthorn shillelagh from its hook and opened the door of the stall, the cudgel in one hand, the lit match in the other. The resulting creak caused the other horses in the barn to shuffle their hooves nervously in the straw. He was a big man, more in breadth than in height, and had been hired by Mr. Milroy because of his experience as an enforcer with the Irish Republican Brotherhood, the Constabulary having turned him down. Crooks, the lot of them, especially since the new policing law came into effect. He was better off working with the horses. They'd never tell on him.

He peered into each of the stalls. Grand. Grand. All of them grand. But in the last one, a filly sired by Dead Shot was gone. A large filly, she was, a two year old, who had run well during her last outing. Holy mother. What was going on then? He flung open the stable door, ready to raise the alarm. The filly was there, standing quietly in the yard. She tossed her head when she saw Williams, her eyes panicked. She was fenced in, with nowhere to go.

"You kicked open the bloody gate, didn't you?" said Williams.

He hooked the shillelagh on his belt and went towards the filly. "Come on then you stupid cappall. Let's get ye inside."

The filly backed away, eyeing him suspiciously.

Williams glanced towards the house. and said softly. "Come on yer damn fool. Get back in your stall." He took another step towards the horse and tried to grab hold of its halter. The horse reared, knocking him off his feet. He hit the dirt with a thump, flat on his back. He got up, rage surging in his guts.

"Get back in the bloody stall, ye eejit," he said, trying to keep his voice down.

Forgetting his training, he went around behind the horse and pushed at its hindquarters. A hoof came up and whacked against his thigh. He fell back, rubbing the bruise, trying not to cry out. "Shite, shite, shite."

The horse sidled away from him, and he followed it, stick in one hand, ready to hit the filly if she misbehaved. She did, rearing up and neighing fit to wake the devil. He looked over at the house, sitting in darkness, then lifted his stick and hit the horse hard across the poll, a two-handed hit. The filly

AN EXCERPT FROM DEAD SHOT

shuffled for a minute, dazed, then went down like a sack of spuds, legs buckling under her.

"Holy Mary, Mother of God...."

He knelt beside the horse and lifted its head. The eyes were dark, lifeless. Even if she wasn't dead, she wouldn't be racing again. This was the very thing he was there to guard against, an eejit like himself. What had he done, for chrissake? Lost himself a job he had.

He poked at the horse with his stick, just to be sure, but nothing.

He squatted beside the filly and cast about desperately for an idea. The stable door was still open, and he could see Dead Shot eying him from his stall. Not able to talk, thank the Lord. But that gave him an idea. He went back inside the stable, hung the shillelagh on its hook, and opened the gate to Dead Shot's stall ever so slightly.

"What's going on...ah, Jesus..."

The stable boy, up early for a change. Williams grabbed the shillelagh of its hook again and walked into the yard, the club behind his back, without a plan.

The stable boy was on his knees beside the filly. "What's this on your head? Did someone hit you?" He rose to his feet and yelled. "Mr. Milroy, Mr. Milroy...murder...mur..."

He was cut off with a swift blow to the back of his head. He went down, frothing at the mouth. Not dead yet. Paddy Williams sighed. It wasn't his fault. But he'd done time in prison back in Ireland, and he had no desire to do that again. He wasn't going to enjoy finishing the job, but it had to be done.

Another whack on the side of his head, and the stable boy was finished.

Inside the stable, Dead Shot whinnied softly. Paddy Williams checked to see if lights had come on up at the house, and then squatted against the wall nearby and waited. His original plan was still the best he could do. He could cast some doubt on the situation. Eventually, the stallion nudged open the gate and wandered out into the yard, stepping over the stable boy. He pushed his nose against the dead filly, urging her to get up. The filly did not move.

Williams wiped the blood of man and beast off his stick. He'd have to lose it somewhere. Throw it in a ditch outside town. The big stallion could have killed both the filly and the stable boy. Not likely, but with room for doubt. And maybe they'd think the two of them had interrupted horse thieves, and he'd been kidnapped. If they were complete eejits they'd think that. He'd best scarper.

He went back to the stall and got his kit. He wished he'd put aside some of his pay…but too late for that. He knew a man down in Palmerston who'd take care of him. He'd best find work there until he had enough to get out of the country, preferably on a farm out of town where he could keep his head down. When he had some cash, he'd leave. Australia was out, unless he went all the way to Perth. They knew him in Melbourne. South Africa might do. But first he had to find himself a horse and head south, get himself some funds.

* * *

Mr. Milroy tapped the bloodied stick against his palm. "I

knew it, I bloody well knew it," he said. "That Williams, he didn't run off because he thought he'd get the blame. He did it."

"But why?" asked his trainer. "What did he have to gain? I mean, clearly this is his stick, and it has blood on it. But I don't understand..." He had arrived earlier with the shillelagh in his hand, having been given it by a farmer he knew, who had found it in a ditch.

"Men like him don't need a reason," said Milroy. "I'll show this to the police and see what they have to say about it, but..."

"You don't think they'll do anything?"

"They've closed the case," said Milroy. "Too much else going on. I wish I could hire someone to look into it. Do we know of a private investigator?"

Chapter Two: The Square

Palmerston North, 10 December 1880

Mette Hardy was finding that marriage suited her very well. Two years since she married her Sergeant Frank - Frank Hardy, a coach driver and private investigator. They had purchased a stud farm and built it up together, working side by side, living temporarily in a soddy, building fences, and removing stumps, and she had loved every minute of it. Her life had changed so much, and Palmerston, her home before she and Frank moved to the farm, had changed as well.

She walked around the Square and marveled at the improvements. As recently as last autumn, the centre of The

Square had been a mass of mud, with train tracks across one corner, a lone man in a buggy offering rides out to Terrace End, and clusters of stores and hotels struggling to make a profit dotting the periphery. Now, buildings were going up at a rapid pace, closing The Square in from all sides. Palmerston was beginning to look like a real town. She'd heard the population was now close to twelve hundred, the numbers boosted by the new chums from England flooding in by the boatload. New Zealand was in the depths of a depression, made worse by the new arrivals, some unable - or unwilling - to work, but you certainly wouldn't know it from walking around the Square.

She stopped at one of the new businesses - Mr. Allingham, a bootmaker who sold ready-made boots and shoes, offering free repairs for any he'd made himself. She'd once had just a single pair of boots, huge monsters reinforced on the soles with hobnails. What had Frank seen in her, wearing such ugly boots? Now she owned two pairs: some side-laced Adelaides and a more practical pair of Balmorals for the farm. She also owned a very nice pair of high heeled shoes, custom-made by Mr. Allingham on the newer lasts designed specifically for each foot, right and left. She'd never worn anything so pretty and yet so comfortable, but the soles had worn through and she'd brought them into town to have Mr. Allingham replace them.

She found the bootmaker bent over a last, stitching a tempting pair of tan-coloured Adelaides. "Good morning Mr Allingham," she said. "Those are beautiful boots. What size are they?" Her feet were large, much to Frank's amusement, and she was ready to pounce on a pair of boots in her size.

"Too small for you Mrs. Hardy," said Allingham, glancing up from his work. Did everyone in town know she had big feet? "But I do have a larger pair of dancing shoes that would fit you exactly. Just a minute and I'll fetch..."

She was torn, but after considering the possibility for a moment, said, "Please don't bother. I mustn't spend more on shoes. I was actually bringing in the pair I purchased from you last summer to have the soles replaced."

He took the shoes from her and eyed the soles. "I'll have to charge you for the leather," he said. "But the work..."

She took out her purse, wondering how long his business would last if he kept up that practice. "That's very kind of you."

"The Square seems very busy today." Allingham took the five-shilling note she proffered. "Is it normal for this time of year?"

"It's just the volunteers, parading up and down," said Mette. "My husband has been drilling them, and after the training they rush off to enjoy themselves in the saloons and billiard halls."

Mr. Allingham shook his head. "Dear, dear," he said. "I left the West Coast because of all the drinking..."

A templar, she thought. She didn't like drinking, and had convinced Frank to limit his consumption of beer to a glass or two a day, but this zeal for insisting that no one should be allowed to drink troubled her. Her sister-in-law Agnete, once a very loose woman, had married a templar and had started accosting strangers in the street with pamphlets. Mette was dying to ask her who had given her the right to bother other people with her opinions, when she had such a flawed past herself.

She left her shoes with Mr. Allingham and went back into the Square to continue her walk. Outside, two men from the Palmerston North Rifle Volunteers, still wearing their caps and belts, reeled towards her stinking of cheap gin.

"'Ullo miss," said one, staggering towards her. "What about a kiss then?"

She sidestepped him easily, and glanced towards the saddlery, worried what Frank might do if he was watching.

"Leave 'er alone then Bobby," said the other volunteer. "She's married to sarge. E'll 'ave yer guts for garters if he sees yer interfering with his woman."

"Sorry miss...missus," said the first volunteer, taking off his cap and clutching it nervously to his chest. "Just got excited...war coming and everyfink. Had to celebrate..."

Mette shook her head and smiled, then walked away quickly. Best not to pay attention. But war coming? She hoped not.

She'd intended to conclude her walk at the saddlery where Frank was buying new racing gear and talking to Mr. Jordan, but the day was fresh and Robinson's Book Shop, next door to the saddlery, called to her. Frank could wait a little longer.

She stopped outside the book shop to look over at Frank, deep in conversation with Mr. Jordan, apparently not having seen the volunteer accost her. He was wearing his full sergeant's uniform, required for his work with the Palmerston volunteers, and looked impressively handsome. He spent one day every week drilling them in preparation for the war he insisted was not coming.

A rough-looking character was standing at the doorway of the book shop and she pushed past him, avoiding his eyes. She could feel him leering at her as she closed the door behind her. A new chum by the look of him, or worse, an Irishman.

"Good morning Mrs. Hardy," said Ernest Robinson as she entered his shop, which he had owned since his father died.

Mette had expected to like Ernest as much as she had liked his father, but that had not proven to be the case. In fact, she disliked him more than anyone she had met in the last three years, other than Frank's nasty son Milo. But that was another story.

"Good morning Ernest," she said. She smiled at him, wondering why he never used her first name. She'd been close friends with his father, and now Ernest was married to Agnete they had lunch at Pieter and Maren's place every Sunday after church. Frank hated it, but agreed to go as long as he didn't have to go to church first.

Ernest Robinson rubbed his hands together and asked, "Is there something I can help you with, my dear?"

Since inheriting the book shop from his father, Ernest Robinson had filled his shelves with penny dreadfuls crammed with stories about pirates and highwaymen and barbers who cut off people's heads and put them in pies. She picked up one with a particularly nasty cover showing a gruesome hanging, and flicked through it. Dreadful. An appropriate term for such trash. "I was wondering if you had my latest royalties?" she asked. "Your father used to give them to me four times a year, and..."

Looking guilty, he took an envelope and something wrapped in brown paper out of a drawer. "Ah, yes, my apologies," he said. "I've been meaning to give this to you...and my father left you a little gift. A book I believe..."

She pushed the wrapped book into her pocket and opened the envelope, not expecting much. She'd started writing books about cooking in the New Zealand bush two years ago, and every now and then Mr. Robinson would give her a pound or two from the sales. Frank called it her pin money, and it had

247

helped her buy, well, not pins, because she hated sewing, but books, and a beautiful fountain pen which made her writing so much easier.

She pulled out the contents, and almost fainted. "What...?"

* * *

From in front of Jordan's saddlery, Frank Hardy watched his wife walking around The Square as he spoke to Mr. Jordan. It was something he never tired of, watching his wife walk. A tall slender woman with a bounce in her step that suited her personality, she had gained confidence in the last two years in a way that had surprised him. She had been young when they married. Was still young. But now she had the bearing of a married woman who knew what she was about.

"What do you think of the filly?" asked Mr. Jordan.

Frank turned, frowning, then realized Jordan was talking about a horse.

"The filly?"

The one Mr. Snelson bought up in Patea," said Jordan. "Have you seen it? A one year old out of Dead Shot."

"Must have cost him a few quid," said Frank. "Dead Shot is one of the best sires in the North Island."

Jordan named a price, and Frank grimaced. "I'd like a filly from Dead Shot," he said. "But not at that price."

"If you have a good brood mare you could take her up to Waitotara, and meet Mr. Milroy, the breeder, there" said Jordan. "Stud fee is five pounds. You could afford that, couldn't you? I heard the government is paying you well for drilling the volunteers..."

Frank wasn't sure if the meager fee he received for volunteer training would help much, but he could probably swing a fiver for a stud fee for his mare Dolores. She fell pretty reliably. "I'll think about it," he said. But it would mean leaving Hemi and Mette in charge of the farm, and he wasn't sure about that. A pity he didn't have a man to take care of things when he wasn't there.

He could see several of the men he'd drilled that morning wandering around The Square, looking totally unprepared for a lolly scramble, let alone a skirmish against trained resisters, like the ones up at the Front in Parihaka. Round-shouldered and pot bellied, the lot of them. Never get taken on by the British army, not one of them. During training he would have them stand in a row, feet out at precisely the same distance, not quite right-angled, bodies erect on the hips leaning forward slightly, in the manner recommended by the drill manual, and the next thing he knew they would square up their shoulders and stick out their bellies, making it impossible for them to hold their weapons.

Then there was the marching itself. They would step out as one, and be out of step within minutes. He'd resorted to bringing cut sticks, exactly eighteen inches long, to enforce the length of the stride, and had made them march one at a time along a line of the sticks as he walked beside each one bellowing loudly. "Hup two three four…"

"Mr. Snelson — Captain Snelson — told me they're going to start training the volunteers on the rifle range," said Jordan.

"Well count me out on that." Frank turned and eyed the Square again. Mette had vanished, probably into the book shop. "Marching straight ahead is hard enough to achieve. Did you see me trying to get them to wheel in formation this morning? Enough to make a man cry in his beer."

"I think he has you in mind for the training," said Jordan. "Weren't you a dead shot, back in the war?"

Frank nodded. "I still am," he said. "All the more reason for me not to train the volunteers to shoot. It'd kill me."

Back in The Square, Mette, came out of the book shop. How horrible for her that her dear friend Mr. Robinson had died and left the shop to his oily son Ernest. Frank had been trying to get Ernest to come out as a volunteer, but Ernest saw himself as part of the gentry, and thought fighting was for lesser beings. She started to walking towards the saddlery.

From fifty yards away, Frank could tell she was in a state of high excitement. So much so that she almost tripped over Hohepa, younger brother of Hemi who worked for Frank. What Hohepa was up to going in to the book shop was a mystery, although Mette had taught him and his brother, Hemi, to read. He was probably intending to shoplift a penny dreadful, as he certainly didn't have enough cash to buy one.

Mette walked towards him, smiling, her face flushed. She was clutching an envelope in her hand. Something important, obviously. He held her gaze, smiling, until she was within a few feet of him, then asked, "Did you talk to Ernest about Agnete's..."

He was interrupted by a bullet ricocheting off the door jamb inches from his head, followed by the boom of a gunshot - a breech loading revolver, by the sound of the echo. A Colt or an Adams probably. He grabbed his wife by the elbows and manhandled her into Mr. Jordan's shop. "Get down behind the counter, Mette." Then he strode out into the Square to find out what the bloody hell was going on.

The answer came quickly. In the centre of the Square, a runaway horse, whose rider still carried a pistol - an Adams, as he had suspected - had been brought to a halt by a heroic bystander. The rider was one of Frank's volunteers, Henry Thompson, a recent immigrant from Southampton.

"What the blazes are you up to?" said Frank. "You almost killed my wife." He took the pistol from Thompson and broke it open. "There's still a bullet in here. Were you intending to kill me as well?"

"Sorry Sarge," said Thompson. "I didn't mean..."

"It weren't his fault," said the heroic bystander in what was clearly an Irish accent. "He had 'is gun pointed at the ground, he did, but the horse stumbled in a pot hole and the gun came up and..."

Frank removed the bullet from the magazine and handed the empty gun back to Thompson. "Never ride with your weapon loaded," he said. "Unless you're in a fight."

"I was thinking about that," said Thompson. "About what it would be like, charging at the rebels..."

"That's not going to happen," said Frank. "Off home with you now." He was going to have to add weaponry to his training, he could see that. The volunteers were useless without it. He turned to the Irishman. "Thank you for your actions. We could have had a disaster. I don't think I've seen you around."

"I just arrived," said the Irishman. "I'm looking for work in Palmerston."

"What kind of work?" asked Frank.

"Horses," said the Irishman. "Anything to do with horses."

"Good timing," said Frank. "I own a stud farm, and I was thinking I could do with some help. What did you say your name was?"

"Williams," said the Irishman, sticking out his hand to Frank. "Paddy Williams."

27

Who is Sergeant Frank Hardy?

This book follows, *Not the Faintest Trace*. However, it is a **standalone**, although with references to events in the previous one. Below is some background information on Frank Hardy and his history. There are **no spoilers**. You don't have to read this section. It's just here to give you a feel for my protagonist.

- **Sergeant Frank Hardy** is an Englishman who was brought up on an estate where his father was coachman. He joined the army and fought in Crimea and India before arriving in New Zealand in the 1860s. He belonged to the 57th Regiment of Foot, known as the Die Hards (Named during the Napoleonic Wars after the Colonel died at Albuera shouting the words, "Die hard the 57th, die hard." They took him at his word and most of them died.)
- **In 1869** Hardy was part of a Colonial New Zealand force who pursued a rebel Maori force known at the time as *Hauhau*, led by a chief named Titokowaru. During that chase he witnessed a Colonial soldier beheading a Maori chief in front of the chief's wife and two small sons. This atrocity later comes back to haunt Hardy in the form of

Anahera, the Avenging Angel, the *Hauhau* warrior. That story is covered in Not the Faintest Trace, with Anahera (the Maori word for angel) making a brief appearance in this book. He is distinguished by *moko*, or tattooing on his face in the shape of an angel.
- The atrocity actually happened, and Captain Porter, who appears in both books, came upon the beheading and stopped more from taking place. As Frank Hardy is fictional he was, of course, not actually present. I have probably been a little unkind to Captain Porter as he turned into a fictional character at some point and developed a personality of his own. In real life he was considered a hero; he married a Maori woman, and became Mayor of Gisborne, where he mingled with my family, the Grahams. I have had a photo of a tennis party that includes his wife on my wall for years, without realizing who she was.
- **By 1877** Hardy is living in Palmerston, in New Zealand and driving a mail coach, unhappy with his life and looking for adventure. Part of the adventure he found involved **Mette Jensen,** a young Danish to whom he is now engaged.
- **Not the Faintest Trace opened in 1869** with the atrocity, seen from the point of view of the wife of the chief who was beheaded, and then **jumped to 1877** with Anahera watching two young Scandinavian men drown in a river. Anahera is out to avenge the events of 1869 and is looking for **Die Hards like Frank** to kill. The story of the young men drowning is true. Paul Nissen was my great grandfather Hans Christian Nissen's brother, and Jens Lund, who remains missing in my books, but was found

with Paul, was his cousin.
- **Recalled to Life** picks up Frank and Mette's story a few months after they become engaged.

Thanks for reading.
Wendy
www.wendymwilson.com